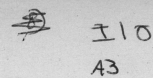
THE SPECIAL ONES

Also by Em Bailey
Shift

Em Bailey is an Australian writer living in Germany with her partner and daughter. Em used to be a new-media designer for a children's television production house and is now a full-time author. *The Special Ones* is her second, much-anticipated novel for young adults. Her first novel, *Shift*, won the teens' choice Gold Inky Award in Australia and was shortlisted for a number of other awards.

When she's not writing, Em is generally getting lost, losing stuff, reading, hanging out with her friends and family, and listening to Radiolab podcasts. She always locks her doors at night.

EM BAILEY

THE SPECIAL ONES

ELECTRIC MONKEY

First published in Australia in 2016
by Hardie Grant Egmont
Ground Floor, Building 1, 658 Church Street, Richmond, Victoria 3121, Australia

This edition published in Great Britain in 2016
by Electric Monkey, an imprint of Egmont UK Limited
The Yellow Building, 1 Nicholas Road, London W11 4AN

Text copyright © Em Bailey
Text design copyright © Hardie Grant Egmont

ISBN 978 1 4052 7591 0

A CIP catalogue record for this title is available from the British Library

Typeset by Sonya Murphy
Printed and bound in Great Britain by the CPI Group

59006/1

MIX
Paper
FSC FSC® C018306

To Matt and Madeleine, the two other 'em's'.

CHAPTER ONE

I hear the main gate slam closed, and I just know from the sound of it that Harry has news. He must have banged it really hard as the gate is a fair distance from the farmhouse. He would only do that, I'm sure, if he was sending me a message. He must have finally found our new Lucille.

Relief floods me. We've never gone this long without one before, not in the whole time I've been here. Finally, we'll have some good news for *him*.

I've drawn the heavy velvet curtains on the windows, but the heat creeps in around the edges anyway. Beneath the corset and layers of petticoats, my body sweats. A heavy wind rattles the windows. *Bushfire weather* – that's how my father would've described it. Fire was something my parents worried about a lot when we lived in our old house, surrounded by trees.

Fire. Family. My old home. Things I don't let myself think about in here.

It will take Harry at least ten minutes to make it from the gate to the farmhouse – longer if Felicity spots him coming – but even so I long to gather up my skirts and dash out of the parlour, outside, to the very edge of the front verandah, and wait for him to come into view. I love watching Harry walk. There's something so reassuring about his unhurried lope.

But I am the Esther, and Esther doesn't dash. Her remembering book is very clear about that. Esther's movements are dignified, considered – especially in the parlour. Esther would never let excitement or nervousness show, or waste time watching people walk.

Sometimes being Esther feels like wearing a Halloween costume. One that doesn't fit. One I can't ever take off.

With great effort I stay in my chair, listening to the daytime noises of the farmhouse and continuing with my work. On the little wooden table beside me are the socks for darning. Clothing repairs are normally the Lucille's task, but the mending has piled up to the point where it can't wait any longer. The sock I'm currently working on is one of Harry's and it has his smell. Hay, earth, sun. As I push the needle through the fabric, I picture him striding across the farm towards me, coming closer and closer. Past the chickens and the area where the crops grow. Past the peach tree completely covered, the Felicity assures me, with promising green nubbles of fruit. Then, finally, between the two lemon-scented gum trees standing like border guards where the farm officially ends and the kitchen garden begins.

When I know he must be close, I strain to hear his steps – and, yes, there they are. Purposeful but not rushed, matching the steady rhythm of his breath.

I am always edgy when Harry leaves the farm. When I first arrived here, *he* made it clear that the farm was the only safe place left in the world. Beyond the gate were innumerable dangers. Security guards, police officers, doctors, teachers, parents, all lying in wait to force us back into lives which didn't really belong to us. And even though I don't believe this any more – not really – I'm always relieved each time Harry returns safely.

The handle of the front door rattles as it turns. There are footsteps down the hallway and finally the parlour door swings open. Harry fills the doorway as air and light flood the dark, stuffy space. He's breathing deeply and when I sneak a quick glance at him, I notice that his wheat-coloured hair forms damp swirls against his forehead. It's hardly surprising, considering the thick trousers and woollen jacket he's wearing.

I put down the sock and hurry (while trying to appear not to hurry) over to the sideboard, where I have a carafe of water waiting. My hand trembles as I pour a glass for Harry.

Slow, considered movements, I remind myself. *He* is probably watching us right now, and he mustn't suspect how tense I am.

Outside the window, the generator whirs. I have questions, lots of them, but I keep them in check. Conversations between Harry and Esther must be as formal as a script. I hand the glass of water to Harry, careful not to let our fingers touch, or our eyes meet. 'Did you see Lucille today?'

My voice is smooth and calm and perfectly Esther, but I'm sure Harry senses my nervousness. Last time the Lucille was renewed in four days. This time it's been almost three weeks. The followers – especially Lucille's – keep asking how much longer it will be before they see her again. And it's only a matter of time before *he* loses patience with us.

Harry gulps down the water. 'Yes,' he says when he's finished. 'I saw her.'

Although it's the answer I was expecting, I can barely keep from flinging my arms around his neck. I refill his glass to give myself time to regain composure. If any of the followers are watching they need to see that we have everything under control – that Lucille has simply gone away and will come back soon, just like she has before.

'How is she?' I ask.

Two dents appear on Harry's forehead, like invisible fingers have pressed into his skin. They're gone in an instant, but I know what they mean. When normal forms

4

of communication are restricted, you learn to gather information in other ways. That slight frown means there are changes to the Lucille. Significant ones.

'Her hair seems straighter, and a little lighter.' Like me, Harry knows better than to let his concerns show in his voice. 'She's obviously been spending some time in the sun.'

Automatically, my eyes flick over to the photograph above the mantelpiece. Gilt-framed. Dominant. The image itself is a little blurry – like it's been enlarged – but it's still clear enough. Four figures stand on the verandah of an old stone farmhouse. Three of them are girls in gloves and long white dresses.

The smallest girl in the photo has thick braids and a cupid's kiss of a face. Above her, written in old-fashioned cursive, is a name: *Felicity*.

Near her is a male and his beard makes him look older than he really is, which is probably no more than nineteen. He has one hand arm protectively around Felicity, his shoulders seeming so broad compared with her tiny child's frame. *Harry*.

To his left is a girl with dark curls and a curvy figure. Her chin is held up in a way that could be proud or defiant, or both. *Lucille*.

The fourth figure, standing near the front door, is a tall, thin girl standing with her hands clasped. Her expression is smooth and unreadable. That's me. *Esther*.

Screwed into the wall beneath the photograph is a little brass plate. I can't read the engraving from here, but I know what it says. *The Special Ones.*

The followers often ask me during evening chat:

*What were you thinking about when
that photograph was taken?*

At first the question frightened me so much I could barely type a reply. I was convinced they'd picked me as an impostor. That they already suspected the girl in the photo was a total stranger to me.

It's hard to remember exactly.

My hands would shake as I typed my reply.

It was so long ago.

Not a great answer, I knew that. But no-one ever challenged me about it and gradually I became more confident. My answers improved.

*When that photograph was taken I was thinking
about how I, as a Special One, can help to guide you,
my loyal follower, through your times of need.*

Sometimes I'd even twist the question around, making it seem like *I* was doing the testing.

What do you think I was thinking?

•

'The sun is good for the soul and its effects on Lucille will soon fade once she's back here,' Harry says mildly. 'And her hair will right itself too.'

I turn to find that he has moved from the doorway and is standing near me now, also looking at the photograph. I nod in reply. Of course, we both know that the Lucille's hair won't really right itself but at least changing straight, fair hair into dark curls will be easy compared with other transformations I've had to make – like the time I had to turn a Felicity's short, dark frizz into smooth, plaitable blondeness. Besides, the greatest challenges with reintroducing a Special One are not to do with physical appearance.

'Otherwise, she's just as she was,' Harry adds, draining another glass of water.

I take this to mean that her height and weight are pretty accurate, which is good news. In Lucille's remembering book, she is described as being taller than Felicity but shorter than Esther. She needs to be soft, but in no way plump.

'And she has that same look in her eye.'

There's the slightest hint of a chuckle in Harry's voice as he says this. The Lucilles always have a particular expression. In her book, this is described as 'being filled with strong emotion', but I have always secretly thought of it as sulky and troublesome. I suspect Harry feels the same. No matter what it is, the Lucille needs to have it. That expression is what the followers will be expecting.

Harry tips his glass towards me as I pour, the water forming a connecting arc between us.

'Where did you find her?' I ask.

'In a food court, eating a hotdog and chips,' says Harry.

'Poison,' I say primly, but my mouth salivates. When was the last time I ate anything like that? Probably when Mum took me to the local shopping centre, soon after we moved. She was hoping, I guess, that the outing would make me see the benefits of our new location. But what fun could I possibly have without the friends I'd left a thousand kilometres behind? Mum dragged me into shops, where I steadfastly refused to try on anything, and then I picked, stony-faced, at the lunch she bought me.

'Poison,' agrees Harry, but I think I catch the tail end of a smile on his face before I hastily look down.

Harry and Esther are not allowed to look directly at each other for more than three seconds at a time. What does Harry make of me in those brief glances? Does he just see Esther – her neat hair, her tightly corseted body, her controlled face? I used to hope that he would see more, or at least sense the things buried deep inside. But then I wondered if this was the wrong thing to wish for. Maybe Harry wouldn't like the real me. Esther is capable, strong. She gets on with things without complaint. She doesn't freak out at the sight of blood or cry when things don't go her way. In other words, she's nothing like I am inside.

There's a long silence until, with a start, I remember that there's another question I'm expected to ask. The most important one, even though I already know the answer.

'Does Lucille remember who she is?'

In my peripheral vision, I see Harry shake his head. 'I would say she's completely forgotten everything.'

'Awareness is sometimes slow to dawn,' I recite. 'After all, it's been a long time since Lucille's old form left us. It's not surprising that she's forgotten a few things.'

Harry nods. 'The renewal process can leave the mind temporarily confused,' he says. Somehow Harry can make the stiffest of his mandatory phrases sound natural, even comforting. 'Once she is safe at home with us, she will soon remember.'

I suddenly hear Felicity's voice, wafting in on the hot northerly wind. She's out in the garden, singing a jumbled song. 'Merrily we roll along, on a cold and frosty morning.' Most songs are forbidden in here, of course, and I am not even allowed to hum – but the Felicity is expected to sing nursery rhymes. For some reason, though, this particular Felicity always gets the words wrong. It makes me uneasy. It's the sort of thing *he* could easily become very upset about.

The song stops and a plaintive voice calls out. 'Is Harry home yet?'

Harry gives a low laugh and I smile too. The Felicities are always so sweet. It's hard not to get attached.

'Yeah, I'm home, Flick,' Harry calls. 'I'll come right out.' He turns to me. I keep my eyes firmly on the ground, although the urge to look at him is always strongest when he's about to leave. 'I'll take her down to the farm and get some ingredients for dinner. Today's word was …?'

'*Rejoice.*'

It worries me that Harry so often forgets the guiding word, as it is supposed to shape everything we do, think and feel each day. In our remembering books it says that the guiding words form the basis of the teachings for our followers; that *he* watches us always, recording everything we do and say, and then the most inspirational – the most Special – moments of our lives are made into short films from which our followers can learn.

When I received the guiding word this morning, there wasn't much to rejoice about. But the news about the Lucille has changed things.

'*Rejoice* – that means meat, if you ask me,' says Harry thoughtfully. 'No chance of getting a rabbit at this time of day, though. How about a chicken?'

I hesitate. We only have five chickens left and their eggs are very valuable. I should say no. Esther is supposed to restrain this kind of extravagance and it's really too hot for roasting, anyway. But the idea of eating fresh meat rather than the boiled potatoes and green sauce I'd been planning is too tempting to resist. Plus there's the added thrill of saying yes to Harry.

'I'll make some mash to go with it,' I say and look at Harry just long enough to see his eyes crinkling at the corners.

'Perfect.' He strides off, whistling, and I feel a pang, knowing I'll be alone in here again.

'Make sure she wears her hat,' I call after him. The Felicity in the photograph has very pale skin. 'And don't let her on that peach tree.'

I don't remember which Felicity broke the tree-climbing rule – the first, or the second? – but I'll never forget her punishment. The image of that tiny figure, lashed to the peach tree for an entire day, crying out for water and forgiveness, still flashes into my mind sometimes.

I doubt Harry will forget it, either. He was the one who had to tie her there in the first place.

I hear Felicity squeal with joy as Harry appears outside and I picture her flinging herself on him, like it's been months since she saw him and not just a few hours. I'm glad she can do this. A child her age needs physical contact – hugs, kisses, tickles – but Esther is not allowed to touch the other Special Ones, and the Lucilles just don't do that sort of thing.

In the kitchen I catch sight of them through the window, Felicity holding Harry's hand as they make their way past the gum trees. A little while later a squawking, flapping noise rises on the wind, gaining rapidly in tempo and intensity until it suddenly cuts short.

Harry's news has filled me with optimism. There is still a lot to do, but I feel strong and capable, energised despite the heat. Soon there will be four Special Ones back here again. This means another person to share the work, to speak with the followers, and to keep *him* happy.

Part of me remains tense, though, because what lies ahead is daunting. Planning for a kidnapping is never easy, even when you've done it as many times as I have.

CHAPTER TWO

In our remembering books, it's called 'collection'. It's described in a way that makes the whole process sound very straightforward – as if all we're doing is bringing someone back to where they belong. What you'd do with anything that's gone missing and has turned up in the wrong place. Like a puppy that's wandered into a neighbour's yard, for instance. Or an umbrella left on a train.

As I go about my afternoon chores, I start a mental list of what needs to be done. The most pressing thing is to start preparing Felicity for what to expect. She has only been with us for six months – in her *present form* – and hasn't gone through a collection before, other than her own and that's completely different. It's vital that everyone reacts the correct way when a Special One rejoins the group.

I'm peeling potatoes at the kitchen table when Harry and Felicity return late in the afternoon. Felicity proudly carries the wicker basket filled with freshly harvested items from the kitchen garden: radishes, baby carrots, silverbeet. The scent of outside clings to them.

Harry triumphantly holds up the headless chicken. 'Dinner!' Blood drips onto the stone floor.

'It's Martha,' Felicity informs me. 'She hardly laid any eggs so it's fair, really.'

'Thank you.' I take the carcass and hang it up over a pan to let it drain with some string Harry gives me. He always seems to have a piece or two in his pocket. We had chickens in the backyard of our old house in the country, but they were pets. The idea of eating them would've horrified me. Now I find myself thinking of all the uses this small chicken can be put to. The feathers can plump up our pillows. The fat can be used for cooking. The bones will be boiled to make stock for soup, and once they're removed and dried I'll grind them into a powder for my medicines. Nothing is wasted here.

Our followers will enjoy this, no doubt, if the scene makes it into one of the teaching films. *Your life seems so authentic, so sustainable and honest*, the followers write to me. I never correct them, of course.

Martha's blood splashes rhythmically into the pan. Funny to think that I used to be fussy about my food. No gristle, no fat, nothing that looked too much like the creature it came from. One lean winter in here and all that changed. Now I eat everything. Eels from the dam, frogs, grubs. Once I even fried up a snake that Harry killed on the verandah steps. It's surprising how anything can taste good, if you're hungry enough.

Outside the window, the leaves of the eucalypts shimmer silver-white in the late afternoon sun. Felicity slides into one of the heavy wooden chairs that Harry made the first year I was here, and watches as I sort through the vegetables. The lettuces are caterpillar-holed but the radishes are red and perfect. Radishes always grow well here for some reason.

'Any news?' Felicity asks me. She knows that Harry has been searching for the Lucille, but she isn't allowed to speak to him about it. Questions of this nature must be directed to Esther alone.

I take a breath and plaster on a smile, making sure I'm turned towards the main camera on the wall. 'Yes. Good news!'

Felicity sits up straight. 'Lucille's coming back?'

'Yes. Wonderful, isn't it?'

'I'm glad. Really, *really* glad,' says Felicity, wrapping herself in her arms.

The Felicities and the Lucilles are generally not very close – the age gap is too big for them to be friends, and the Lucilles are not exactly the motherly type – but I understand why Felicity is pleased. It feels unbalanced here when one of us is missing. Like a table minus a leg.

Now my smile is genuine. 'Me too.'

I send Felicity to fill a bucket with water from the well. 'It's a bit murky,' she says apologetically when she brings it into the kitchen. She's right – the water is muddy, a sign the well's getting low. It's concerning, but now is not the time to dwell on it.

I plunge the vegetables into the water and begin to wash them. 'Now, Felicity,' I say. 'You know that Lucille may seem a little confused when she first returns.'

'Will she?' says Felicity. 'Why?'

A small black beetle loses its grip on a leaf and begins swimming in desperate circles. I fish it out and deposit it on the windowsill. It's nice to be able to save a life once in a while.

Meanwhile, Harry picks up his cue. 'Remember the last time Lucille was renewed, Esther?' he says. 'She didn't remember any of our names when she came back – even her own!' He shakes his head as if this were simply a funny anecdote.

Felicity's face scrunches. 'I don't remember Lucille going away before. Do you mean before I got here?'

Her mistake makes me freeze, but Felicity doesn't realise she's slipped up. Even worse, I see another question forming on her lips. Harry lunges at her and she screams as he scoops her up and tickles her with a furious intensity, making her small body squirm.

'Oh, Flick, you're such a joker!' Harry says loudly. 'Pretending you don't remember the last time Lucille was renewed. And pretending that you haven't *always* been here!'

Felicity wriggles away from Harry and gives him a reproachful look. 'That's more ouchy than tickly, Harry.'

But she doesn't say anything more. Either she's forgotten the topic or she's remembered that *before* is a subject she should avoid.

When the vegetables are clean, I reward her with the biggest and reddest of the radishes, and then begin to slice. My favourite knife is the one Harry gave me last year, on the first anniversary of my arrival. He carved the handle himself, so touching it is almost like touching him.

I glance at Felicity to find her watching me again, the radish still in her hand. She gives me a smile, the same one she uses when we're being verified. The sort you put on when you know someone is watching you. I give her the same smile.

I wish I could reach over and stroke her hair, reassure her that everything will be fine. But I can't, and instead I find myself noticing the things about her that need attention. There's a rip at the hem of her pinafore, and her dark roots are starting to show again. My insides pinch. More things to do.

'We all feel a little out of sorts without our Lucille,' I say, speaking clearly so the mics can pick up every word. 'That's why it's such good news that she'll return soon.'

Felicity makes tiny mouse-like marks in the white flesh of the radish. 'When will she be here?' she asks.

'Tomorrow,' says Harry, as if there's no possibility of anything going wrong. Maybe it's genuinely how he feels. I wish I did.

'I'm going to make up a song for her,' Felicity announces. 'A welcome home song.'

'What a lovely idea! That will make her feel glad to be back,' I say, then take the opportunity to sneak in another little warning. 'And before we know it – maybe in just a week or two – Lucille will be back to her old self again.'

For a second I catch Harry's eyes, and I'm pretty sure I see in them the same thing I'm thinking.

Let's hope so. For everyone's sake.

CHAPTER THREE

For the rest of the evening, my mind splits off in two directions. One path leads me through Esther's usual routine. Cooking dinner. Clearing up, and putting the bones of Martha the chicken (who was delicious) in a pot of seasoned water to make stock. Getting Felicity into bed as quickly as possible so that she can snare a few hours' sleep before evening chat begins.

But the other path is an imaginary trip through tomorrow and the days that will follow, the steps defined by prior experience. Do I have the necessary supplies to correct the new Lucille's appearance? Will her clothing fit, and if not do I have what I need to make the alterations? And through all of this I'm steeling myself, trying to become impervious to the pain and stress that are heading our way.

But maybe I'm worrying unnecessarily. Maybe this time won't be so difficult. The first two collections were the worst, back before I'd realised there was a difference between what our remembering books said would happen and what I saw happen. Before I'd properly learned to control myself and hide how I really feel.

An unwanted memory flashes into my mind of home. Of my exasperated father, telling me, 'You have to stop all this crying!' when I appeared for breakfast with my eyes red and swollen. It had been several months since we'd moved to the city by then, and my parents must have decided I'd had enough time to adjust.

'You can't be so soft and sensitive about everything,' my mum said. 'You'll give off victim vibes.' I suppose they were worried I'd get bullied, though you don't get bullied if no-one notices you're there.

The shadow girl. That's how I felt in that huge school. How can you be so completely alone when you're surrounded by hundreds of other people? Somehow I managed it. The girls at my new school seemed only to talk about music I'd never heard of, and fashions I had no interest in. One glance at me and they knew I'd have nothing to contribute.

I sat by myself in class, walked alone down endless corridors, spent breaks in the library, developing a taste for books about looming environmental disasters. I knew how the polar icecaps felt. I too was melting, becoming a little less solid each day.

But I'm not like that now. These days I'm a girl of stone.

•

Most evenings after dinner Harry goes back out to check the rabbit traps, or I'll hear him behind the house, chopping firewood. But tonight, when I return from putting Felicity to bed, he's at the table in the kitchen, smoking his pipe and repairing one of Lucille's boots.

I also have tasks. It's been six sunrises since I last made *his* tonic, for one thing, so I take the purple glass bottle from its shelf in the kitchen cupboard and bustle about gathering ingredients. Once I have them – the seven green herbs, the powdered mushroom, the chicken bone – I begin pounding them together in the mortar and pestle that I keep solely for this task.

The one good thing about having no Lucille is that I've had Harry to myself in the evenings. Often we don't even talk much, it's just good to have him near. But today my worries are churning too much to enjoy his company. What if something goes wrong with tomorrow's collection? Something big? What if the new Lucille realises what's going on and panics, or causes a fuss? A security guard might spot Harry loitering and become suspicious. Or a police officer might wander by at the wrong moment.

'Don't worry, Esther.' Harry's face is turned slightly towards me, enough that I can catch a glimpse of his slow, sun-cresting-the-horizon smile. 'It's going to be fine,' he murmurs.

And though they're just words I instantly feel calmer. Harry knows what he's doing. He wouldn't put us in danger.

He points to my slipper. 'Your heel's worn out. Pass it here and I'll fix it for you.'

I slip off the shoe and hold it out to him. Harry takes it in his hand, this thing that just a moment ago was pressed against my skin, which has moulded to the shape of my body. Heat scorches my face and I quickly return to my work, grinding and pounding the ingredients in my mortar until they are a fine paste, not lifting my eyes again until I can tell by the colour of the evening sky that it's time to prepare for evening chat.

Quickly but carefully I scrape the paste into the purple bottle and add twenty drops of cactus juice. Then I place the bottle in the middle of the kitchen table.

The chat room is right at the back of the house, next to the changing room; the rooms are separated from the kitchen, parlour and bedrooms by a long corridor. The chat room is always locked, other than when we go to answer followers' questions, and in the morning, when I receive the day's instructions. If someone needs to communicate with *him* at any other time – to report one of the others for breaking a rule, for instance – they need to ask me to unlock it. So far, no-one ever has.

The farmhouse is made from wood and stone, the surfaces smoothed by use and time. Light is provided by candles, which Lucille and I make out of beeswax collected from our hives. Life in here is blurry, indistinct. It flickers.

The chat room, in many ways, is like every other room in the farmhouse, but there are small differences that somehow make going in there like stepping into another dimension. The lock on the door is jarring: modern and chrome rather than rubbed-worn brass like every other doorhandle in here. And then there is the way the room sounds.

Elsewhere in the farmhouse, the noises are all natural ones. The floorboards expanding or contracting. A possum scampering across the roof. The wind outside and birds singing in the trees. But in here during a chat session, the dominant sound is the hum of the computers. Incessant, alluring – the song of another life.

Freshly renewed Special Ones mistakenly believe that the chat room will help them. They think it offers a way of contacting people on the other side of the gate. But there's no search engine on these computers. No access to social media. There aren't even any clocks. Everything is blocked. There's a wall around our internet use which is much wider and higher than the physical wall around the farm. The chat-room computers can only be used in the way *he* intended: to speak with our followers or sometimes to him.

Like almost everything else on the farm there is a ritual to how things are prepared for a chat session. First I turn on Harry's computer, and then the one I use. Lucille's is next in the line and it will remain blank for another evening. Felicity's computer goes on last. As the chat interface appears on each screen, I can see the followers who are already there waiting, their usernames blinking impatiently.

Some of the names are very familiar. Tru-to-self-92 is here every night. And Cobble_IT is also a regular. But there are new names every night too. The list of those eager to chat never seems to stop growing.

I wonder, as I do almost every night, who all these people are. What do they look like? Are they young or old? They seem so unsure of themselves, needing advice on every tiny aspect of their lives. Don't they have family they could talk to? Or friends? But with a guilty lurch I remember that I felt like this myself once – like there was no-one in my life who understood me.

My remembering book says that no matter how banal their questions sound, how trivial, we must respond to each follower with kindness and patience. We must always model the virtues of the Special Ones. If we fail in this there will be repercussions, for *he* is always monitoring us.

As I'm checking everything, I hear a high-pitched ringing tone that fills me with dread. I smooth my skirts and nervously pat my hair – a ridiculous gesture, considering I am sure he can already see me – before I slip into my seat to accept the call.

'Good evening, Esther.'

It's hard to believe that this voice belongs to a real person – someone with a body and a face and blood pumping through his veins, with emotions and thoughts. The tone is soft and unmodulated. Robotic. *What must it be like, inside his head?* I quickly push the thought away. That is definitely not somewhere I would ever want to be.

'Good evening.'

'I gather that Lucille's collection is taking place tomorrow?' It's framed as a question, but of course he already knows the answer. Not just to this, but to everything we say and do. When I first got here, I actually found that comforting.

'Harry will bring Lucille back from the shopping centre tomorrow afternoon,' I confirm. 'We have been rejoicing at the news.'

If I'm expecting to earn some praise by using the guiding word, I'm mistaken. He doesn't even seem to notice.

'Remind Harry to stay vigilant at all times. All police are criminals – violent and evil. If they catch Harry, they will kill him. Then they will come to the farm and begin shooting, and then they will set the place on fire. They would show no mercy to any of you, Esther. Not even Felicity.'

It's a speech I've heard before, one that still makes me sweat, even though I no longer really believe it. The trouble is I can picture the scene so clearly – the ringing shots, the fire, the panic, the deadly confusion. And even if I no longer think that the police are our biggest threat, I do know that what

Harry is about to attempt is very risky. I tuck my trembling hands out of view. Esther doesn't show fear, not ever.

I take a steadying breath before replying. 'I'll warn him.'

'Has my tonic been made?'

'Yes. It's on the kitchen table.'

The call ends abruptly.

Conversations with him are always like this. Short and sweat-making.

After this, I wake Felicity. Fortunately, she's used to getting up quickly now, and she wriggles back into her petticoat and pinafore without a word of complaint. She understands the urgency surrounding chat – the importance of being there every evening, of looking exactly how we looked the evening before, showing no signs of fatigue. We are not supposed to change. We, in our perfection, are meant to have risen above all bodily needs.

When Felicity is ready, we hurry down the hallway to the chat room. Harry is already in his seat and flashes a grin at Felicity. I am certain it is meant for me too.

'Ready, everyone?' he says.

I take my seat. 'Ready.' Then I turn to my screen and type the same words I always do at the start of evening chat:

Good evening, follower. I'm Esther.
What would you like to know?

•

The chat session is very busy, and my head and wrists ache after an hour of endless question-answering. Esther's area of expertise is healing, mainly through nutrition and home medicine, but also through the power of positive thinking. I'm even busier than usual because Lucille's followers are currently directed to me for help and I'm not nearly so familiar with her tips on bringing beauty to the world. Harry can't help me, either, though he usually gets fewer questions than the rest of us – he only advises on self-sustenance and farming tasks.

The followers of curvy, pretty Lucille are more likely to veer off topic than my own and, although it must be clear from the teaching films that I am nothing like Lucille, they are not deterred from asking forbidden questions, saying filthy things.

What are you wearing tonight?

Have you ever had a boyfriend?

I want to –

Harry is very quick to react when I point these out to him and he deletes the follower immediately, but it adds to the stress of the situation.

There's one good thing about this session, at least. When the inevitable question arises — *When is Lucille back?* — I'm able to give an answer. *She's on her way back already.*

●

I often drift into an almost-trance during these sessions — it helps me think like Esther. But this evening a question arrives that jolts me awake.

Are you real?

This sort of query pops up from time to time, and it always makes me edgy because it feels like a test. After a long pause, I write back.

Why would you doubt it?

A reply pops up almost immediately.

*Well, your answers sound a little robotic,
to be honest. Tell me something about who
you are. What your life is like.*

My fingertips twitch. What would happen if I wrote the truth? *I'm pretending to be the reincarnation of someone in a photograph because some crazy guy thinks I'm an immortal being. But it's only a matter of time before I slip up, and when that happens he'll probably kill me.*

But instead I supply a line of Esther's, one almost threadbare from overuse.

You must have faith.

And then I move on as quickly as I can to another question.

Is it true that I can make myself feel better simply by smiling, even if I have nothing to smile about right now?

Yes, I write back, the words flowing easily now I'm once again in familiar territory. *Smiling is the gateway to happiness and is the most powerful medicine of all.*

When Felicity stifles a yawn, I realise that it's time to end this session. 'That's enough for tonight,' I say.

Harry leans back in his chair and exhales. I feel my own shoulders start to sag, and force them back up. 'It seemed busier than usual tonight,' I remark.

'Word of the Special Ones is spreading,' Harry replies. Often with Harry, I can't tell if he means something as a good thing or not.

Harry takes Felicity back to her room and I set about putting everything in order. The computers crackle as they power down, and then there's silence.

CHAPTER FOUR

Despite my exhaustion, I have trouble falling asleep and lie in bed, listening to the night noises. After a hot day like today, the old floorboards in the hallway creak as they cool. It sounds like someone slowly pacing up and down.

When I first got here I was tempted to sneak out when I heard these noises, to see what was going on. But we are forbidden to leave our rooms overnight except in special circumstances.

I look around my little bedroom. The ceiling is low – barely high enough for me to stand under – and the two closest walls are just an arm span apart. There's just enough room for a narrow iron-framed bed and a small chest of drawers. On the floor is a rag rug, woven by a Lucille. Tonight I've left the window open and a breeze occasionally inflates the white cotton curtains like lungs. Outside, the leaves of the trees rustle and shift.

An urge to check on my secret thing comes over me, even though I know how risky it is. On nights like this, when the moon is full and high, it must be very easy for *his* cameras to see me lying here under the thin sheet. But I suppose even he can't see beneath it.

My fingers creep down the mattress until they're level with my hip. Using the smallest movements I can manage, I slowly wriggle my finger into the little hole in the seam there, pushing until I feel it. My secret thing, hidden deep within the mattress.

It's soothing, and for a moment my anxieties loosen a little. At least I still have something from before. Something that proves there really was a before.

I slip into a dream about translucent figures in billowing white skirts. They drift down the corridor towards me, complaining in whispery, rustling voices.

'You didn't protect us.'

'I did my best!' I protest weakly.

'It wasn't enough,' they hiss, moving closer and closer.

I'm jolted awake, heart thumping. Someone's knocking at my door. Lurching into a sitting position, I croak out some words. 'Who's there?'

'Esther, it's just me, Harry. Sorry to scare you.'

I swallow. 'It's okay. Is everything all right?'

'Yes, everything's fine. I received a message. We're doing a sharing tonight.'

I've swung my legs out of bed before Harry's finished speaking, before I even feel the rush of dread this announcement always brings.

'OK. You go and wake Felicity.' My voice is almost back to normal. 'I'll meet you in a few minutes.'

I've already lit the candles in the parlour when Harry appears with Felicity, her face dazed and dream-fogged.

'Tired?' I whisper, needlessly. We are all of us permanently tired.

We stand together in the middle of the parlour, only three points of a square, and bow our heads. First, we say the affirmation.

'He is the floor beneath our feet and the roof above our heads. He is the walls around us. He is the window through which we see into ourselves and the door that leads to a better understanding. He is always watching, protecting us. We follow him so we in turn can be followed ...'

Then it's time to offer up our failings. 'Felicity,' I murmur. 'You go first.'

'I dropped an egg,' Felicity says loudly as the candles flicker around us. 'I wasn't being careful in the henhouse, and an egg fell out of my hand and smashed.'

This is the first I've heard of it. I try to catch her eye, but Felicity won't look at me. Maybe because she feels bad. Or maybe because it isn't true.

Then there is a silence as Harry and I wage an invisible battle over who will share next. I want to go last, but the seconds drag on so long that finally I can't bear it. Silences are dangerous. They suggest someone has forgotten what they're meant to do.

'I lost the fruit bowl – the one you carved, Harry,' I blurt. 'And also another dishcloth.'

I hang my head in genuine shame, and not just because I know what Harry will do next. In here, I am constantly losing things. Sometimes they turn up again, tucked away in the wrong cupboard or obscured behind some other object – but usually when things go, they go for good. It bothers me that I have become so absent-minded, especially when we have so few possessions. I am sure I used to be a lot more careful.

Harry follows quickly. His sharing is about the lettuce crop, which has been poor so far this year. I long to jump to his defence and point out that the weather has been hotter and drier than usual but we're forbidden to interrupt others sharing. 'I could've done better,' he keeps muttering.

Harry's sharings are always like this. He offers up things that either seem trivial or that he couldn't rightfully be blamed for. He'll say he took too many breaks, or that he didn't work long enough hours, when to me it seems like he never stops working. He is so hard on himself, so hard that I wonder sometimes if it can possibly be genuine.

After sharing comes the judgement. Whoever has committed the worst transgression will feel their guilt becoming heavier and heavier, until it pushes them down to the ground. But no matter how trivial Harry's sharing appears, his guilt seems to push him to the ground before anyone else.

It took me too long to realise what he was doing. Harry sinks first to protect the rest of us. Since I twigged to that, the sharings have become a slightly ridiculous competition between Harry and me to confess last, and to get to the ground first. It would almost be funny if it wasn't so awful.

Sometimes I manage to beat him, but not tonight. Harry collapses to his knees the moment he's finished sharing.

'No, Harry!' protests Felicity. 'Not you again. It's not fair!'

'Shh!' I warn her. Even in the middle of the night, *he's* watching. I doubt he ever sleeps.

'But what I did was way worse than what Harry did,' Felicity mutters. 'What you did was worse, too.'

'That's enough, Felicity,' I say sharply, so it doesn't look like I'm indulging her. 'Go and get the punishment wheel.'

Felicity gives me an agonised look, which I meet with a stern stare until she runs to a wooden box on the mantelpiece, just below the Special Ones photograph. Inside it is a wooden disc with a pole through the middle. It looks like something from a children's game.

The disc has been engraved with lines, dividing it up like slices of cake, and on each slice is a different word. *Whip. Knife. Tree. Cellar. Stove. Hunger. Work.* There's a tiny red arrow engraved into the central pole. Felicity hands me the wheel.

'Thank you. Now return to bed, please,' I say.

I can tell she's considering arguing, but I am determined that she won't see this tonight. I fix her with a glare so fierce that she takes off. There's the sound of her feet hurrying up the corridor, her door pushing back, and the creak of bedsprings. My mother used to tease that I couldn't even scare a mouse. Those days are long gone.

I hold the central pole steady on the floor in front of Harry, and spin the wheel. It rattles as it turns.

Please stop on work, I beg the wheel. It often seems to land on this and Harry is used to hard labour. *Or hunger.*

Going for a week on just flour and water is easy for Harry, especially as I usually sneak a little honey or fruit juice into the mixture.

The wheel slows until finally it stops. I lean forward to see where the arrow is pointing. *Whip.* My ears sing, as if I'm about to pass out. It's never stopped on this before.

'Harry,' I whisper, unable to help myself. 'I can't do that to you. I just can't.'

He lifts his bowed head for a brief moment. 'That's okay. I'll do it myself.'

Immediately, I regret being such a coward. I would have carried out the punishment on Harry far less harshly than he will on himself.

'It's okay, Esther,' says Harry again. 'Just get the whip for me.'

I nod and drag myself over to the chest near the door. It creaks as I open it. The whip is near the top, curled in on itself like a snake. My hand trembles as I get it out, and then I walk slowly back to Harry.

'Thanks,' he says as I hand it to him.

How can he remain so calm? The tail of the whip is as thin as a blade.

'You go now, Esther. And don't worry. I'll be fine.'

As he begins to unbutton his shirt, I turn mechanically and walk out of the parlour, not daring to speak. As I close the door behind me, I hear the sound of leather cracking against bare skin.

●

My first task every morning after washing and dressing is to receive the guiding word. Sometimes I go to the chat room to receive it, and sometimes there's a note. Like today. The envelope, marked *Esther*, is propped up against the purple bottle on the kitchen table. I slit open the envelope, which is thick and creamy and smells oddly of flowers, and remove the card within. The guiding word is written on it in old-fashioned script: *Transform*.

Automatically I start considering how this will impact on my tasks and routine. It's an easy word to apply to our food, at least. Bread is *transformed* into toast when it's held over a fire. And it works well with my chores too. After all, tidying and washing are types of transformation. And then, of course, there's the big event of the day: the collection. That will also involve transformation – both for us and the girl. If everything goes according to plan, that is.

The kitchen is how I left it last night, except that the purple bottle is now empty and clean. It's strange to think of *him* standing in our kitchen, washing it. Or maybe there are two and he swaps the empty one for the full. I put the bottle away, trying not to dwell on the thought of his having been here during the night. Was it before or after our sharing session? Or was he there as it happened, watching us through the keyhole? The idea makes me shiver, despite the heat which has already started to build.

As I'm preparing our breakfast Felicity appears, dressed and stifling a yawn. 'Where's Harry?'

'He's already working.' Harry gets up extra early on collection days so that he can do his chores before heading off.

Felicity sips at the glass of frothy, fresh goat's milk, which I've poured from the canister Harry left by the front door. 'Can I go with him today? To collect Lucille?' she pleads.

I'm surprised – shocked – that she would even ask. 'You know that's impossible!'

Felicity puts her elbows on the kitchen table, supporting her chin in her hands. 'I just want to help him.'

I'm sure she means it. But I'm also sure it's not her only motivation. She wants to go *out there*. 'Absolutely not,' I tell her. 'You'll stay here with me.'

Felicity doesn't cry, but her mouth quivers and I feel like a monster. I probably didn't need to say it so harshly. If only I could hug her, or even just pat her shoulder so she could see I'm not like this really, that it's just an act.

'We'll have fun today, I promise,' I say, softening my voice. She doesn't look at me. Doesn't respond. But I persist. 'How about we make some biscuits while we wait for Harry and Lucille to return?'

Felicity chews her bottom lip. Finally she peeks up at me. 'You mean like a welcome-home treat?'

'Exactly!' I say. My voice is a little too loud for Esther, but I'm happy to be winning Felicity back. 'We could have a party.'

I know too well that when the new Lucille arrives, the last thing she will want to do is celebrate. But that's irrelevant. The main thing is that, for now, Felicity is happier.

Harry appears for breakfast. His whistle is as bright as ever but his eyes, when I sneak a look at them, are rimmed with dark shadows. I wonder if he slept at all last night.

I also wonder how his back must look, after being lashed by the whip.

He sends Felicity off to collect the eggs so the two of us can run through the day's plan.

'What time will it happen?' I ask.

'The gate will be unlocked directly after lunch,' says Harry. I am not exactly sure how *he* communicates with Harry. I think it's mostly done via the computer, although I know that Harry, like me, sometimes finds instructional notes awaiting him in the mornings. 'The Lucille told her friends she'd be shopping after school. She arranged to meet them at four in the food court.'

This shopping time will be Harry's only chance to carry out the collection. Once the girl's friends turn up, it will be too dangerous.

'Make sure you get her phone,' I remind him.

One collection was nearly derailed when the girl sat on her mobile and it rang someone. Harry managed to get it before anyone picked up, but it was a warning to us both. Accidents can happen so easily.

'Have you locked the windows?' Harry asks.

I get up and do it immediately, so there's no chance of my forgetting later.

'And your lure?' I ask. Harry must have something that will entice the girl to come with him. Something so tempting that it makes her abandon all those years of stranger-danger warnings and decide that he is worth the risk, though I have no doubt his warm brown skin and gentle eyes go a long way with that.

'I'll probably use the talent-scout one again,' says Harry. 'She looks like the theatrical type.' He gets up, preparing to head back outside.

'Harry?' There's one more thing I need to say. Partly because I've been instructed to, but also because it's part of our collection-day ritual. 'Look out for police officers, won't you?'

Harry smiles, but his eyes are serious. 'I always do.'

•

After the morning's chores, the three of us eat a silent lunch together in the parlour, everyone caught up in their own thoughts. As I start to clear away, Harry stands. 'Well, I'd better go,' he says.

I know that the main gate is only unlocked when it's time for someone to pass through, and none of us know how long it stays open. Missing that time window would be terrible.

We walk through the kitchen and out onto the side verandah. I go with Harry to the very edge and slip him a neatly written list of things we need. Black hair dye. Tinted contact lenses. Some spools of cotton thread. Harry tucks my list into the pocket of his jacket.

Not for the first time, I wonder where he'll get the money to buy the things on that list, or whether he'll simply steal them. I have no idea how he gets into town, either – I used to assume that he rode a bicycle or caught a bus, but then once I heard the distant, foreign sound of a car engine soon after he'd gone.

As Harry starts to walk down the steps, Felicity clutches at his arm. 'Don't go,' she begs. 'I've got a bad feeling in my stomach about it.'

Harry puts an arm around her shoulders. 'Young lady, you've got a bad feeling in your stomach because you ate too much lunch,' he says, teasingly. 'Esther will make you some fennel tea and you'll feel fine.' He tweaks one of her plaits. 'I'll be back before you know it, Flick. With Lucille. Now, how about you walk with me to the gate?'

Felicity turns to me. 'Can I?'

'Of course,' I say. It's a relief to be able to say yes for once. 'But come straight back afterwards so we can bake those biscuits.'

Felicity nods, happy again. Or happier, at least.

Harry salutes and almost, but not quite, looks at me. 'Back soon,' he says.

I want to wish him good luck, but Special Ones aren't supposed to need it. 'I'll be here,' I say. 'Waiting.'

I watch from the front door until Felicity and Harry disappear past the gum trees and into the farm. Even then

I remain where I am, as if the whole mission depends upon my staying in place for as long as possible. It's only after I hear the gate clang closed that I return inside, my stomach hollow. It's begun.

•

It's far too hot to be baking, but I can't go back on my word. Besides, it's a good opportunity to do some maths with Felicity: how many quarter cups of flour, how many tablespoons of sugar – that sort of thing. I slip on my apron. In the pocket I put a pillowcase. I'll need it later.

When the dough is ready I divide it in half, giving us a ball each. I roll mine flat, planning to use my favourite knife to cut out some shapes. But the knife is not where I thought I'd left it. It's frustrating, all these missing items, and worrying too. I'm starting to think there's something wrong with my brain. Then I remember the note resting against the purple bottle this morning, and another possibility occurs to me. *He* took the knife. But why would he do that?

Felicity is chatting to herself as she shapes the biscuit dough into letters with her fingers. 'E for Esther and H for Harry. L for Lucille. I'll make it very curly and fancy because she'll like that.' The tip of her tongue pokes from her mouth as she works, making her look even younger than she is. 'And for me, a very funny little Z.'

I freeze, the missing knife forgotten. 'You mean an F. Felicity starts with an F.'

Shock fills Felicity's face as she registers her mistake. She snatches up the Z and squishes it so the dough squirts out between her fingers. 'Sorry,' she whispers. 'I – I just forget sometimes.'

'We need to work on your letters,' I say, managing to smile, but although she nods I know I've scared her badly.

I wish I could explain that I'm just trying to protect her. But even if we could speak freely, what would I tell her I'm protecting her *from*, exactly? If I said 'from renewal', she would only be confused. After all, aren't we currently baking biscuits to celebrate just such an event? Maybe later on today, when Harry and the new Lucille return and she sees what renewal is actually like, she'll understand.

In the meantime, we can only hope that with the Lucille's collection today, *he* will be in the mood to let a little girl's error slide.

I try to cheer Felicity up by joking around and being silly – or as silly as Esther can be. At first she refuses to be won over, but I finally get her to laugh even though I suspect she's only doing it to please me. When we put the biscuits into the black cast-iron stove, Felicity goes to check on the animals and I start tidying up.

I can tell from the position of the sun outside the window that it's around four o'clock. The time Harry said the girl was meeting her friends. If everything's gone smoothly he will already have her by now.

But the problem is the *what if*s. What if the girl changed her plans and didn't show up? What if a friend joined her earlier? What if Harry realises that she isn't right after all, and the whole search process must begin again? That would mean more lies to the followers, more stalling, more sleepless nights.

Then there's the biggest *what if* of all. What if Harry doesn't come back this time? He must have at least considered running away during a collection. Who wouldn't?

He makes it clear that our followers are everywhere, and that if we ever 'got lost' they would quickly find us. What would happen next is left unsaid.

Maybe it's fear that motivates Harry to return, but I'd like to think he comes back because of us. Because of me.

The smell of burning biscuits brings me back into the present moment, and I rush to pull the tray out. The oven is a temperamental brute. It took me many weeks and ruined dinners to work out how to use it. I've got the hang of it now, but sometimes it still likes to incinerate something, just so I don't think I'm in charge.

This time I've managed to get the tray out before too much damage is done, although one of the Ls Felicity made for the Lucille is completely blackened. I try not to see it as a bad omen.

Felicity suddenly bursts inside. 'They're back! Harry and Lucille – I can hear them coming!' She is jumping up and down with excitement.

'Good,' I say, my voice smooth and light. But my chest constricts, like invisible hands are pulling the strings of my corset.

'It's *so* great,' says Felicity joyfully. She runs to the door and flings it open. She has no idea what is about to happen.

I linger in the background. 'Can you see them?'

'Yes. They're coming into the kitchen garden.' Suddenly, Felicity stiffens.

'What's wrong?' I say, although of course I know.

'Lucille looks different,' she says slowly.

'Well, of course she looks a little different. She's been away for so long.'

Felicity shakes her head. 'She looks *completely* different. Like she's not the same person at all.'

CHAPTER FIVE

Harry opens the door and comes through. 'Come on in,' he says to someone behind him. 'We're home.'

There's a brief pause and then a girl steps into the house, almost stumbling, although there's nothing there to trip on. Her face is flushed and she has that glazed, slightly wild look that new Special Ones always have when Harry brings them here.

It's always the clothes that are the most out of place, especially with the Lucilles. This girl is wearing a short, filmy skirt and a loose shirt that slides off one shoulder to reveal a neon-pink bra strap. Out there there'd be nothing unusual about her outfit. But in here she looks indecent – almost naked. I'd love to reach out and touch the fabric of her skirt. It reminds me of butterfly wings, brightly coloured and paper-thin compared with the heavy, handmade, coarse materials I've become used to.

Although Harry had warned me, I'm a little shocked by the fine, blonde straightness of the girl's hair. I just hope it's not the sort that refuses to hold a curl.

The girl looks around. She's not yet afraid. 'Is this all part of the set?' she says.

'Yep,' says Harry. 'This is where it all happens.'

The girl sways forward like a drunk, and runs her hand along the dark wooden bench. 'It's all so realistic!' she exclaims loudly, her words slurring.

Behind her, I quietly lock the door and slip the key out of sight. The girl doesn't notice. She's examining Felicity. 'I love your costume. And your cute hairdo. You're like a doll.'

Felicity is staring back at her with equal curiosity. 'How come you look so different?' she asks, stretching out a hand and touching the girl's hair.

The girl pulls back, frowning. 'Hey! Keep your sticky little mitts off me.'

Felicity's expression darkens. 'You're not really Lucille,' she says loudly. 'You don't look like her at all. And you smell funny.'

The new Special Ones always bring with them odours we don't have in here. Commercial washing powder. Shampoo. Deodorant. The scents are so strong they sometimes give me a headache. It's hard to believe I must have smelled like that once too.

The girl puts her hands on her hips, swaying like a wheat stalk in a strong wind. 'My name is Sasha, and I do *not* smell funny.' She swings around to Harry, nearly toppling. 'Is that little girl a bit soft in the head?'

'She's just curious about you,' replies Harry. His voice is soothing and friendly but a look comes over the girl's face, like she's just remembered that heading off with a stranger is generally considered a bad idea, no matter how nice or good-looking he is. She squints at Harry. 'Where's the film crew?'

It's time for me to step in. I move over to her, a wide smile on my face, my arms outstretched, although I have no intention of embracing her. 'Welcome home, Lucille!' I say. 'We've all missed you so much.'

The girl stares at me and her breathing quickens. Then her eyes begin to dart around, searching, I guess, for possible exits. 'You're a bunch of weirdos,' she says, but I hear the crack of fear in her voice.

I keep my fake smile on full beam. 'We're so glad you're back, Lucille. Sit down. Let me make you a cup of tea. We baked you some welcome-home biscuits and Felicity is going to sing for you.'

'I'm not singing for *her*,' mutters Felicity.

The girl isn't listening. 'I've had enough of this!' She turns to lunge at the door, but Harry grabs her arm.

I come up on her other side, not touching her, but close enough that I can whisper in her ear. 'There's no point fighting. Just co-operate.'

She goes nuts. She shoves me away, her eyes now wide with undisguised panic. The shock of being touched stuns me, even though I know this often happens during collection. The place where her hands pressed against me burns.

'Get away from me!' the girl yells. 'You're freaks, all of you!'

She staggers towards the door and discovers it's locked. Next she rushes to the window – also locked – then back to the front door. It's like watching a bird trapped indoors, crazed and desperate to escape.

I've witnessed similar scenes too many times to be upset by this. But that's not true for Felicity. She's so young that she has mostly forgotten her own renewal, so this ugliness is clearly confusing for her. She jams her hands over her ears and squeezes her eyes closed. 'I don't like this! I don't like this!'

Beside me, Harry slowly draws in his breath and I know what it means. It's time.

He produces a rope from behind a chair and, with a single deft movement, lassos the girl. He binds her hands as I pull out the pillowcase from my apron pocket and slip it over her head while she shrieks. It felt brutal the first time I did this to a new Special One, but generally it calms them down.

This time, though, it has the opposite effect. The hooded girl struggles even more. 'My uncle is a judge!' she screams. 'You'll all go to prison for this!'

Felicity is pressed up against the wall now, shaking and white. I should've made her stay outside, down on the farm with a task to keep her occupied, like I've done with the other Felicities.

The girl thrashes wildly. 'You can't do this to me!'

I glance questioningly at Harry. He nods. We must get the Lucille into the changing room as quickly as possible.

'Take some biscuits,' I instruct Felicity, 'and go to your room.' Felicity flees.

Harry bundles the girl into the corridor and I move ahead to open the doors. She fights him every step of the way, swearing at the top of her lungs. It's a long time since I've heard language like that. My entire body is taut.

Should Harry have given her a stronger dose of whatever it is that he gave her? Or have we made a terrible mistake this time? The Lucille is meant to be strong-willed but this one seems *too* strong, too resistant. I can't imagine her sitting in the chat room, answering the followers' questions about beauty and love.

When Harry finally gets the girl into the changing room and I've locked the door on her, all I want to do is slump to the floor. The girl is still in panic mode, screaming for help. I hear her throwing herself at the door, falling to the ground, staggering to her feet again. It's awful.

Shame is a feeling I've mostly learned how to stifle. But sometimes, like now, it rises in an uncontrollable wave.

Harry must guess how I'm feeling. 'We've done the right thing, Esther,' he murmurs. 'We did what we had to do.'

He sounds so sure that I feel a little less evil. For now, at least.

He takes his pipe out of his jacket pocket and leans against the wall. 'Let her tire herself out.'

●

Unlike the rest of the farmhouse, the changing room is made from stone. It has no windows, just a couple of slits near the ceiling and a mesh grate set into the door. It's always dark and cool in there, and I often think that it would make a good place to keep our food supplies in summer. Maybe that's what it was designed for originally. But it's also a good place to keep a newly collected girl. The thick walls almost entirely block the sound of screaming.

Harry smokes his pipe by the locked door while we wait for the girl to calm down. Normally at this time I would be in the kitchen, preparing our dinner, washing potatoes and greens for a simple meal. My stomach rumbles. But in these early stages of reintroduction, it's crucial to stay nearby.

Instead, I work on my mental to-do list and the step-by-step strategy for turning this girl into a passable Lucille. The clothes should be easy enough. The previous Lucille's things are already waiting in a pile on a chair near the bed. Obviously the girl's hair will need dyeing and curling, but there's no point attempting that for at least a couple of days. Acceptance needs to come first, or despair. Either will do.

The girl is still moving around the room, raging and yelling, but she's slowing down now, and her voice is husky from overuse. My own tiredness builds as I watch her through the little grate in the door. She's a mechanical toy – faltering, skipping, failing. When she finally crumples to the floor, it's sudden and shocking – as if someone has yanked out her spine.

I give her a minute, and then when Harry nods I unlock the door. We walk in together and I pull the pillowcase from the girl's head. Her face shines from a smeary combination of heat, snot and tears.

Our new Lucille.

I reach out a hand and lightly pat her shoulder, allowing myself a small moment to enjoy the rare sensation of touching another human being. It's restricted and closely monitored during a collection, but Esther is allowed it.

Lucille pushes my hand away and gives me a look of stony hatred. Her eyes, I notice, are blue. Another thing that will have to change.

I sit down on the floor in front of her, my heavy skirts bunching around me like a deflated hot-air balloon. 'Are you okay?'

'Of course I'm not *okay*,' spits the Lucille. She lifts her bound wrists and points a trembling finger at Harry. 'He kidnapped me!'

Harry gently corrects her. 'I brought you home.'

'Lucille,' I say. 'You are back with us now. With the Special Ones.'

'You're insane,' she snarls.

Harry crouches beside her, the fragrance of pipe tobacco wafting up from his hair and clothes. 'Come on, Lucille,' he says softly. 'Don't you remember us? Don't you remember what happened?'

She doesn't answer.

'You were with us, then you left for a while,' I say. When I'm doing this – *reminding* a girl of who she used to be – I speak in a singsong way, like I'm telling a bedtime story. 'Then Harry found you and brought you home. Our dear, beloved Lucille. Don't worry if you can't remember it all yet. It'll come back to you soon.'

The girl shakes her head savagely. 'I know exactly who I am. I'm –'

I shush her. 'No, Lucille. You're confused. Your soul is still settling. False memories are blocking the pathway to remembering who you really are. But the knowledge will return soon, I promise.'

There's another small shift in the Lucille's expression then, so subtle that only Harry or I would be likely to spot it. Doubt. This is good, as uncertainty opens up the opportunity for a new version of the truth to be slipped into a person's mind. The version that is needed to survive in here. But obviously there's still a long way to go.

'Who exactly do you think I am?' she asks. Her speech is still slightly slurred, but it's rapidly getting sharper. We need to work fast. The hours after Harry first brings someone back is when they are the most open to having ideas implanted. The ideas burrow deep into the still-groggy mind and begin to grow.

Harry hands me a small-scale copy of our photograph for Lucille. I show it to her and tap the dark-haired figure on the left. 'This is you here,' I say. 'Your name is Lucille.'

Beneath the streaks of tears and snot, her face is very pale. 'That photo must be a hundred years old. How could it possibly be me?'

I lean forward. If I say the right thing now it could mean the difference between an easy transition for this girl and weeks of hardship for everyone. 'You are special, Lucille,' I say in my lullaby voice. 'You are one of *the* Special Ones. Just like Harry, Felicity and me. We live here on the land together, away from all the evils of the modern world. We are spiritual farmers who lovingly tend to our followers, shepherding them through the difficult times.'

'They worship us,' puts in Harry.

The girl lifts her eyes to him. 'Worship?' It's clear she likes the word. The Lucilles always do.

'Yes,' says Harry. '*Worship.*'

She looks back at the photo again. 'That can't be me,' she whispers, more to herself than to us. 'No-one can live that long.'

She's resisting it – of course she is – but at least she's listening.

'Imagine pouring milk from one glass into another,' I say. 'The milk stays the same, doesn't it? It's just the glass that has changed.'

The Lucille gives a tiny, almost imperceptible nod. I suppress the smallest flare of triumph.

'Well, your soul has always lived here with us,' I explain. 'But your glass needs changing over time. Each time the glass renews, it messes with your memory for a little while. Kind of like the bubbles of froth you get in milk after pouring. They go away and the surface steadies again, doesn't it? It's a natural part of the process. Inside you're still our Lucille. You'll see.'

I've recited this passage many times. More times than I care to think about.

Lucille's eyes are wet. 'But what happens to my – to the other soul? Which was already in this body that Lucille has now been *poured into*?'

'There was no other soul,' I say, allowing a note of sadness into my voice. 'That body was just a shell. It moved and talked, but there was nothing real inside. Not like now.'

Lucille is shaking her head, but I can tell I've struck a nerve. We all have that sense of emptiness inside, but it's worse for some of us than others. It goes deeper and stays longer. It's what Harry saw in the food court. It's what *he* recognised in me.

I stand up, smooth down my skirts. 'You'll see how different you feel in a day or two, Lucille, as your soul clears.'

'We're really glad to have you back,' Harry tells her and he sounds so genuine that I have another momentary flicker – is it possible Harry believes all this is actually real?

When he offers her a hand, the Lucille allows him to help her up off the cold stone floor. I smile to myself. Harry's charm is hard to resist. He leads her to the small cot in the corner and she sits down with a snuffle, raising her bound wrists to wipe her nose.

Then Harry gently takes the picture from my hand and shows it to Lucille again, pointing to the other figures. 'That's Felicity,' he tells her. 'The little girl who was in the kitchen before. She helps her followers remember what it's like to be a child. How to play, how to laugh, how to be filled with lightness and wonder.'

Poor Felicity. She didn't look so full of light and wonder when she fled to her bedroom. I will have to make an extra effort to be kind to her over the next few days.

'I'm Harry, obviously,' he continues with a smile. 'I work on the farm and produce the food we eat, teaching our followers how to harness the sacred bounty of the sun, earth and rain to provide sustenance.'

'Don't forget kidnapping,' the Lucille says, coolly. 'You could teach them about that as well.' And then suddenly she looks at me. 'Did he kidnap you, too?' she asks. 'Is that how you ended up here?'

I look away, my face flushed. Harry laughs good-naturedly. 'It's called a collection,' he says. 'Your soul is still settling into its new form. You'll remember everything soon enough.'

Lucille swallows, and looks at the photograph again. She points a finger at the central figure. 'And this is you?' she says to me.

'Yes, I'm Esther,' I say. 'I teach our followers how to heal themselves with natural remedies and how to find inner harmony and balance.'

Lucille leans closer to the image. 'She does look a lot like you.'

I smile serenely. Esther's verification smile. 'She *is* me.' I sound like I believe it. 'And you *are* Lucille.'

The Lucille bites her lip, staring at the image. 'She's a little like me, I guess,' she admits. But then she shakes her head vigorously, as if trying to stop something from taking hold. 'But it can't be –'

'Yes, Lucille,' I say firmly. 'That girl *is* you. You're Lucille. You help your followers bring beauty to the world, to their homes and to themselves. You teach them how to find love by teaching them how to love themselves. Your followers need you. They've been *waiting* for you to return.'

For a moment, Lucille's dirty, tear-stained face is transformed by a tiny smile. I lean even closer, seeking out her gaze. 'I know you want to help them,' I say softly. 'That's what we do. We are the Special Ones.'

Lucille closes her eyes. She doesn't agree, but she doesn't argue either. I glance at Harry and he nods. The process of reintroduction is a bit like repainting a house, and today we've begun to sand back the top layer.

When I look back at Lucille, she's stretching out on the cot, bringing her hands under her head like a pillow. The extreme heat, her emotional exhaustion and whatever Harry's given her have taken their toll. Within a few minutes, she's fallen into a deep sleep.

When he's sure she's out, Harry gently unbinds her wrists. She hardly stirs, though her skin is rubbed raw in places.

'I'll leave you to it,' he whispers, winding up the ropes, and I unlock the door so he can leave the room.

Once the door is relocked, I remove the girl's clothes. It's difficult to do because she is a dead weight, and yet I need to be quick and careful to avoid waking her. Also, I know *he* still frowns upon my touching skin if I can help it, even today.

I check that she is decently covered by the sheet as I bundle her into Lucille's long white nightgown. When I leave the room, I take her clothes with me and put them directly into the stove.

CHAPTER SIX

There's no sound from the Lucille during the night, and when I press my ear against the door at sunrise the next morning there's still silence. It's not until we've almost finished breakfast that we hear a muffled thumping from down the corridor.

'Ah,' says Harry cheerfully. 'Someone's finally woken up.'

I peer through the grate in the door to find Lucille standing there completely naked, the nightgown a shredded heap on the ground. She stares back at me defiantly, the hazy look from yesterday gone. 'Let me out, *right now.*'

'Lucille,' I say calmly, 'we're happy for you to join us when you're dressed and ready.'

'Where is my stuff?' she says through gritted teeth.

'On the chair next to you.'

Lucille kicks the chair so viciously that it topples. The clothes tumble to the floor. 'Those aren't mine!'

'Of course they're yours, Lucille,' I tell her. As I move away from the door, something whacks against it from the other side. Probably the chair. I sigh quietly. It looks like she's decided on the slow and painful path. That's so typical for a Lucille.

For an entire week she refuses to get dressed, or even get up. The tactics that usually help in this situation – withholding food, threats – don't seem to affect her and it crosses my mind that she might be prepared to die rather than do as we ask. Something else occurs to me too. Maybe the problem actually lies with me. Maybe I'm losing my ability to pull off this sort of transformation.

One morning I come in to find that she's tipped a full bedpan onto the ground and smeared the contents everywhere. Any sense of triumph or relief I had at this girl's arrival here has long vanished. I feel her glaring at me as I silently clean up the disgusting mess.

I fetch a basin of hot water and hand her a sponge and some soap. She eyes these with displeasure. 'I want a shower.'

'Sorry,' I tell her. 'This will have to do.'

'Where do you get this horrible soap from?' she says, examining it with a frown.

'It's homemade. From fat and lavender.'

Lucille drops the soap like it's crawling with maggots. 'I'm not washing myself with *fat!*'

'That's up to you,' I say mildly. Given the state of her hands, I'm confident she'll change her mind. She does, eventually, and when she's finished I pass her a cloth to dry herself with.

'Are you going to bring me my clothes now?' she says. 'My *real* clothes I mean, not that stupid costume.'

I stand up and sigh dramatically. 'Fine,' I say. 'You win.'

I leave the room, locking it behind me, and go to the kitchen stove, where I scrape a little of the soot into a bowl. I bring it back to Lucille. 'This is what's left of them,' I tell her.

The Lucille clenches her jaw like she's trying not to scream. I'm surprised. Up until now she hasn't held back on anything.

'Please just let your soul settle, Lucille,' I tell her. 'The Special Ones and our followers are eagerly anticipating your return, but your soul needs to fit comfortably beneath your skin first.'

I leave her standing there and lock the door behind me. I'm growing tired of her childish behaviour, and I'm also getting worried. What if we never transform this girl? What then?

•

When I walk in the next day, I'm astonished to find Lucille wearing her pantaloons and petticoat, the corset in her hands.

'How do you put this thing on?' she asks, holding it out to me.

'I'll show you,' I say, hoping she can't see how relieved I am she's given in, how close I was to despair.

'It's so uncomfortable,' she complains as I tighten the laces.

'You get used to it,' I say, cheerfully. I'm pleased. The clothes fit perfectly. Harry has judged her size well.

'What were you like when you first came here?' she asks me, curiously. 'I've been trying to imagine it – you at high school, or at the movies with friends – but I just can't. How long were you locked up in this room for? Did it take long for you to – you know – *accept* it?'

I turn away, so she can't see the tremble in my hands. 'I have always been here,' I say, as calmly as I can.

Luckily Lucille has already lost interest in the question and turned her attention back to herself. 'Can I see myself in a mirror?' she asks.

'We don't need mirrors here,' I tell her.

She gapes at me.

'The Special Ones watch only their *inner* selves,' I explain. 'The outer self – the glass – is irrelevant. Don't you remember that from when you were here before?' Lucille shakes her head. 'Well, you will. And you'll soon find that life is much more meaningful and rewarding when you're not obsessed with trivialities like physical appearance.'

This is a classic Esther line. It's also a lie. Lucille stands utterly still and silent as I help her into another petticoat and then her skirt and blouse.

I step back to evaluate my work. 'You're already looking a lot more like yourself, Lucille,' I tell her.

Lucille snorts under her breath. 'I bet I still look like me,' she mutters.

Unfortunately, she's right. There are many other changes required yet. Her hair, for instance. And her eye colour. Until the new Lucille looks just like the one in the photograph, I can see it'll be hard for her to fully accept her new situation.

The queue of followers wanting to speak to Lucille grows every night. I keep assuring them it won't be much longer now, hoping that it will be true. And then one evening I log on to find the followers buzzing with news – something we have heard nothing about. *He* has sent them all a message saying that Lucille will rejoin the house in ten days' time.

My stomach lurches. The Lucille is far from ready. But time has run out. In desperation I actually consider tying Lucille up while she's asleep and doing her hair that way. But I know that wouldn't work. Lucille needs to accept what is happening. She needs to believe in it.

●

It's a huge relief when I unlock the changing room the next morning to find Lucille fully dressed and, by the look of her face and hands, clean. Maybe that's why the message was sent to the followers. Perhaps he sensed a change in the Lucille that we had failed to see.

'How big is this place?' she asks. 'There's a garden or something isn't there? Where does it end?'

'The farm is a few kilometres wide,' I tell her, putting down her tray of food, which includes some tiny, very sweet strawberries that Felicity proudly presented to me yesterday. The guiding word is *growth*.

'Hang on. We're on a farm?'

I laugh. 'Didn't you notice the animals outside on your renewal day?'

The Lucille shakes her head. 'I don't remember much at all about getting here. I'm pretty sure that guy drugged me. You know, because for you lot it's bad to look in a mirror but it's okay to spike someone's mango smoothie.'

'We have chickens and a couple of goats for milking,' I tell her. 'We had a cow too, for a while.' I'm glad she doesn't ask what happened to the cow. She'd probably never use the soap again if she knew. 'Harry and Felicity grow all our vegetables and fruit out there too.'

I feel Lucille's sharp gaze on me. 'Is there a fence?'

'Yes,' I say. 'A really solid one with barbed wire on top. Only Harry can go through it, when it's opened by *him*.'

'I guess it's a high fence, right?' says Lucille, her eyes dulling.

'Oh yes,' I say. 'We are very well protected in here.'

The last Lucille tried to climb the perimeter fence. I'd just dozed off one night when I was woken by screams – the sound of someone in extreme pain. Then there was the sound of Harry thundering down the corridor. I waited in my room, heart thumping, until I heard Harry return.

'Esther!' The tone of his voice let me know that this was one of those *special circumstances* when it was okay to leave my room during the night. I ran down the corridor to find Harry standing in the kitchen holding Lucille, hysterical and covered with blood.

I moved around briskly in my nightgown, grabbing my herbal ointments and making bandages from old sheets while Harry soothingly told the Lucille that everything was fine, everything would be all right.

But everything wasn't all right. The very next morning, the Lucille's renewal notification arrived.

'Do we ever get to go out?' asks Lucille. I turn and fold up her nightgown – a replacement for the shredded one – so she can't see my face as I answer.

'No,' I say. 'There's no need. Only Harry goes out sometimes.'

'What makes him return?'

It's startling to hear her voice the exact question I've had in my own head so many times. 'He returns because he belongs here,' I say, Estherishly. 'Just like you belong here. Our four souls are intertwined.'

'Well, I definitely don't belong in this awful room,' says Lucille, looking around the tiny, dark space with hatred. 'When can I go into the rest of the house?'

My heart leaps – she's never shown the slightest interest in doing this before – but I must be careful not to share how desperately we need her out there.

'Once you've finished your transition,' I say, firmly. 'Then and only then.'

Lucille pulls a face. 'You mean dye my hair, don't you? And wear those clothes?'

'That's part of it.'

'So once I've *transitioned*,' she says, rolling her eyes, 'then I can go to the farm, right?'

I shake my head. 'Only Felicity and Harry are allowed into the farm. Your territory ends at the garden gate.'

Lucille's face creases into an expression of resentment and annoyance that is becoming all too familiar. 'But that's not fair! Why don't *I* get to go to the farm?'

'Because your area is the house and garden.'

'But I want to go wherever I like!' She pouts. I half-expect her to stomp her foot.

'Want has nothing to do with it,' I shoot back. This girl should be happy that she at least gets to go into the garden. My territory ends with the verandah.

●

Lucille sulks for the rest of the day.

'Leave her be,' says Harry, when I tell him. 'I think she's close to coming round.' He doesn't mention the countdown for Lucille's expected re-entry to the house, but I am sure he's thinking about it just as much as I am.

I am not so optimistic, but when I take in her evening meal, she asks me what Lucille is supposed to be like. 'I need something to help me remember,' she explains.

I hurry to the bookshelf in the parlour and bring back Lucille's leather-bound remembering book. My hand is shaking a little as I open it to the section covering the sorts of questions Lucille takes during evening chat sessions.

What is true love and how can I find it?

What makes someone beautiful?

Why am I always so lonely?

Each question is accompanied by various Lucille-esque responses to select from, depending on the nuances of the situation.

Lucille flips through the section, the gilt-edged pages glimmering. Then she looks up at me. 'Am I expected to learn all this off by heart?'

'Yes,' I say and wait for the inevitable eye-roll or face-scrunch.

But they don't come. Instead, Lucille simply stretches out on her bed, the book open before her.

●

Later, when Harry asks me how the day has been, I tell him that I think Lucille is starting to accept who she is. I can hear the surprise in my own voice.

'That's fantastic,' says Harry, clearly relieved. It's not just that Lucille is expected back in the house in only a few days. We're also overdue for a verification, and when that comes Lucille will need to be perfect.

●

The following morning when I go to the changing room to give Lucille her breakfast, I'm almost excited. How much of her remembering book will she have read?

I unlock the door and go in. 'Lucille?'

There's a whooshing sound and a terrible pain in my head that crumples me to the floor. The room whirls, ceiling and walls spinning wildly. I look up, skull throbbing, to see Lucille leaning over me with one of the bed's wooden legs in her hand and a venomous smile on her face. She jumps over me and runs out the door into the corridor.

'Lucille!' I've bitten my tongue and my mouth is thick with blood. 'Come back. Don't be stupid.' There's no reply.

She doesn't get far. Harry overpowers her before she's even reached the kitchen. Despite my thumping head I manage to stagger out to help him, and together we tie her up again, rapidly passing the rope between us as the Lucille thrashes and sobs. Felicity sits eating her breakfast in the kitchen, watching us impassively. The girl's hysteria doesn't seem to bother her any more.

'She's not Lucille, you know,' Felicity says just as we finish tying her up. 'She'll never fit in here.'

I frown at her. It's dangerous to speak like this. But secretly I think she's probably right.

•

Only when Lucille is safely back in the changing room does Harry untie her. Immediately she drops to the floor like a dead weight, all the fight seemingly drained from her. I sit outside her door for a while, running my fingers over the sore bump on my skull, even though I have lots of chores I should be getting on with. Maybe I'm hoping my being here will help. Maybe I'm just too exhausted to do anything else. I sit there for hours, watching as thin slits of light slowly trace a path across the floor and wall of the corridor.

We can't go on like this, I think. *We'll have to start again with a new girl.* But this is such a terrible, overwhelming prospect that I squash the thought immediately. We have to make things work, however impossible that seems.

I'm so deep in my gloom that when Lucille abruptly taps on the grate of the door, I'm startled.

'I'm ready,' she says. There's something different about her – I notice it immediately. Her voice has changed.

'Ready for what?' I say, getting up and looking at her through the grate.

Lucille's eyes meet mine. 'For transition.'

CHAPTER SEVEN

After it's washed, I discover that Lucille's hair has a natural wave to it that, she admits, she usually blow-dries out. It should be easy to encourage it into ringlets, especially when it's been wrapped in rags overnight.

'See?' I tell her. 'That's even more proof that you really are Lucille.'

Lucille nods slowly.

I dye her hair over a basin that I bring into the changing room. Lucille bends her head over it without saying a word. She also submits to the brown contact lenses without a fuss. The change these two alterations make is astonishing.

'*He* will be so pleased with you!' I tell her.

Lucille's eyes may be brown now, but they're as sharp as ever. 'Who is *he*, exactly?'

I slip into the familiar chant. '*He is the floor beneath our feet and the roof above –*'

Lucille cuts me off impatiently. 'Yeah, I read all that in the remembering book. But who is he really? Does he live here at the farm somewhere?'

'Of course not!' I say. 'He lives out there, on the other side of the fence. But he sends us messages and watches over us.'

'So none of you have met this person?'

Her questions make me nervous. It'd be so easy to slip up and say something wrong. 'Not in person,' I answer cautiously. 'Look, your memories of him will return with time. The only thing you need to know right now is that he is there to guide and protect us.'

'But protect us from what?'

I give her the best answer I can manage. 'From everything *out there.*'

●

Four days before Lucille is due to rejoin us, Harry and I decide to bring her out for a test run. When I tell her that she can have breakfast with us the next morning, her face lights up. 'I can leave this room?'

'Yes.' It's nice to see her look happy for once. But I still have my reservations. 'Make sure you're ready when I knock tomorrow.'

She nods. 'Don't worry. I will be.'

And, sure enough, when I unlock the door the next morning Lucille is sitting on the edge of her bed, dressed and with her dark curls neatly pinned back. Her hands are folded in her lap, her expression demure.

'Ready?'

'Ready,' she says, sounding excited and a little nervous. When I bring her into the kitchen, Felicity's eyes widen with amazement.

'You *are* her, after all!' she breathes and then astonishes everyone by running over and hugging her. Lucille doesn't try to push her off. Possibly she's too stunned.

Harry stands up and pulls out a chair for Lucille. 'It's great to have you here with us,' he says gallantly.

'Thank you,' she says.

For a moment, my eyes meet Harry's and we exchange a grin. So far, so good.

Today we are having scrambled eggs cooked in the butter I made yesterday. Using the churn is hard work but I find it strangely enjoyable. I love the way the cream transforms – separating and solidifying, becoming something utterly different from what it was before.

Lucille looks down at her plate, frowning. 'Can't I have toast instead? I don't like scrambled eggs.'

'Today's word is *quiet*,' I tell her. 'Toast is too noisy.'

'What is *that* supposed to mean?'

'Every morning *he* gives us a word to guide us through the day,' I say as patiently as I can. Lucille should already know about this from her remembering book. 'Today's word means that we must eat quiet food, speak quietly, have quiet thoughts.'

'But that's so dumb!'

Felicity eyes her disapprovingly, putting a finger to her lips. 'Don't you *know* what quiet means?'

My heart begins to pound as Lucille pushes away her plate. 'I can't believe you all just accept this stuff,' she says loudly. 'You just go along with it all. We should be able to walk wherever we want. There's a big fence around this place, right? It's not like we can go very far.'

'Lucille!' I hiss warningly. It's not just herself she's endangering; it's all of us. What must *he* be thinking, watching this scene? My hands begin to sweat.

Lucille goes on as if she hasn't heard me at all. 'My remembering book is so full of rules – and most of them are so ridiculous! Like that one about none of us being allowed to dance.' Lucille shakes her head. 'I mean, seriously? If we're so "special" how come we're not allowed to have any fun?'

Harry seems as calm as ever. But I'm not Harry and I can't stand this any longer. I jump up and grab the Lucille by the arm.

'What are you doing?' she screeches.

'You're going back to the changing room!' I tell her. My fingernails dig into her skin as I drag her back. I can't believe she would be so stupid. She knows better than to fight me, at least – but she keeps complaining about the ridiculous rules even after I've slammed the door in her face.

When I return to the kitchen, Harry says to me, 'You did the right thing,' but I am not so sure he means it. I peek at his face and it's ashen. It's clear that he has the same concern that I do – that there's no way Lucille will be ready to join us by the end of the week.

•

It feels like I've only just drifted off to sleep when I wake again with a start, my heart racing. I can hear something out in the corridor. Someone calling.

'Esther? Are you awake?' Even when I realise, with a flush of relief, that it's just Harry out there, my heart still pounds.

'Is something wrong?'

'I received a message,' he tells me, his voice just on the other side of my door. 'We're doing a sharing tonight.' Before I can say anything, he adds, 'Lucille has to be there too.'

'Really?' I can't imagine Lucille standing there and confessing to the mistakes she's made. I doubt she thinks she's made any.

'Yes,' says Harry. '*He* was very definite about it.'

I get up. 'I'll go and get her,' I say. 'You wake Felicity.'

●

Lucille sits up as I walk into the changing room with a candle held high.

'What's going on?' she says. There's a glimmer of fear in her eyes. *Good.* This is what she should be feeling. It's what I feel myself.

'Get dressed and you'll find out,' I tell her. 'And make sure you behave yourself. Believe me, you don't want to make any mistakes tonight.'

Lucille dresses quickly and silently while I wait. Her breathing is rapid, unsure.

When she's done, I lead her down the corridor to the parlour where Harry and Felicity are already waiting, hands folded in front of them. Lucille hovers in the doorway. 'What's going on?' she says.

'We're doing a sharing,' I tell her. 'It's when we four come together and share with the others the mistakes we've made. The things we're feeling weighed down by.'

'And then what?' Lucille asks, suspiciously.

'Then we wait to see who feels the burden of their guilt the most,' I say. 'And that person ...'

Harry finishes the sentence for me. 'They are given a chance to have their burden taken away from them.'

I glance at him. I suppose that's one way of putting it.

'What if I don't feel guilty about anything?' says Lucille.

Harry smiles. 'I'm sure you'll think of something.' He stretches out a hand towards her. 'Come on, Lucille. Come and join us.'

Lucille doesn't accept his hand, but walks over to where he and Felicity are standing. My insides squeeze together at the thought of what I must share. *I grabbed Lucille by the arm and dragged her back to the changing room.*

'Should I go first?' asks Felicity.

I start to say yes, but Harry holds up a hand. 'No. Lucille must start.'

Lucille crosses her arms angrily. 'I'm not saying anything!' she says, her voice cracking at the edges. 'Why should I? It's all of *you* who should be feeling guilty about what you've done to me, keeping me locked up, not feeding me properly, not letting me shower or speak to my family.'

She pauses for a moment, swallowing and shaking her head. 'I'm the innocent one! You have *no* idea how hard this has been for me.'

'I know you don't really feel like that, Lucille,' Harry says gently. 'I reckon you're actually feeling pretty bad about how you've been acting.'

Felicity gives a little squeak of anxiety and I can tell she's expecting what I'm expecting. That Lucille will completely lose it now.

But Lucille doesn't say a word. When I tilt my head, I'm shocked. She's *trembling*.

Harry's eyes are fixed on her. 'This has been hard for you, hasn't it?' he says softly. 'Letting go of everything you thought was true. Finding out who you really are. We've all been through it too, don't forget. We're not mad at you.'

I am, I think.

'We just want you back,' he continues. He sounds sincere. Perhaps he is. We're under a strict deadline to reintegrate her, after all.

Lucille suddenly lets out a low moan. It's a shocking sound, something that seems to come from deep within her. I hear Felicity's breath catch.

But Harry seems unfazed. 'It's okay, Lucille. What matters is that you accept the truth now. And you do, don't you? You do accept that you are a Special One.'

Lucille chokes again and nods, her tears falling freely.

Harry moves so he is standing in front of her. 'Poor old Lucille. You feel bad, don't you? Bad about fighting the truth for so long.'

'Yes,' wails Lucille.

'It's heavy, isn't it, that guilty feeling?' says Harry quietly. 'We've all felt it.'

'It's pushing me down,' says Lucille, panicked. 'I can hardly stand up!'

Harry places his hands on her shoulders. 'Let it push you. Don't fight it.'

Lucille collapses to her knees, head bowed, chest heaving.

I turn to Felicity. 'Get the wheel.'

Felicity hurriedly fetches the box on the mantelpiece. She doesn't look *pleased* exactly as she hands it to me, but she definitely doesn't look as sorry as she does when it's Harry who's about to receive punishment.

'You can go,' I tell her, as I remove the wheel from the box and set it up on the floor.

'No, let me stay,' she pleads. 'I want to see what she gets.'

I start to argue but Harry stops me. 'Let her stay.'

I spin the wheel and Felicity crouches down beside me. Lucille remains where she is, motionless. Even her trembling has stopped. Felicity watches the spinning wheel intently. The candle on the mantelpiece makes the wheel form strange, amoeba-like shadows on the floor.

'Cellar!' announces Felicity, as the wheel finally stops.

Cellar. The worst one of all.

Lucille doesn't react. It's just a word to her at the moment. She'll find out what it means soon enough. Harry and I go over to the rug and roll it up together, revealing the trapdoor in the floor. Harry pulls on the worn brass ring.

With a shudder the cellar door lifts, releasing a whoosh of stale air from deep below the house.

Harry goes over to Lucille and holds out his hand to help her up. 'Come on, Lucille,' he says. His voice is so kind and patient. Almost loving.

Lucille looks up at him and, after a slight pause, takes his hand. I think for a moment that Harry is going to get down into the cellar too, but just at the edge he stops.

Lucille stops too and looks down. 'I have to go in there?' she says. She sounds very young, very small.

'It won't be for long,' Harry reassures her. I hand him a jug of water from the side table and he in turn holds it out to her.

I keep waiting for Lucille to wake from her strange, trance-like state and start yelling that we're crazy if we think she's going down there. I almost *want* her to. But Lucille just nods and takes the jug. Then, daintily lifting her skirts, she descends obediently into the cellar.

The trapdoor slams down over her and Harry fixes the catch in place. He makes an odd noise and I think at first it's from the effort of manoeuvring the door, which is heavy and awkward. But then I glance at his face.

'Harry?' I whisper. 'Are you all right?'

'I had to do it,' he mutters. His voice is so strange suddenly, so fierce! 'Going down there is her only hope now. And ours, too.'

I'm not sure I understand exactly what Harry means, but I recognise the emotion. The survival urge forces us to do things we don't want to do. Sometimes terrible things.

I nod slowly. 'We had no choice,' I murmur.

CHAPTER EIGHT

The cellar punishment can only end when *he* sends a message to Harry. Usually no more than a single day passes before it arrives, but this time a whole two days go by without a word. I start to get concerned. Lucille is meant to move into the main part of the house with us in the next couple of days. As I walk around doing my chores I imagine her below me, alone, without food and with nothing but spiders for company. I spent a day and a night in the cellar once, for forgetting to leave the tonic out on the kitchen table. It felt like I'd been there for a year when the trapdoor finally opened and I was released. Time goes very slowly in the pitch-black.

Another day passes and my thoughts become darker. How long could Lucille last down there with that single jug of water? How much longer will the punishment last? Has *he* forgotten about her? Then something truly terrible occurs to me. Maybe she's being abandoned down there. Left to die.

The more I think, the more certain I am that this is what's happening. I'm not sure what to do. Pull up the trapdoor and let her out? Smuggle some food and water down to her? Or leave her to her fate to protect myself? *I'll wait one more day*, I think, hating myself for being such a coward.

And then, after breakfast the following day, Harry comes up to me and says, 'It's time to let her out.'

'Really?' For a moment I'm trembly with relief, but almost immediately fear clutches at me again. For the first two days I had heard the occasional noise from below the floor, which I assumed must have been Lucille moving around. But there were hardly any sounds yesterday and nothing at all so far this morning. I'm terrified of what we might find when we open the trapdoor.

Felicity wants to watch but there is no way I'm letting her see what might be down there. I shoo her off to collect the eggs.

Harry and I roll back the rug again and then he pulls open the trapdoor. I peer into the blackness, hoping that Lucille will stampede up the stairs. There's no sound from down there.

'Maybe she's dead,' I whisper. Dead from dehydration or hunger. Dead from a spider bite – or one from a snake. Dead from loneliness and fear.

Harry shakes his head. '*He* wouldn't let that happen.' Does he really believe it? I can't tell.

I lean over the dark square, plunge my head into it. 'Lucille?' I call. 'You can come out now.'

There's silence. Nothing.

'I'll go down and look for her,' says Harry, his face grim despite his mild tone. 'Maybe she's asleep.' But suddenly there is the sound of footsteps – very, very slow ones – and I glimpse a flash of white in the darkness.

My heart stops as a figure floats from the gloom. *Of course it's Lucille*, I tell myself. And it is, but she's different. A layer of dust and dirt has settled on her, fading her hair, covering the colour in her skin. She looks older. Drained.

She climbs the stairs rigidly, mechanically, like a thing that's been wound up and has no choice but to go, go, go. Even her expression has changed. The glimmer has left her eyes. Now they're blank.

Harry reaches a hand to help her out, but she doesn't seem to see it.

I hold out a glass of water and a hunk of bread and butter I have prepared for her. Something bland but filling. 'Here.'

She accepts the water silently, drinks it, then hands back the empty glass. 'Thank you, Esther,' she says. Her voice makes me shiver. It doesn't come from her body now but from somewhere far away or long ago. 'I need to go and clean up,' she says. Then she floats off down the corridor. I glance at Harry. He looks relieved.

'It's happened at last,' he says. 'She's one of us now.'

I nod but, inside, I'm not so sure that's really what's happened.

●

I look up from laying the breakfast table to find Lucille standing there, making me jump. She has washed, changed her clothes and redone her hair.

'What can I do to help, Esther?'

'Nothing, just sit down!' I say, my voice overly cheery as I attempt to cover my ill ease. 'Ah! Here's Felicity with the eggs.'

Felicity stops just inside the doorway when she sees Lucille there. 'You're out of the cellar,' she says. She sounds a little disappointed.

'I'll take those,' says Lucille, holding out her hand for the basket.

'No, really,' I say. 'It's fine. I'll take them.'

Lucille shakes her head stiffly. 'It says in my remembering book that Lucille should assist Esther whenever she can during mealtimes.' She takes the egg basket and goes to the pantry.

Felicity looks at me, eyes meaningfully wide. I make mine big in return. Harry walks in, grinning.

'What do you think, Esther?' he says, sitting at the table. 'Is it time for Lucille to move out of the changing room and back into her bedroom?'

He makes it sound like there's an alternative. Today is the deadline for Lucille to rejoin us. Still, Lucille doesn't know that and it won't hurt her to think we have some power over what happens to her. I turn to Lucille. 'Would you like that? To live out here with the rest of us?'

'Only if you think I'm ready, Esther.'

Her new voice gives me the creeps. I force myself to smile. 'You're ready. I'll show you your room after breakfast. It's just as you left it.'

•

Lucille's bedroom is the biggest one, and has the best view. From her window it's possible to see out over the kitchen garden, and also to catch a glimpse of the world beyond the perimeter fence. *Outside.*

Jutting up on the horizon, far beyond the fence, is a brick tower – tall and cylindrical, although slightly narrower at the top. It looks like it might belong to a factory, and although it's probably no longer used I still find myself checking it for smoke or steam whenever I'm in Lucille's room. I've never seen any, but on bright days I can just make out lettering on the tower, written with different coloured bricks – *OWN.*

Maybe it's a fragment of a word, or they're simply someone's initials. But for me they act as a constant reminder: *You are on your own.*

Lucille doesn't notice the tower when I take her in later that morning. There are too many other things to absorb, especially after so many days in the changing room and then in the cellar.

She walks slowly around the room, picking things up and putting them down again. She lifts the small vase of flowers I sent Felicity out to pick and breathes deeply, her eyes closed.

Felicity hovers in the doorway. 'Do you think she likes them?' she whispers and I nod.

Lucille stands in front of the picture I've hung near the door. It's a watercolour of a young girl sitting in a garden, sewing. 'This isn't right,' she says, suddenly. I'm not sure what she means. Lucille swings around and faces me, frowning. 'It's not right,' she says again firmly, and then points to the opposite wall. 'This picture would look much better over there.'

I suppress a smile. 'You can move it,' I say. The Lucilles always like to make minor adjustments like this. 'I'll ask Harry to hammer in a nail for you.'

It's Lucille herself who suggests she join evening chat that night. 'My followers have gone for long enough without my guidance,' she says, tucking a glossy ringlet behind her ear. 'And I'm sure *he* must be wondering what's taking so long.'

I examine her face, trying to work out if she's sincere. I'm still not sure what I think of this new Lucille.

'She's got a point, Esther,' says Harry. 'It has been a very long wait for the followers.'

'Well, okay,' I say, making it seem that I'm the one allowing it. 'I guess we can try it.'

Lucille looks genuinely thrilled and Harry shows no sign of concern, but the uneasy feeling in my chest continues to grow.

I take Lucille to the chat room early so I can explain how everything works. She reacts as everyone does when they see the sleek modern glow of the computers – with disbelief and excitement. 'How do they work? I thought we didn't have any electricity.'

'We have a solar generator,' I explain. 'Harry looks after it.'

'Why don't … can you remind me why we don't use it for other things? Like lights and refrigeration?'

It's something I've often wondered about myself. How much easier my work in the kitchen would be if I could put things in a freezer, or keep milk fresh for more than a single day in hot weather! But making life easier has never been the focus here. As it says in our books, *hard work is our greatest teacher*.

'The generator is just for the computers,' I tell her.

'So which one is mine again?'

I point. Lucille sits down in front of it and stares at the blank screen.

'Remember, the chat is monitored,' I tell her, a warning note in my voice. 'If you say anything inappropriate to the followers, there will be repercussions. And not just for you.'

She turns her head. Smiles her new, unnerving smile. 'Oh, Esther. You don't need to worry. Have you forgotten who I am?'

•

The chat session goes well – better than it usually does with a freshly renewed Special One. When I glance over Lucille's shoulder to check her answers, I can see she's writing with the ease of someone who's been doing this all her life.

I find myself noticing how similar she is to the previous Lucilles. The Lucilles always have a particular way of sitting at the keyboard during chat – their backs ruler-straight, eyes intently focused. They all twirl a lock of hair around their index finger when they're thinking, too.

When the session ends, Lucille is glowing. 'They were all so desperate to talk to me! They really *valued* my opinions and advice.' She flicks back her hair. 'We're kind of like gods, aren't we?' she muses, more to herself than anyone else.

Did I feel like this after my first chat? Probably, back when I still believed I really was Special. I definitely don't feel like that now. Now I live in constant fear of making a mistake and exposing myself as a fraud.

'Like gods?' I say lightly. 'Well, yes. Exactly.'

●

With Lucille living among us, life on the farm finally returns to normal. She takes over her allotted duties and I'm free to get on with the tasks that have been mounting up: pickling vegetables for winter, giving the cutlery a thorough polish. And, of course, the followers fall over themselves with delight at finally having the four Special Ones back together again.

I feel myself relaxing, just a little. I should know better.

'I've had a message from *him*,' says Harry one morning, between mouthfuls of porridge. 'It's verification day.'

I knew we were due for this, but all the same I instantly lose my appetite. 'Today?'

'Oh no,' whispers Felicity. 'When?'

Harry calmly takes another spoonful of porridge. 'Directly after breakfast.'

'Verification,' says Lucille. 'That's when we stand underneath the photograph in the parlour. To check that we haven't changed.' She has developed a way, I've noticed, of asking questions that sound like statements. It's a clever tactic.

'Exactly,' I say.

I'm glad she doesn't bring up the topic of what happens if someone *has* changed. If they've become too tanned, lost weight, or put it on, if their hair has become lighter or darker. Maybe the eyes look more tired than in the photograph, or more afraid.

As I clear away the breakfast things, my eyes flit over Felicity, checking for faults. I've been so focused on Lucille recently that I haven't been as vigilant about checking her appearance. Luckily I fixed her roots a couple of days ago, but she is getting tall – worryingly so. Her hems should've been let down in an attempt to disguise her growth. But there's no time for anything like that now. No time to do anything but hope she'll think of bending her knees slightly under her skirt during the check, to shrink her height a little.

We file into the parlour. 'Try and match the photo,' I murmur to Lucille.

Lucille snorts and without a word she goes and stands beneath the photograph hanging above the mantelpiece. Almost instantly her face assumes the exact expression of Lucille in the image. It's amazing how well she does it. A little disturbing, in fact.

Harry, Felicity and I take our places too, and I try, as always, to channel Esther's face – that blank unreadability. We are so silent that I can hear the buzz of cicadas outside.

Directly in front of us is the window, the curtains drawn. I focus my eyes on the place where the two drapes of material meet and overlap.

The most difficult part of verification is knowing how long we are meant to stand in position. With some things we are given very detailed information on how a thing must be done, but it's the opposite with verification. There's no flash of a camera, no voice or bell that rings to let us know when our time below the photograph starts or ends.

At first I made everyone stand in position for hours – sometimes for the entire day – until we were all dropping from fatigue. Eventually Harry gently suggested that it probably wasn't necessary to stay there quite so long. Now I wait until I have counted to a thousand in my head.

A numbness creeps up and around me as I stand there. I start to feel lighter and lighter, until it's as if I've left my body altogether and am floating somewhere near the ceiling. I look down at the four of us standing there, so eager to please our invisible director, hoping that he will continue to cast us in the roles we've been selected to play.

Nine hundred and ninety-eight, nine hundred and ninety-nine ...

'That's enough, everyone,' I say, and we all take in a breath at the same time.

Lucille looks around expectantly. 'Now what?'

'Now we get on with our normal tasks,' I say. I'm already on my way to the door. I've got a lot to do today and less time to do it in than usual.

Lucille frowns. 'But we need to find out if we've passed or not.'

'*He*'ll let me know tonight,' I tell her. 'Before evening chat.' I hurry out before she can ask anything else.

CHAPTER NINE

There are no messages waiting when I log in.

'You passed,' I tell Lucille. 'We all did.'

'Sometimes we fail, though,' she says.

I think about the first Lucille. The one whose weight loss I'd been unable to disguise, despite the padding stuffed into her corset.

'Yes.'

'And then we are renewed.'

I turn away from Lucille, wiping dust from a shelf to hide my expression. 'Yes. Then we are renewed.'

Lucille is silent for a moment, then shrugs. 'Well, I've only just been renewed. So that wouldn't happen to me again so soon.'

She's wrong. It doesn't matter how long it's been since your last renewal. It can happen at any time. But I keep quiet. Let her feel safe, for a while at least.

●

The Lucilles always like to rearrange things in the house and, sure enough, by the end of the week all the furniture in the parlour and kitchen has been subtly reorganised. I don't mind. The adjustments bring a freshness to the farmhouse. Lucille is in the *eager to learn* phase, and that's fine by me too. With each skill she acquires – *re*acquires – my life becomes a little easier. She quickly masters the basics of mending and darning, and goes into battle against the dust with a determination I've never seen in a Lucille before.

'Hard work strengthens our minds as well as our bodies,' she tells me one day. Her eyes shine with the light of the newly converted. 'Hard work is our greatest teacher.'

●

When she's ready for it, I unlock the fabric cupboard and show her the contents. Lucille runs her hand down the bolts of cloth. 'Harry brings this for us,' she says.

'Sometimes he does,' I say. 'But sometimes it just appears in there.'

Lucille narrows her eyes. 'Just *appears*?'

I nod, like there is nothing strange at all about a cupboard that fills itself. 'Yes. Sometimes when I get up in the morning, there will be items we need waiting for us on the kitchen table. Sometimes things are already locked away in the cupboard. Never food or water, though. Just things we can't make here.'

'But how does it get there?' Lucille persists. 'Does *he* bring it?'

I think about the night-time noises, the creaks that sound so much like footsteps. The prickling sensation I feel thinking that someone's out there, prowling around. The way the purple bottle empties overnight. 'I don't know,' I admit, because there's nothing in any of our books that explains the things that appear. Or disappear.

There's a silence. '*He* takes care of us,' says Lucille, eventually.

'Yes,' I say. 'He does.'

Lucille runs her hand down the cloth bolts. 'This is for me to use,' she says. 'To sew things we need.'

'That's right,' I say.

'I've … *forgotten* how to sew,' says Lucille, chewing her bottom lip. Another Lucille characteristic.

'That's okay,' I say. 'I have a simple project that will help you remember.' I hand her a rectangular object made from white cotton.

She turns it over and over, puzzled. Then she looks up brightly. 'It's an eye mask!'

'It's a sanitary napkin,' I tell her. I know it's mean to laugh, but it's hard not to at the horrified look on her face.

'I don't want to make *sanitary napkins*!' she objects. As her voice rises in pitch and volume, I catch a glimpse of the girl she was when she first arrived. It's somehow reassuring to see she hasn't completely disappeared.

'Fine by me,' I say. 'But you're going to need them.'

Lucille looks down at the napkin in her hand as this information sinks in. 'How many do I need to make?' she asks, finally.

'That depends,' I say, 'on how frequently you want to wash them out.'

She blanches. 'Can't I just throw them away once they're used?'

I pull a shocked expression as I open the door to the parlour and usher her inside. 'Of course not. That would be terribly wasteful.'

When I look in before dinnertime, there's a tall pile of napkins on the table beside Lucille. 'Not bad!' I say, examining them. Her stitch work is surprisingly good.

'It had to be done,' she says, as if her objections from this morning never happened.

I smile at her, pleased and a little astonished at how well she's handled it. 'We need to start on some new clothes too. Maybe tomorrow?'

Lucille nods her head. 'Yes, of course.'

A few days later, she presents Felicity with a skirt. It's very simple and slightly wonky, but Lucille has clearly spent a lot of time on it. She's even embroidered little bluebirds around the hem.

Harry is full of praise for her work. 'She's changed so much,' he marvels to me, later.

And it's true, she has. But although I'd never say it to Harry, this new obedient, rule-following version makes me nervous. Unlike with the loud, angry girl who first arrived, I have no way of knowing what she's thinking.

•

Although life in the house has settled down, there are still things on my mind. The heatwave, for instance. The garden is rapidly wilting and turning brown. The trees look limp and tired. Felicity mentions that it's taking her a long time to pump water out of the well. Bushfire thoughts steal hours of sleep from me. What would we do if everything outside started to burn?

He *would rescue us*, I tell myself. *He'd open the gates and let us out. We are the Special Ones, after all.*

But there's always another voice in my head that persists in asking, *But what if he doesn't?*

Harry returns one evening with a look I recognise. Something is wrong. He doesn't say anything while Felicity and Lucille are there, but when we are alone in the kitchen after dinner, he leans against the sink as I do the washing-up.

'The main water tank is almost empty,' he says quietly. 'I'm not sure how much longer it'll last, even if we're very careful. I'm giving the animals water from the creek but that's almost dry too.'

I've suspected this for a while now – the water Felicity brings in has been getting progressively murkier. But when I actually hear Harry say it, I feel a squeeze of panic. 'What can we do?'

Harry breathes out slowly and, for once, he has no reassuring words. 'We just have to hope it rains.'

I say nothing. We both know from experience that relying on hope is pointless.

That evening during chat, I find myself doing something I haven't done for a long time – fantasising about asking the followers for assistance. *We are about to run out of water. Please help us.*

Maybe someone will come to our rescue. But there's no question that *he* would see what I'm writing, and I would end up being punished, or renewed. It's strictly forbidden to complain to the followers, or ask for assistance.

I force the thoughts from my mind and busy myself answering a follower's question about curing her insomnia – *you need to listen to your inner voice and then reassure it* – instead.

Another week passes with no rain. Then another. Every day I get up and look out the window to be faced, yet again, with a smooth, blue, cloudless sky, the air more stifling than the day before. One by one the chickens die of heat exhaustion, then – even worse – one of the goats. I salt the meat, wrap it in cloth and hang it in a dark cupboard to cure.

We stop using water for anything other than drinking and even that is strictly rationed. Everyone's hair and skin takes on a greyish-brown tinge. My tongue develops a furry coating.

I dream of water – especially of the fountain in the park near where I used to live. In the dreams I am standing in the fountain's base, my head tilted back to watch the shining ropes of water arc up into the air. Droplets tumble down towards my outstretched arms and opened mouth but disappear before they touch.

Harry stops whistling, but works just as hard as ever. 'The rain will come,' he promises every time he catches me staring out the window at the sky. 'Don't fret.'

We have another sharing night, and this time Felicity manages to drop to the floor first, for the heinous crime of keeping a tomato all to herself one day. 'I was thirsty,' she admits.

My heart aches for her. But she seems pleased. 'This time you don't get punished,' she whispers to Harry.

When she spins, the arrow lands on *knife*.

Harry shakes his head. 'No. Spin it again.'

It lands on *knife* again.

'Let me do it,' says Harry, taking the spinner. The result is the same. Felicity protests but Harry insists on trying once more. *Knife.*

'Let her receive her punishment!' says Lucille, exasperated. 'It's clearly what *he* wants!'

Felicity places her small hand on Harry's arm. 'It will be okay.'

I get up and go to the chest in the parlour, unwrapping the punishment knife from its dark square of velvet. Its handle is carved from bone and its hooked blade gleams.

Felicity's hand trembles, just a little, as she takes the knife from me. 'Not too hard,' I whisper. 'It doesn't have to be hard.'

Harry seems frozen, his eyes fixed on Felicity. She lays the knife across both her palms and then squeezes her fingers tightly around it. Her eyes shut and a moment later there's a trickle of blood from each side of her clenched fists. The blood drips onto the kitchen floor.

Two minutes isn't even long enough to boil an egg. But right now, it feels like an eternity.

The moment I've mentally counted to 120, I say, 'Time's up, Felicity. Let go now.'

Her hands are a mess of dark blood but her face is radiant. 'Now it will rain,' she says. 'I've fixed it.'

The certainty in her voice makes me want to cry.

•

I dream about being cornered by a large dog, growling and baring its teeth at me. As it's about to bite, I see that it has the face of a man – someone I've never seen but somehow recognise.

Then there's a loud crack, and I wake just as the room is illuminated by a flash of light.

At first I don't dare to believe it. *A storm?*

There's a knock on my door. Harry. 'Esther! Come out and look at the rain!'

'But we're not allowed to leave our rooms during the night –'

'It's okay,' says Harry. 'These are definitely special circumstances.'

I pull on my robe and rush to the kitchen just as the rain starts to fall, drumming on the verandah roof. Harry is already there and Lucille and Felicity join us a moment later. Together we gather around the window and stare out.

'I knew the cut would work,' says Felicity triumphantly, clasping her bandaged hand against her chest. 'I just *knew* it.' She turns to me, her face bright with a sudden idea. 'Can I go outside and run in the rain? I'm so hot and sticky.'

'Yes,' I say quickly, before I can think of a reason why she shouldn't.

Lucille shakes her head disapprovingly. 'You shouldn't let her do that.'

'Felicity shows our followers how to take a childlike joy in the world,' I point out. 'And what could be more joyful right now than playing in the rain?'

'It's not appropriate behaviour for a Special One,' says Lucille.

'I disagree,' says Harry, suddenly. There's a smile in his voice. 'Come on, Felicity. Let's go together.' He hooks an arm through hers and they head outside.

'Well, don't expect me to help if you ruin your clothes,' Lucille calls haughtily after them.

But I doubt they even hear her. The rain drowns out every sound.

I press my nose against the windowpane and watch them in the moonlight – Harry, so tall and broad, and Felicity's small frame. Both of them are completely drenched. They dash around crazily, spinning and leaping and whooping.

'Dancing is forbidden,' Lucille states.

'They're not dancing,' I say, although I'm not really sure about that. 'You should go out there too. Cool down and wash off some of the dust.'

'I'm not dusty,' says Lucille indignantly, but I am sure I catch longing in her voice. 'I will wait for the morning and wash in the proper way.'

I go outside and stand right at the edge of the verandah – the limit of Esther's territory – enjoying the cool breeze. The wind blows some of the rain in my direction, peppering my skin. The lightning continues to flash, the thunder to boom.

Harry turns towards me, his eyes focused on a point just above my head, a broad grin on his face. He beckons. I laugh, shaking my head. He's teasing, of course. He knows as well as I do that Esther is not allowed to leave the house. But it's a beautiful idea, twirling in the rain with Harry.

'The sky looks so beautiful!' cries Felicity, her face turned upwards.

'I used to love lying outside, looking at the night sky,' I tell her, though I shouldn't talk about before. Still, I doubt *he* could hear me over the sound of the storm. 'It seems to go on forever, doesn't it?'

When I glance back at Harry, he's stopped moving. I'm surprised by how sad he suddenly looks. But a moment later, Felicity calls to him and then he's smiling again, swinging her around.

I feel like I've been holding my breath for a month and have just let it go. I picture the tank and the dam steadily filling with water, up and up and up.

When Harry and Felicity finally come back inside, I find towels for them and then the three of us go to the kitchen window again, somehow unable to drag ourselves away from the sight of so much water. Lucille stands a little way behind, periodically reminding us that it's time we all went to bed, that we'll be exhausted in the morning.

I know she's right, but I stay anyway. The rain shows no sign of stopping – if anything, it's getting heavier. I'm glad. I hope it rains forever.

There's a sudden clap of thunder so loud that the house shudders and Felicity yelps. 'Hmm,' I say thoughtfully. 'That was a sign.'

Felicity looks at me, eyes wide. 'A sign of what?'

'A sign that you should go to bed, young lady!'

Felicity protests, but I can tell she's actually glad to go. She's almost tripping over from tiredness and she knows as well as I do that there will be no sleeping in.

'Don't be scared by the storm,' I say as I tuck her under the covers, being careful not to touch her.

'I'm not,' she says, yawning. 'This is my storm. I made it happen.'

●

In the morning the air is fresh and cool. There's a small puddle of rainwater on my floor, shining like silver. I get up and look out at the garden, marvelling at how sparkling and clean everything looks. The leaves of the eucalyptus trees gleam. Even the old factory tower on the horizon looks new, its lettering more distinct than usual.

There's a magpie warbling somewhere nearby and I suddenly feel a rush of something I haven't felt in a very long time. *Joy.*

Everyone is in a good mood over breakfast, and Felicity skips off happily to the farm with Harry, although she must still be very sleepy. I tidy up and put on a loaf of bread for lunch (the guiding word is *fresh*).

I'm just settling down to help Lucille put darts into the bodice of the dress she's making, when I catch sight of Felicity hurrying up from the farm. She does this occasionally. Sometimes she's forgotten something, and sometimes there's good or exciting news to report – newly hatched chicks, for instance. But it's clear from her face that the news she's bringing today is neither good nor exciting.

Harry, I think instantly, my stomach dropping. I'm already at the door when Felicity bursts through, straight into the parlour.

'What's wrong?' My throat constricts.

At first Felicity is too breathless to speak. She holds out something in the palm of her hand. Two small peaches, green and hard. 'The peach tree was struck by lightning last night!' she blurts, between gasps. 'It's split in half. Right down the middle!'

I steady myself against the doorframe. This is very bad news. The tree has always produced impressive amounts of fruit. We eat peaches almost every day in summer, and I preserve as much of the excess fruit as I can for winter.

I realise Felicity's eyes are on me. 'It'll be okay, won't it?' she says.

'Of course it will.' I force the words out. 'Everything will be fine.'

She nods, but I suspect I've offered her no real comfort.

Harry is determinedly cheerful during lunch, but it's different when he has a chance to speak to me privately. 'The storm has done a lot of damage,' he mutters. 'All the tomatoes are gone, the wheat is pretty much destroyed. Some of the carrots will be edible, maybe the potatoes. Not the beans, though.'

I keep my lips pressed tightly together, afraid of what might gush out if I open them. This is my fault for hoping the rain would never stop.

'Hey, it's okay,' says Harry, glimpsing my face. 'We'll survive it. The important thing is that we're together.'

I know he's trying to cheer me up, but I wish he hadn't said this. It feels way too much like tempting fate.

●

We'll survive. We'll sort it out. We'll make it work.

I keep repeating these sentences to myself as I go about my tasks. If I think it enough, maybe it'll come true. There's still a month or so of reasonable weather ahead. Time enough to plant new vegetables, Harry assures me – quick-growing things. And *he* wouldn't let us die, would he? Maybe he'll take pity on us and I'll wake one morning to find emergency food rations on the kitchen table, just to tide us over until the new crops grow.

And at least we have water now, I keep reminding myself.

But I carry with me the feeling that something terrible is about to happen.

One morning I wake slightly later than usual – the morning light is already halfway across my windowsill – so I hurry directly to the chat room to receive my instructions. The guiding word is *reduce* and I walk back to the kitchen, wondering how to model it for the followers. How can I reduce anything from the little we have left? I jump when I see Harry standing there – still and silent – with an open envelope in one hand and a card, smelling of flowers, in the other. His eyes brush past me and there's something in that glance, something so primitive and chilling that I freeze.

'Harry? What is it?' But I know. Harry hesitates for a moment and then turns the card around so that I can see it. The writing is formal and elegant, like you might see on an invitation to a fancy party.

Harry, please commence preparations for your renewal.

CHAPTER TEN

When I first read about renewal in my remembering book, before I'd actually witnessed one, I thought it must be like having a makeover. I figured that when a Special One was renewed, they would go away for a couple of days and come back with a new outfit or hairdo or something.

But then the first Felicity was renewed. When her replacement arrived, I realised in horror that I was expected to pretend this terrified stranger was the same person who'd left a few days earlier, just that she looked a little different and had *forgotten* who she really was.

I know only too well what happens to the new ones who are brought here. Gradually they are convinced to change, moulded to be who we tell them they are. But there's another unanswered question: *What happens to the ones who leave?*

At first I tried to convince myself that they simply returned to their old lives. But I know that can't be true.

He is many things, but merciful is not one of them. It would be too dangerous. Their families would want to know where they have been. The police would become involved. The girls might be able to figure out the location of the farm. There is no way he would risk that. The much more likely explanation is that renewal means death. And once I realised this, I decided that renewal was something to avoid, no matter what.

I started keeping a list in my head of what kinds of actions or mistakes seemed to trigger a renewal. I decided that if I could pinpoint the causes I could somehow protect myself – and the others – against it. Many things were obvious. Neglecting chores, for instance, or doing them poorly. Dancing. Sleeping in. Talking about life before coming here. Doubting or questioning anything to do with the Special Ones.

But I knew that avoiding renewal had to mean more than just sticking to the rules. It meant being like Harry. Harry, who never loses his temper or complains. Harry, who follows the rules without a blink, no matter how crazy they seem. Harry, who, if he doubts the purpose of the Special Ones, never lets it show on his face. And something dawned on me.

He's acting. Doing it to survive.

I decided I'd follow his lead. Be the perfect Special One. Do what was asked of me without question or complaint.

I buttoned myself into my Esther costume and threw myself into the part. This, and only this, would keep me safe.

But Harry's renewal notice has changed that. Its arrival means that I was wrong. Because if someone as faultless as Harry can be renewed, then clearly none of us are safe.

●

Esther must announce the news of a renewal to the Special Ones as soon as possible. But at breakfast I can barely speak, let alone deliver this terrible information. I can tell Harry is waiting for it, but he doesn't push me either.

Lucille and I spend the morning doing the first half of the weekly clothes and linen wash – a mammoth task that takes all our time and energy. There's no chance of discussing Harry's news and, besides, we all need to be together.

Harry and Felicity return for lunch, Harry doing a good show of being as cheerful and calm as ever. Felicity and Lucille don't seem to notice anything different, but I can hear the tension in his voice.

In the kitchen, Felicity hands me a basket full of hard, greenish peaches. 'That's all we could save,' Harry says apologetically. 'I hope they will see you through for a couple of weeks at least.' His carefully chosen words are painful to hear. *You*, not *us*.

As we sit down to eat Harry asks, 'Any news?' He's prompting me.

I shake my head. *Not yet,* I think. Saying it out loud – *Harry's being renewed* – will make it official. I sit and stare at my plate. I can't eat. Can't talk. My hand shakes as I raise my glass, and the water tips onto the table. I jump up to grab a cloth and catch Harry's kind eyes watching me, his face full of sympathy. After a couple of seconds he looks away.

I am suddenly ashamed of myself. I'm such a coward.

'Esther.' Harry's voice is surprisingly firm. 'It's time to tell them.'

Lucille latches on instantly. 'Tell us what?'

Usually I plaster on Esther's *good news* smile when I make a renewal announcement, but I can't manage it this time. 'Harry has received his renewal notice.' The words are a string of thick sausages being pulled from my mouth.

Felicity's chair clatters to the ground as she leaps up and flings herself onto Harry. 'No! You're not allowed to go.'

'Renewal is a necessary process, Felicity,' Lucille says disapprovingly. 'It's a reason to celebrate.' I want to hit her. She gets up and walks over until she's standing in front of Harry. 'Congratulations, Harry,' she says loudly, one hand on his shoulder. 'I look forward to seeing you again in your new vessel.'

Harry nods at her. 'Thanks, Lucille,' he says and pats her hand.

What does it feel like, being touched by Harry? His skin is probably a little rough from all the hard labour he does, but I imagine it being warm and also somehow soft. A feeling rises inside me – tingling and very un-Esther-like.

Lucille withdraws her hand and gives Felicity and me a disdainful glance. 'This is a moment of great happiness for Harry.'

Rage flares up in me, strong and bright. *Happiness?* And before I can stop myself – 'Are you really that stupid, Lucille?'

Lucille's eyes bulge. 'You can't talk to me like that, Esther!' she says, spluttering with indignation.

'Can't I?' I shoot back. I know I'm close to losing control and, even more dangerously, I don't really care.

'Esther, calm down,' Harry says. I know he's looking into my face, and I keep my eyes averted. But in my peripheral vision, I see him stretch a hand towards me as if he's planning to touch my arm.

I freeze, wondering if he'll dare. Perhaps he's decided that it wouldn't really matter now that he's being renewed. His finger hovers there, close enough for me to feel (or at least imagine I can feel) the warmth from his hand.

'Harry!' gasps Lucille.

Harry doesn't answer but he puts his hand down again. 'Esther,' he says softly. 'You trust me, right?'

'Of course I do,' I mutter.

'Then you must believe me that everything will be fine. I'm promising you.'

I nod, feeling calmer, even though I know what he says can only be wishful thinking. Because how could everything be fine? I've seen so many renewals and I know exactly what will happen. At evening chat tonight, we'll announce to the followers that Harry will be going away for a short while. *For spiritual revitalising and soul cleansing.* We'll pretend that it's nothing more than a health check-up.

Tomorrow, Lucille and I will start preparing a set of clothes for Harry – the ones he'll wear when he leaves. We'll all behave like nothing terrible is going to happen. In a few days, the second message will come – the one announcing that today is *the* day. Harry will dress in his renewal clothes. We will share a last meal together. Then Harry will walk out the door and I will never see him again.

●

Time begins passing in morse-code moments: some long and drawn-out, others passing in a flash. Harry and Felicity work on the farm from first light until sunset, planting new crops. I am sure Harry is trying to pass on as much information as he can, and Felicity will try her best to absorb it all – but she is far too young to replace him on the farm in any real way.

It's always been Harry's task to find the new Special Ones when someone is renewed. But who will find the new Harry? *The new Harry.* It's impossible to accept this concept.

One night, as I lie awake in bed, Harry knocks on my door. 'Come out here,' he says. His voice sounds different. 'I've got something I want to show you.'

Quickly I tie my robe around me and hurry to the door. Harry is standing in the hallway, dressed in his day clothes.

'What's wrong? Is someone sick?'

'Everything's fine. I just want to show you something. And before you ask, yes – you can leave your room.'

He turns and walks off down the corridor. I pad along behind. He leads me through the parlour, and when we arrive at the front door Harry opens it wide and walks through.

'Where are we going?' I'm having crazy thoughts. *Harry is planning to run away and he wants me to come with him.* Would I go?

'Don't worry, we won't break any rules,' he says. He steps out onto the verandah, the wooden planks creaking as he walks across to a blanket that has been spread out across the boards. Harry sits down on it and pats the space beside him. 'Come and sit,' he says.

I hesitate. I am fairly sure that *he* has not really given me permission to be out here in the middle of the night with Harry. And although I've never spotted any cameras out here that doesn't mean they're not there.

'Don't be nervous,' Harry says in a low voice. 'I won't do anything … *forbidden*, I promise.'

I feel a strange flip in my stomach, but I'm not sure if it's relief or disappointment. I walk over to the blanket and sit down at the far edge of it.

'Now,' says Harry. 'Look up.'

I tilt my head up and gasp. A hole has been cut in the roof of the verandah – about the size of a large door – and through the gap I can see the sky, black and cloudless, strewn with stars.

'What do you think?' says Harry. He seems nervous and so adorably shy that my heart pirouettes.

'Did you do this?' I whisper. 'For me?'

'Yes.'

'But why?'

'Because you said the other night that you used to like lying down and looking at the night sky,' he explains. He sounds a little embarrassed. 'I wanted you to have the chance to do it again, before I left.'

I begin to laugh. 'So – you destroyed the roof just so I can see the stars?'

'Well, I didn't *destroy* it,' says Harry, laughing too. 'I just removed some of the galvanised iron. It'll be easy enough to put it back on later.'

What Harry's done is crazy, and here crazy usually means dangerous – but that just makes it more beautiful. A gesture like this could easily make a person cry. But I manage, somehow, to keep myself together. 'Thank you,' I whisper.

'My pleasure,' he whispers back. 'Now, look up and enjoy the view.'

It sounds boring, I know – lying on hard, rough, splintering floorboards, staring up into blackness. I'm sure the me from *out there* would've thought so. But I could have stayed there all night, watching only the tiny flickering and pulses of light from the stars.

Harry doesn't try to talk to me, and at first I'm silent also. Then I discover that my face is wet, and I'm crying.

'Esther?' Harry says in a low voice. 'Are you okay?'

I close my eyes, willing the right words to come. 'I'm just so happy for you and the journey you're about to take,' I manage to whisper. There are tears spilling into my hair. 'The process of renewal strengthens the soul. I'm … looking forward to meeting you again.'

I've never been able to speak freely with Harry. And soon he'll be gone, without even knowing my real name. But I hope, harder than I've ever hoped for anything, that right now he understands how much he's meant to me. How I'll never forget him.

Out of the corner of my eye, I see Harry open his mouth, like there's so much he wants to say. Then he closes it again. 'Me too, Esther,' he says finally. 'Me too.'

●

I'm not sure how long we lie there – maybe a couple of hours, maybe more – but finally Harry sits up. 'You'd better go to bed,' he says, regretfully.

'Yes, probably.' I sit up too, but neither of us stands. Out in the darkness, I hear a bird begin to sing. Dawn must be near.

'Harry?' I say. 'Thanks.'

He turns and looks at me for the count of three, and I'm startled by how strong the expression is in his eyes. He seems frustrated and angry – things I've never seen in him before. Finally, he looks away. 'It's nothing,' he mutters. 'You deserve way more.'

When I go out onto the verandah the next morning, the galvanised iron is back in place on the roof, with no sign of the hole.

It crosses my mind that it didn't really happen. But then Harry emerges, humming 'Twinkle, Twinkle, Little Star', and I know it was real.

●

I feel stronger after the star-gazing night. More able to cope. And there's plenty of work to distract me from my darker thoughts, too. Lucille has to make Harry's renewal outfit but as she is still *remembering* how to do it, Esther is allowed to help. I end up doing a lot of it myself.

There is a drawing in my remembering book of how everyone's renewal outfits should be, and Harry's consists of dark trousers, a waistcoat and a white shirt. I draft the pattern from this and, sitting in the changing room together, Lucille and I cut material and begin to sew.

It's strangely soothing to work on these clothes, despite what they represent. I linger over the details and take extra care that the seams won't irritate or rub, that everything is perfect. Lucille clearly finds my involvement a challenge to her skills, and makes a big show of checking everything I sew, pouncing delightedly on any tiny mistake.

But her behaviour can't touch me. My head is full of other things, like my increasing obsession with trying to decide what it was that Harry did to trigger this renewal. Was it because he encouraged Felicity to jump around in the rain the night of the storm? Was it because of the chicken he slaughtered after he finally found the new Lucille? Or was there something else that happened that I don't know about? Maybe something happened that he never told me about. Exhausted, I try to block the thoughts, but they creep in anyway.

Finally, the news I've been dreading comes. 'The second message arrived,' says Harry one morning, showing me that hated creamy envelope. 'I'm leaving tonight.'

He says it in the same way he might say 'I'm off to milk the goat', but I can tell he doesn't really feel that way, no matter how well he hides it.

Lucille raises her hands above her head. 'Let our joy rise up and take flight!'

I fight the urge to throttle her. How can she be so naive? Harry catches my eye and winks at me. *Don't worry,* the wink is saying. *Don't be sad.*

But how can I not worry? How can I not be sad? I rise silently and go to the changing room to finish working on Harry's shirt.

●

Harry spends the entire day down on the farm, not even returning with Felicity at lunchtime. 'He's got too much to do,' she reports and I try not to feel hurt that he doesn't want to spend every last moment he can with us. With *me*.

He joins us for dinner, clearly exhausted but still managing to smile. I bring out some of the dried goat's meat and place it in front of him.

'Who's hungry?' he asks, lifting the plate and offering it around.

I shake my head. I couldn't eat anything. Felicity also refuses.

Lucille accepts two slices. '*He* doesn't like food to be wasted,' she says piously.

I clear the table and wash up mechanically. *Don't think, don't feel …* It's the only way I'll get through this.

Then we gather in the parlour, standing in the four points of a square, heads bowed, eyes closed. Lucille, Felicity and I begin to recite. '*We are sending Harry on his journey today. We wish him well …*'

I try to disconnect myself from the words, pretending I'm back at high school – my old one, from before we moved – performing in the end-of-year play. I have no doubt that *he* will be watching us carefully right now, zooming in on our faces to check that we have the right expressions, that we look as if we're happy and excited. Then Felicity and Lucille sing the renewal song, the only song that Lucille is allowed to sing: '*Oh, you Special One! Your journey starts today. Make haste with your return …*'

I keep my head bowed throughout, throat tight. For once I'm glad I'm forbidden to sing.

Afterwards, Harry goes to the changing room, where Lucille has laid his renewal outfit out on the cot. There are no specific clothes for the rest of us on renewal day, but

Felicity wants to put on the bluebird skirt that Lucille made for her. Unfortunately, it's nowhere to be found and she has to select something else.

Lucille, Felicity and I wait outside the closed door. Lucille knits her fingers together. 'I just hope they fit,' she keeps saying, as if she alone made them.

Harry steps out of the changing room a few minutes later, straightening his collar. The clothes fit perfectly. I knew they would. 'How do I look?' Harry asks, sounding a little self-conscious.

All I want to do is stare at him. Fix him in my mind. He is so familiar and so *there*, somehow, that it's impossible to believe that in a short time – just a few minutes – he will be gone. 'You look just right,' I manage to say.

And then it's time. The final farewell. We must, as always, stay calm and controlled, no big displays of emotion are permitted, because we must all pretend that a Special One leaving for renewal is just a temporary thing. That they will soon return, the same – if not better – than before.

At the front door Felicity and Lucille hug Harry goodbye – Lucille in a stiff, formal kind of way and Felicity so tightly and for so long that Lucille finally reaches over and peels her off him. I step forward, my hand outstretched to take Harry's. The cameras will surely pick up my nervousness, but I can't help it. This will be the first – the only – time I can touch him.

There is another reason I'm on edge. I have something to give Harry. I prised it out of my mattress this morning and I've been carrying it around with me ever since, waiting for this moment. It's the twenty-dollar note that I've managed to keep hidden ever since I first arrived here. It had seemed like such a lot when it was still in the mattress. But once I fished it out, it suddenly seemed like nothing. I'm still determined to give it to Harry, though. Maybe it will help with whatever he finds waiting on the other side of the gate.

Harry's hand slips into mine and I press the folded bill into his palm with my thumb. I see surprise flash momentarily on his face. Then his thumb curls in just enough to secure the gift and he looks me steadily in the eyes. *Thanks*. Two seconds. Three. Four. Five. He squeezes my hand tightly in his.

His skin feels just as I thought it would – a little rough but also warm. I was worried I would cry at this moment, but I feel strangely calm. 'I'll miss you,' I whisper.

His eyes are shiny. 'I'll miss you too.'

'That's long enough,' says Lucille.

I'm hoping Harry will ignore her, but after one last squeeze he pulls his hand from mine. The money is carefully hidden from view and he slides it into his pocket. A moment later he removes his hand and presents me with something. 'For you.'

It's a small comb with very fine teeth, smooth and pale, carved from bone.

Lucille frowns. 'We don't give gifts for renewal,' she says, but both Harry and I ignore her. My fingers curl around the comb. I can still feel the warmth of his hand on mine, encasing it in a glow.

'I'll see you again soon,' Harry says. His voice has taken on an urgent tone. But that's probably not so surprising, considering these are the last words he'll ever say to me. 'We're connected.'

He suddenly grabs my hand again, his eyes looking directly into mine. 'Esther. Remember that, won't you? *We're connected.*'

I nod, swallowing hard.

We all walk with Harry to the verandah. This is as far as I can go. Although it is late, the sunset lights up the garden like a stage set. I stand at the edge of the steps and watch as the rest of them walk as far as the garden gate, where Lucille stops. Harry looks back at the house for a moment and I watch him, glowing like an ember. Then he takes Felicity's hand again and walks with her through the gate.

I watch until they disappear out of view into the farm, and then I can only listen as their voices fade. Finally, faintly in the distance, I hear the main gate bang closed.

My entire body prickles like I've been dunked in icy water. It's happened. Harry's gone. Inside, I feel something swing loose, then break.

CHAPTER ELEVEN

For the first few days after Harry's departure, I struggle to move. Even the simplest of tasks – combing my hair, peeling potatoes, nodding – suddenly seem to require monumental effort. I drag myself through the day, cripplingly tired, but also dreading the moment when I go to bed. Bed means having no tasks to distract me.

In quieter moments, I catch myself composing letters to Harry in my head, filling him in on every tiny detail. *I made jam out of the ripest of those peaches you salvaged after the storm. It was a little sour so I stirred some honey into the mixture and it helped. Felicity is being brave, but I know it's hard for her working on the farm alone. She really misses you, Harry. So do I …*

The night-time noises seem to grow louder and more frequent, although maybe it's just that I'm hardly sleeping anymore. Almost every night I think I hear footsteps, which often seem to stop just outside my door. Worst of all are the times when I think I hear the sound of heavy breathing too, coming through my keyhole. *It's just the wind,* I tell myself over and over as I lie there, picturing a hand reaching out towards the doorhandle, grasping hold, starting to turn. I try to work up the courage to fling open my bedroom door, but I can't. I'm afraid of what I will – or won't – find out there.

●

One night after evening chat I linger in the chat room alone, dreading the thought of going back to my room and the night-time noises. I draw out the routine of shutting down the other machines for as long as possible, polishing every surface until it gleams. Then, when there is absolutely nothing left for me to do, I sit down in front of Esther's screen. Stare at it. It looks like a piece of the sky, that unwavering blueness. Something you could float off into.

Just when I'm finally, reluctantly, about to turn it off, I hear it – the ping of a message arriving. This happens sometimes – a follower sees that I'm still online and tries to sneak in a question. Normally I'd ignore it, but tonight I'm eager for distractions. The username – Piper – is not familiar to me.

Esther. A close friend recently gave me twenty dollars and I'm not sure what to do. Should I save it?

I stare at the message and feel a little pulse of hope. *It's Harry,* I think. *He's alive.*

But it might not be Harry. It might be from a normal follower, just asking an innocent question. It might also be a test from *him.* Maybe he saw me slip the money to Harry.

It's too much to fathom and my hand darts out and turns off the screen. I can't answer it now. I need to think. I climb into bed and lie there, heart pounding and the covers pulled up to my nose, trying to decide what to do.

I want with all my heart to believe the message was from Harry. *He's asking if you want him to come and rescue you,* my tired, overly stimulated brain keeps insisting. But I also know that this is very unlikely. It doesn't make sense that anyone could survive renewal. *But maybe he did, maybe Harry's the exception. The only one who made it through.*

Just before dawn, having not slept at all, I get up and dress. I want to go to the chat room before the others in case the message is still there – or any more have arrived. I still haven't decided what I am going to do.

Outside, two kookaburras go through their morning song routine, accompanied faintly by the rooster down on the farm. The house has the stillness of very early morning. I pad down the corridor, instinctively stepping over the squeaky floorboards. I unlock the chat-room door and go inside. The room seems charged, the way the air feels before a thunderstorm. I hold my breath as the screen comes to life. And then I deflate when I see what's there.

Nothing. Absolutely nothing.

The message has disappeared. Maybe it was never there. I bow my head in my hands and nearly burst into tears. I'm so tired.

A voice speaks behind me, making me almost leap from my chair. 'Esther? What are you doing?' It's Lucille, still in her nightgown, watching me from the doorway.

'Just getting on with things,' I reply. In my attempt to pull myself together, I sound terser than I intended.

She leans forward, squinting at the screen. 'Are you about to write a report?' she asks. Without realising, I've opened the form that is used to contact *him* if someone has broken a rule. 'Have Felicity and I done something wrong?'

I quickly close down the report form. 'There's nothing to report,' I tell her. 'Nothing at all.' I click on another icon, one that opens up the most recent message from him. 'Your word today is *trust*.'

•

Why didn't I reply to that message? The thought torments me throughout the day. Of course it's possible that the message was a test from him, or a genuine question from a follower. But now that it's gone I feel almost certain that it was from

Harry. I should've taken the risk. Because what other options do I have now? I'm not safe in here, no matter how obedient I am. Harry's renewal has made that clear.

After evening chat, when Lucille and Felicity have gone to bed, I sit down in the chat room and wait. Hoping what happened last night will happen again, but not daring to believe that it will.

Which is why when the message from Piper appears, long after the chat session has finished, I feel my breath catch in my throat.

Are you there, Esther?

I'm really worried about my twenty dollars.

I think something bad might happen to it, if it stays where it is.

But maybe it's better off there — I'm not sure.

This time I don't let myself think. I just begin typing.

That twenty dollars is at risk. You should save it.

CHAPTER TWELVE

The next message appears almost immediately.

Yes, that's what I thought too.

I can't write anything direct. I can't ask if it's really Harry and, if so, how he managed to survive renewal. But it's not as hard as it could have been. Harry and I have always had to talk in code.

Do you have a savings plan in mind?

It's not a typical topic for discussion with a follower, but *he* has always stressed that we should answer all genuine questions with respect.

Not yet. But I'm working on it. I just wanted to hear if you thought it was a good idea. Something you'd approve of.

I shut my eyes as I type.

It sounds like a wise idea to me. And I'd do it sooner rather than later.

The conversation is making me dizzy, light-headed. Another message appears.

I have to go but I'll contact you again once I've decided on a savings plan.

Just keep being you, Esther. Don't change, whatever you do.

I stare at the final two sentences. They contain a warning, that's very clear. But is it from Harry, telling me to keep my head down and not do anything stupid, or is it from *him*, letting me know that he has his eye on me, even more intently than usual?

Piper logs off before I have a chance to reply.

•

The conversation buzzes in my head, devouring almost all other thoughts. By late the next day I'm convinced I've made a terrible mistake. When I log on to my computer, I am fully expecting to see a message from *him*, telling me he knows what I've done and that I'll be punished for it. Renewed, even. But there's nothing there. Still, I need to be careful.

Obey the rules and act like nothing has changed, I instruct myself. *Just keep being Esther.*

But it's hard. I'm so exhausted, so completely drained. I spend hours awake each night, unable to shut off my thoughts, falling asleep just before dawn – only to wake up as the sun streams in through my window.

Except that one morning it doesn't stream through. Or maybe it does, and in my exhausted state I roll over and fall instantly back asleep. I don't remember.

The next thing I am aware of is Felicity's voice calling to me. 'Esther? Are you all right?'

I open my eyes to see her small face peering at me anxiously. Lucille is behind her, hands on hips and eyes narrowed.

I sit bolt upright. 'I'm fine. Sorry. What time is it?'

'Well past dawn,' says Lucille, scrutinising my face. 'What's going on, Esther? Are you sick?'

'No,' I say. Not that being sick would be an excuse for me to stay in bed, anyway. There have been times in here when I've been almost delirious with fever or weak from flu, yet I've dragged myself from my bed and done my chores as usual. Sickness is described in Esther's remembering book as a sign that the spirit is restless and possibly in need of renewing. I've learned to smother every sneeze, suppress every cough.

'Then get up!' Lucille orders. 'We can't even choose what to wear if we don't know the guiding word.'

I swing my legs over the side of the bed. I say nothing to Lucille, partly because she's right and partly because I've scared myself.

Harry told me to hang in there until he came to get me out, but sleeping in past dawn is one of the primary rules Esther mustn't break. It makes me fear that my self-control – the one thing I've always had in here – is starting to slide away.

CHAPTER THIRTEEN

Felicity and Lucille hover outside the chat room as I check for the guiding word. My nerves flicker as I turn on the screen. Maybe my sleeping in will have already produced a renewal notice. But all I find is the guiding word. *Dare.*

We've never had a word like this before and I'm not sure how to interpret it. As a challenge? A threat?

'What is the word?' calls Lucille from the doorway.

I turn around so I'm looking directly at her. '*Dare,*' I tell her.

Lucille frowns. 'That's a very strange guiding word. Are you sure?'

I gesture to the screen. 'Come and have a look for yourself.'

She hesitates and I know she's weighing up her desire to catch me out in a lie against the risks involved in breaking a rule by coming in here during the day. 'No,' she says eventually. 'I trust you wouldn't lie to us.'

I make a *daring* breakfast – soup rather than the bread or porridge we usually have. Then Felicity goes off to the farm and Lucille goes to the parlour to sew, leaving me alone in the kitchen with a mess to tidy up.

The sleeping-in incident has left me on edge, like I can't really trust myself. Practically every task on the farm has rules or rituals attached to it. There's an order to how the floor must be swept ('from the far right corner to the far left') and how dishes are washed ('first cutlery – largest to smallest – then plates, bowls and pots'). Even the porridge must be stirred in a particular way – twenty times to the left and then twenty times to the right, swapping hands with each direction change. There are so many opportunities for mistakes.

I stare at the pile of breakfast dishes and decide there are too many dangers to start with this task first. I need to do something more straightforward, with less room for error. I look around. The stove. Cleaning it is back-breaking and exhausting but it's also one of the few tasks where there's very little that can go wrong. You stick your head in it and scrub. Maybe by the time I've finished it my mind will have sorted itself out.

I tie on my most worn-out apron and look for the green headscarf I always wear to protect my hair from the grime. But I can't find it, and have to make do with another scarf instead. My chest pinches. *He*'s taking things from us, I'm almost positive now. It's just not possible that I could be so continually careless.

I scrub and scrub, determined that every surface will be spotless by the time I've finished. Despite my tiredness it feels good to be working hard. It keeps my fears at bay. As I work, a chant starts up in my head, going around and around in time to the movement of my scrubbing brush: *Get me out of here. Get me out. Get me out of here. Get me out.*

'What are you doing?'

Lucille is standing behind me, a pair of Felicity's woollen tights dangling from one hand and a darning needle clamped in the other.

'I'm cleaning the stove,' I say.

Lucille folds her arms. 'You were singing. I heard you singing.'

'No, I wasn't,' I say but I'm not sure. Maybe the chant that I thought was only in my head had begun leaking out.

'You *were*, Esther!' she says roughly. 'And you're strictly forbidden to sing. I'll have to report you. Give me the key to the chat room.'

I stare at her, shocked. No-one has ever reported another Special One. There's always been an unspoken agreement between us: we do whatever we can to protect each other.

'You don't think I'm serious, do you?' Lucille hisses.

'Yes, I do,' I say. 'But I'm hoping you'll change your mind. Please, Lucille. Don't do it.'

It's very un-Estherish to beg like this, but I don't have a choice. There's a very, very slight possibility that *he* didn't hear me singing. If I can talk Lucille out of writing the report, there's a chance I'll survive just a bit longer in here. Long enough for Harry – if it *is* Harry I've been writing to – to figure out a way to rescue me. I don't allow myself to think about how unlikely all of this is. 'I've never done anything like this before, Lucille,' I tell her softly. 'You know that. And I promise I won't do it again.'

Lucille hesitates. Maybe she feels sorry for me. Or maybe she's enjoying being the one with the upper hand, watching me grovel like this. She sighs dramatically. 'I won't write it *yet*,' she tells me. 'But that doesn't mean I'm not going to do it at some stage. I'll be watching you, Esther. You'd better be careful.'

I am careful. I do every chore with a self-awareness I haven't required since I first arrived at this place. I check and double-check everything, think carefully before I complete the simplest thing. I've stopped trusting myself. Every action feels like it carries the danger of a mistake. The constant checking slows me down, stresses me out – but it's the only way I seem to be able to function.

It's late in the afternoon, not long before Felicity is due to return, when I hear a scream from behind the house near the woodpile. It's a horrible sound – terrified and pain-filled.

Lucille comes running from the parlour. 'What was that?'

'It's Felicity,' I say, my blood turned to ice. 'Go and see what's happened.' I long to run outside myself. But I can't, I can't. All I can do is pace the kitchen floor and wait.

Finally there are footsteps – slow, staggering ones – on the verandah. I run to the door and fling it open. Lucille is standing there with Felicity bawling in her arms. Both of them are covered in blood.

CHAPTER FOURTEEN

'She's cut herself with the axe,' says Lucille, her voice stuttering with shock.

Felicity's skirt is a mess of dark red and ripped material. She starts shrieking as I carefully lift the layers back to reveal a deep, nasty gash in her thigh, about the length of my palm. Blood wells from the wound.

She needs to go to the hospital, I think immediately, but that's not possible.

I turn to Lucille. 'We have to stop the bleeding. Right away.'

Felicity's whole body trembles as she sobs. Her lips are a frightening shade of blueish grey.

Lucille is frozen in the doorway, her face stricken. 'I don't know what to do!'

'I'll guide you through it,' I say. 'Put her down over here.' I push two of the kitchen chairs together to form a kind of bed. Then I rush around, preparing things. Strips of material. Boiling water. A very sharp needle and thread.

Felicity's eyes are still squeezed tight when I return, but now she's crying so hard she can barely breathe. I crouch down next to her, trying to keep the panic out of my voice. 'Felicity? You don't need to worry. We're going to look after you. You're going to be fine.'

My heart is pounding so hard it hurts. It's one thing to have someone disappear through the gate never to be seen again. It's quite another to have them die here in the kitchen in front of you.

'Felicity, please,' I say, as I jump up and remove the needle and thread from the boiling water. 'You have to calm down.'

Felicity nods but the racking sobs keep pouring out of her. 'I'm *sorry*,' she wails, bunching her hands into little fists.

I take another look at her thigh, where the blood is still gushing, and the fear makes my voice boom. 'Stop it, Felicity!' I command. 'Calm down, *right now!*'

She chokes into a whimper, and lies there, shaking. I loop some thread through the needle's eye and show it to Lucille.

'Wash your hands,' I instruct her. 'You'll have to stitch up the wound.' Lucille shrinks away from the needle. I drop my voice so that Felicity can't hear. 'Lucille, if you don't do it, she could die.'

Lucille shakes her head, fear and stubbornness combined in her expression. 'She can't die. She's immortal.'

I've never had the urge to shake someone as much as I have it now. I thrust the needle in Lucille's face. 'Do it!'

'I can't,' she whispers, her face almost as pale as Felicity's. 'I'll – I'll pass out. I know I will.'

I can see that this is a very real possibility. Reluctantly I realise I have no choice. I'll have to do it myself.

I kneel down beside Felicity and gently lift her arm out of the way to start wiping the area clean with soap and water. Her eyes fly open and she starts to writhe with terror, but I hold her down firmly until she makes a low, shuddering sound and is still.

Behind me, Lucille gasps. 'You're not allowed to touch –'

I cut her off. 'I am the healer, Lucille. Go and make the pepper tea, please. Extra strong, with lots of honey.'

'But I –'

'Lucille!'

She turns and reaches for the kettle.

Felicity begins to whimper as I pinch the two edges of the wound together and push the needle through, and then she's screaming again. I pull the thread tight, and glance up just in time to see her eyes roll back and her tiny body go limp. I never thought I'd feel grateful for causing someone to pass out, but I do. It's better this way. Easier.

I work quickly. Felicity's skin puckers and pulls as the needle passes through it. Four stitches, five, six. It's such a long, deep cut that it feels like I'll never be able to sew it all up but, finally, after ten stitches, it's closed. As I bandage the wound, Felicity's eyes flutter open and I talk to her, trying to coax her into calmness before the terror takes hold again. 'You were so brave, Felicity! It's all over now and you're going to be fine.'

I want so desperately to gather her up in my arms, but instead I rock back on my heels and take a few deep breaths, wiping my hands on my apron. Then I start tearing bandages into strips to dress the wound.

'What were you doing with the axe out there, anyway?' I ask as I work.

'Chopping firewood,' she whispers, her eyes brimming as she looks at me. 'I thought I could do it. I've watched Harry use the axe lots of times.'

I'm wrapping the strips around her leg when Lucille comes back, a steaming cup of tea in one hand. 'I found a biscuit too,' she says, 'but snacking is –'

'Great idea,' I say, plucking it from her fingers. 'Something sweet is exactly what she needs.'

Lucille's hand is trembling as she holds the cup of tea, and her face is still smeared with blood. I suddenly feel guilty for being so sharp with her. She's probably also in shock.

'Thanks, Lucille,' I say, forcing a cheerful tone. Felicity's leg is now covered in an enormous bundle. 'You did a great job of bringing her inside. I know it must've been awful.'

But Lucille isn't paying attention. She has just noticed the blood on her clothes. 'Well, these are now ruined,' she says in a huff.

I roll my eyes at Felicity, who manages a watery smile in return.

•

My chores fall by the wayside for the rest of the afternoon as I tend to Felicity, encouraging her to eat and drink. There are many things to worry about – infection, for instance, how much blood she lost – but I try to keep the anxiety out of my voice. I even find myself thinking crazy things – like if *he* saw what happened, then maybe he'll send an ambulance to collect Felicity. But I know this is very unlikely.

I am vaguely aware of Lucille coming in and out of the room but I'm too occupied with Felicity to pay her much attention. When Felicity has a little more colour in her cheeks, I carefully remove the dressing and check the wound. The skin around the stitches is an angry-looking red and the cut itself is weeping slightly.

'It's going to be okay, isn't it?' says Felicity.

'Yes,' I say. 'Of course it is.'

Lucille has come back into the kitchen again and is hovering in the background, like she's expecting something.

She has changed into a new dress, one that makes an impatient-sounding *swish* as she moves.

I stand up, suddenly exhausted but knowing I still have things to do. 'You must be hungry, Lucille,' I say. 'Sorry there's no proper dinner tonight, but there's still some bread and I can boil some eggs.'

Lucille holds out her hand. 'I want the key to the chat room,' she says, stiffly.

'What!' I can't believe it. 'Why?'

'Firstly, you were humming. Then you touched Felicity. You've been really snappy with me and now you haven't made dinner, which is one of your primary chores.' Lucille folds her arms. 'I have to report you, Esther. You've run out of chances.'

Felicity struggles into an upright position. '*No!*'

'It's okay, Felicity,' I say, surprised by how calm I feel. It's like Felicity's accident has changed something in me. Like I'm no longer scared of what *he*'ll think. Or maybe I'm just too exhausted to care any more. I pull the chat-room key from the chain I keep it on, walk over to where Lucille is standing and hand it to her. 'You go and write your report.'

I drop the key into her open palm. She looks at me, frowning. 'Aren't you scared of being renewed?'

'The process of renewal strengthens the soul,' I say, poker-faced. Then I turn my attention back to Felicity. I'm aware of Lucille standing motionless behind me and then, wordlessly, she marches off down the corridor. A few moments later I hear the rattle of the key in the chat-room door.

Felicity begins to cry. 'You did a good thing. You helped me. *He* won't renew you for that.'

'Exactly,' I say soothingly. But I know enough about him to realise that helping Felicity won't have made any difference.

●

I have no idea what will happen after Lucille's report, and I hardly have time to think about it that evening as I am busy with Felicity. But when I go down the corridor later to prepare for evening chat, I start to feel a little tense. The last late-night message instructed me to *just keep being Esther.* I couldn't have done a worse job of hanging in there if I'd tried.

I start to wonder, with an inner lurch, if I've just lost my only chance of survival. But then again, what else could I have done? Let Felicity bleed to death in the kitchen? I don't regret what I did. Not for a second.

Still, my hand shakes a little as I turn on my own screen. There's nothing there, though. No message from *him*. No renewal notice. When it's time for chat, I go and check on Felicity. She's pale but awake, and struggling into her clothes.

'You should rest,' I tell her, but she shakes her head.

'If I don't go you'll get in more trouble. And it's my leg that's hurt, not my hand.'

I can see there will be no convincing her otherwise.

I find it hard to concentrate during evening chat. I keep looking sideways to check how Felicity is going, but I also keep wondering if he has read Lucille's report yet. I catch Lucille looking at my screen, probably trying to see if I'm writing un-Esther-ish things to my followers. But I don't even care. I just want the session to finish so I can find out whether I'll get a message tonight.

When the session finally ends (and I'm careful not to close it down a moment earlier than I should), I put Lucille in charge of helping Felicity back to bed. She looks at me suspiciously. 'Why can't you do it?'

'Because I have to close down the screens,' I say, in my patient, Esther voice. 'And Felicity will need some help.'

Reluctantly, Lucille leads Felicity off and the moment they're gone, I look back at my screen, willing a message from Piper to appear. And when one does – *how are you, Esther?* – I want to rush to reply. But I need to think my words through carefully. I don't want to make *him* suspicious, should he be looking in on our conversation, but it's important that I make the seriousness of my situation clear.

My role as healer was tested today. Perhaps my soul has grown restless.

The reply is a very long time coming and I feel the panic start to rise. Maybe I'm not communicating with Harry. Maybe I'm talking to some creepy old guy who knows nothing about my situation. The type of person who lurks online, ready to prey on the innocent and the naive – or the desperate, like me.

In the corridor I hear footsteps. The swish of a skirt. *Lucille*. I've got less than a minute left.

> *Piper? What should I do?*

I'm not expecting the reply that comes.

> *This is good, Esther! Renewal is the solution to everything.*

My stomach drops. It's exactly what *he* might say. *No!* I want to write back. *Come and get me out of here straight away! I can't stay in here another moment.*

But there's no time for more writing, even if I dared. Lucille appears in the room and I only just manage to flick off the screen before she comes up beside me. 'What is it, Lucille?' I say. 'What do you want?'

'I've come to help you close down,' she says.

'Only I am allowed to do that,' I tell her. 'You know that.'

Lucille gives a tight-lipped smile. 'Actually, that's not true,' she says. 'I checked in your remembering book. All it says is that Esther must open and close the chat-room door. It says nothing about whether one of us can help with the screens and tidying the room.'

I keep my remembering book tucked away underneath my bed. 'You went into my room?' I say, shocked.

Lucille meets my eye, defiant, unashamed. 'I thought at least one of us should be paying attention to the rules.'

The anger builds inside me, but before I can do or say anything Lucille lunges across and flicks my screen back on. I try to turn it off again but it's too late.

'There's a message there!' she practically screams. 'Who is it from? Who are you talking to? I know you're up to something, Esther! Stop trying to hide it!' Wildly, she kicks at my chair, knocking it over so I'm sent sprawling to the floor. Then she clicks open the message on my screen.

'It's nothing to do with you, Lucille!' I hurl at her as I scramble to my feet. 'It's just a late question from one of my followers. You've got no right to read it.'

But Lucille is staring at my screen. 'It's not from a follower,' she says. Her voice has become strangely soft and she steps away from my screen, allowing me to read the message myself.

She's right. It's not from a follower. It's from *him*. The room is suddenly way too bright for me to bear. I close my eyes and feel my pulse thrum in my ears.

Esther. Prepare for renewal.

CHAPTER FIFTEEN

For a moment neither Lucille nor I say a word. We stand together, staring at the screen in silence. Then finally Lucille turns to me and nods her head. 'Congratulations,' she says, stiffly. 'You were due for it. *Over*due.'

I don't answer. I'm tingling from the news. *It's happening.* The thing I've dreaded and tried so hard to prevent for two years. I always worried that if I got this message I'd collapse on the spot. But I don't. All I keep thinking is that I'll finally be walking through the front gate of this place. And of the small chance that Harry will be waiting for me on the other side.

For the moment I'm not even concerned about what will happen next. I shut down the screen and leave the room, vaguely aware that Lucille is trailing along behind me, talking nonstop. Her words float by unheard. *I'm leaving,* I think. *I'm actually leaving.*

That night, for the first time since Harry left, I fall asleep almost the moment I get into bed and sleep soundly, deeply, undreamingly until first light.

●

It's not until I have to break the news to Felicity the next morning that I start to feel twinges of concern about what's about to happen. She looks pale and drawn when she appears at the table and barely eats a thing. Later, when I change her bandages, I see with concern that the wound is slightly infected. I clean it up as best I can and then try to deliver my news softly, but the moment Felicity hears it she starts to cry.

'Please don't go,' she begs.

I sit beside her, feeling awful. 'It'll be okay,' I say, weakly.

Felicity shakes her head. 'No, it won't. Who'll look after me?'

'I'll still be here, don't forget,' says Lucille, who is loitering in the doorway.

Felicity isn't comforted by this and I'm not surprised. It's hard to imagine Lucille telling her stories or jokes when she's sad.

'You won't come back!' sobs Felicity. 'Harry hasn't and I bet you won't either.'

'Of course she'll come back,' says Lucille, in a tone that is probably meant to sound reassuring. 'And Harry will too. And they'll be all fresh and full of energy.'

Felicity doesn't say anything but a look comes over her face that makes me realise she doesn't believe this. I feel bad for her, but I actually feel bad for Lucille too. It's true that she did her best to get me renewed, but I suppose she was only doing what she thought she had to do. Life will be much harder for her once I'm gone – although she doesn't yet realise it.

My renewal will almost certainly happen in just a few days and there's a lot to do before then. I want to prepare things for Lucille and Felicity, stock up on supplies for them to use after I've gone.

Felicity brings me the last of the tomatoes – a huge effort, given that she can barely walk – and I make as much pasta sauce as I can, sealing it into glass jars and stacking them in the storage cupboard. After that, I bake – biscuits sweetened with dried berries and honey as well as hard, salty, rusk-like bread sticks. The rusks are not exactly tasty but they'll be filling, at least, and it reassures me to know that I'll be leaving behind enough food to keep Lucille and Felicity going for a while.

Whenever I can snatch a moment I write detailed notes, listing all my tasks and explaining how to carry them out. I record the sort of information that I would've found handy when I first arrived. I record most of the recipes I've developed, as well as explaining how to do battle with the stove. I make a detailed explanation of how to set up and shut down the chat room. The notes are for Lucille, as she'll have to take over from me when I go, but they're also for whoever eventually comes to replace me. It's a strange thought – someone else filling my role, wearing my clothes, being the Esther. Maybe, I think ruefully, she'll be better at it than me.

Over the next couple of days I veer from emotion to emotion – nervousness, excitement, terror. The strangest part is how sad I feel. I find myself looking around at the all-too-familiar details of the house and wanting to cry, although that's so stupid. How can I feel unhappy about leaving a place I've felt trapped in for so long? I'll miss Felicity, of course, and I'll worry about her. Her wound seems to be getting worse, no matter how often I wash it or how much herbal ointment I apply. But it's not just that. I've been playing the role of Esther for so long that I'm not sure I'll remember how to be me again – should I even manage to survive the renewal process. But I don't allow myself to think about that.

Time disappears rapidly. Each day evaporates, rising in a cloud of smoke around me. I float along – not yet free, but not the prisoner I was before, either. There are no messages from Piper. I spend the first couple of days hoping Harry will burst through the door and that together we'll get the other two to safety. But as the days pass, I have to admit to myself that this is very unlikely. *He'll be there when you leave the farm*, I tell myself. *It's the easiest way to rescue you.*

Lucille is clearly struggling to finish my renewal dress, so I begin working on it with her. I don't ask her if she needs my help and she doesn't tell me not to. We sit across from each other in the changing room, for hours at a time, heads bent. Lucille has barely spoken to me since my renewal notice arrived but I'm glad for the silence. It gives me a chance to think about what still needs to be done and to continue the silent conversation with Harry I've been holding in my head.

I tell him about my worries. *Felicity is getting weaker and weaker. She needs to see a doctor, take some antibiotics. What will happen once I'm not here? How will Lucille manage? She thinks she knows it all, but she really doesn't.*

One time, as I'm deep in conversation with Harry, I'm startled by a loud sound from Lucille. I look up to see she's burst into tears. 'Lucille! What's wrong?'

She shows me the piece she's been working on – one of the sleeves. 'It's much shorter than the other one,' she sobs. 'And I don't know how to fix it.'

'Hey, don't worry,' I say, coming to sit down beside her. 'We'll just shorten the other one.' For some reason this makes her cry even more.

•

Later that day, Felicity becomes feverish and I put her to bed, even though I know that *he* would not approve. But I don't care. She can barely stand. There's no question of her working, even though this means the animals will not be fed. I am not at all surprised when I log on that evening to find a message from him.

Esther. Your time in your current bodily form is over. Leave the house at dusk tomorrow evening. Walk through the garden and the farm until you arrive at the main gate. Open it and pass through.

That's it. There's no *thanks for the last two years*, or *I'll miss you*. But then, there wouldn't be. I'm not scared, as I thought I might be. I'm relieved. Felicity can't get out of bed, and Lucille can't go into the farm to tend to the animals or collect the vegetables. If there's to be any chance of any of them surviving beyond the next couple of days, I have to get out of here.

I stay in Felicity's room that last night, trying to keep her fever down. In the morning she seems a little better – or, at least, she's exhausted enough to sleep – and I rush around tidying up, removing all traces of myself from the farmhouse. I strip my bed and boil the sheets and all my clothes except the things I'm wearing, and then hang everything out to dry on the verandah. I scrub my bedroom floor, the walls and the window. I give my 'things' – my bristle toothbrush, my apron, my ribbons – to Lucille. I only keep one thing for myself: the comb from Harry.

For my last meal I prepare a vegetable soup, hoping that I can tempt Felicity to eat some. She insists on sitting up at the table and valiantly swallows a couple of mouthfuls before shaking her head apologetically.

None of us eat much. I put the remaining soup in a jug and leave it covered, in the coolest corner of the cupboard. With luck it will still be fine to eat tomorrow.

Lucille helps me into my leaving dress. 'Is it okay?' she asks as she fusses over the layers of heavy skirts.

The sleeves are a little on the short side and the waist is roomy, but it's wearable. 'It's wonderful, Lucille, thanks.' Any anger I once felt towards her has gone now. It seems pointless.

'You need gloves, of course,' says Lucille and it's while she's searching for some that I notice a pair of scissors on a chair behind her. Shielding the chair from whatever cameras may be watching, I quietly pick them up. I'm not sure what makes me do it. It's just reassuring to slip my hand deep into my pocket to feel the smooth, cold metal.

•

Felicity is exhausted from being up for dinner and doesn't protest too much when I insist that she go back to bed.

Even Lucille says nothing. Maybe it's dawned on her that if Felicity were to die, she'd be completely alone in here.

Felicity starts to sniffle when I say goodbye and covers her face with her pillow. I kneel beside the bed, my own tears rising as I give her the only hug Esther is allowed to give – the one that means goodbye. I can feel the heat of her feverish skin through the fabric of my leaving dress. 'Just hold on a bit longer, Felicity,' I whisper into her ear. 'I'll come back for you.'

She uncovers her face. 'Really?'

I wish I could tell her what I'm hoping will happen. *Harry is waiting for me on the other side of the front gate. We'll get you out of here as soon as possible, I swear.*

But I can't say any of this so instead I simply nod and wipe her sweaty forehead with a damp cloth one more time.

The late summer sun is already half-set when Lucille and I walk out onto the verandah. I feel her watching as I take off my slippers and place them near the door. Esther doesn't have any boots – she's never needed them – so I will make the journey to the gate bare-footed. Then I turn to Lucille and smile. 'Shall we?'

Lucille nods. She looks tense.

Together we walk down the steps. My legs tremble – maybe from excitement. The steps have been the edge of my territory for so long that I half-expect to feel some invisible barrier rise up. But nothing happens, and a moment later I'm standing on the ground, the earth pushing up against my feet.

Almost immediately, I topple over. The ground is uneven and spongy and my legs, already wobbly with nerves, fail me. Lucille bursts out laughing as I pick myself up, and I laugh too. The mood changes.

The evening air brushes across my bare arms and face like silk. The smell of the plants and the soil, the colour and height of the sky, the sound of my own breathing: everything seems brighter, stronger, more intense than I ever remember it being.

At the wall that separates the kitchen garden from the farm, Lucille stops. It's as far as she can go. 'Come back soon,' she says, all stiff and formal and Lucille-ish again, but then her lip quivers.

I hug her, probably a little too tightly for an official hug. 'Take care of Felicity,' I say and Lucille nods. 'Everything will be fine,' I promise, before giving her one last smile. Then I walk past the eucalyptus trees, leaving her, and the house, behind.

I look around curiously as I make my way through the farm. It's simultaneously familiar to me and completely unknown. There are the vegetable beds where the Felicities pick the tomatoes, radishes and beans. Behind them are the beehives, five of them, lined up side by side like dolls' houses. In the distance, straight and golden, are the few stalks of wheat and oats that survived the storm. I see where the peach tree once was, the stump still pale and fresh. There is where the one remaining goat sleeps and, over there, the empty chicken coop.

And suddenly there's the gate – its metallic surface gleaming, loops of wire at the top. I've only seen it once before but it's somehow very familiar. It's appeared in a lot of my dreams, especially recently, although in them it always remains closed, no matter how hard I push. It's hard to believe that soon it will be unlocked and I'll be able to walk through and find out whatever it is that's waiting for me on the other side.

I turn to look back in the direction I've come. Lucille is standing between the sentinel trees, still as a statue, although when I wave, her hand flutters back at me. Behind her, catching the sunset on its shingled roof, is the farmhouse. It's been my prison for the last two years, but it's also been my home and, while I haven't felt safe there for a long time, in this moment it seems far more secure than what's out *there*.

Fear seizes me – a kind of panic. I can't go. Harry might not be there waiting for me. It's likely – very likely – that I'm about to die. I should stay. Stay here, where *he* is always watching over me, protecting me, suffocating me. Except that he doesn't want me here any more.

I have to go.

My hand is trembling as I push against the gate – so much so that I'm not sure I'll be able to open it. There's a noise too, like a distant drum, but then I realise it's the sound of my pulse in my ears. My breath comes in short, jagged bursts, catching in my throat with each inhalation. The gate swings open easily.

I think for a moment I might fall again, my legs are shaking so much. But I force myself to take a step. And another. And then another until I am through.

CHAPTER SIXTEEN

Esther stands just outside the front gate, no more than a few arm lengths from where I am crouching in the shadows, balaclava on, blanket in hand. Tucked in my back pocket is the gun. I watch her carefully, noting every little detail. The way she holds her body suggests that she's somewhere between fear and excitement. This is not surprising. She knows that she is about to come face to face with me.

As I stare at her, I notice something that makes my heart race. Usually the ones who come through the gate look grey and empty, their souls already detached and off searching for their next bodily form. But Esther doesn't look like that. She glows just as brightly now as she did the first day I laid eyes on her.

She has always been the perfect one. The one who was the most like me. Which is why her recent behaviour has been so difficult to fathom.

A single glance and I know whether someone is good or bad, whether their life will mean anything or if their existence is pointless. When my brother was born, for instance, I remember leaning over his crib and sensing how weak he was. I wanted to help but my parents didn't understand, and wouldn't let me do what was needed to make him strong.

The first time I saw Esther, I understood everything about her. Anyone who shone like that must be truly good, truly pure. But she's made so many mistakes lately. Broken so many rules. I have been tolerant, but there must be a limit.

I inch a little closer to her, put my hand on the grip of the gun, just in case. I only ever have one bullet in it, and even that is not really necessary. They always obey me without question. They practically climb into the boot of the car without me needing to do a thing.

It's tempting to step from the shadows right now. Reveal myself. But waiting is an important part of renewal. It's best if they relax, just a little.

Esther is still very tense. Her breathing is shallow and her head swivels constantly from side to side, inclined slightly in that bird-like way of hers. I know every detail about her, every mannerism. Some nights I've examined her sleeping face so intensely that her skin and bone have melted away and I've been able to look straight into the thoughts flickering in her mind. My favourite places to watch are the hollows on each side of her head, where the flesh dips inwards. How often have I imagined pressing a finger against those indentations, to feel the thoughts pulsing beneath the surface. Esther: the only person I can think about touching without feeling repulsed. The only person I've ever *wanted* to touch.

Not that I need to make physical contact to tell what she's thinking about. I know that already. I shape her everything, her days and her nights. I am the negative space around her. The air. The molecules. When she moves, she moves through me. I am unavoidable. Inevitable.

Each time she turns her head it's as if a stream of tiny stars is released, billowing out around her. She looks so beautiful in her white renewal dress, the final traces of daylight in her hair. An urge comes over me – strong and raw. It's like the one I had that Christmas when my brother and I were given a puppy. My father placed it directly into my arms. 'It's your responsibility.' I remember the feeling inside me so clearly – the scrabbling and scratching sensation, like something was trying to free itself, feelings that were so much like the puppy's own movements. It was so confusing that I squeezed and squeezed, trying to control it all until the puppy finally stopped moving.

My heart is beating so rapidly that it takes considerable effort to slow everything down. *Leave her standing there for one more minute*, I tell myself. *Wait until your breathing has calmed.*

Like everything, renewal is about control and timing. These were difficult things for me when I was younger.

Even now I still feel impatience flare sometimes. There's so much stupidity and ignorance in the world. So many people sleepwalking through their lives. Sometimes I long to scream at them to wake up. But I've trained myself to wait, to hold back.

The secret is breathing, and I take a deep inhalation now. Focus my energies on the task ahead. It's disappointing and inconvenient that things have come to this with Esther. I've enjoyed watching her in this current form. But it's just a body, after all, a non-permanent shell. It is, like everything else, only temporary.

Esther takes an uncertain step forward. Stops. It's so quiet that I can hear the rapid in and out of her breath. It's time for me to appear. But before I can there's a rumbling noise, growing rapidly louder. It's something driving, very fast, towards us. A moment later, around the curve of the track, a motorbike roars into view. It pulls to a stop just metres away from Esther, dirt and pebbles spraying from beneath the wheels.

At first, I'm simply annoyed. But then the driver pulls off his helmet and I reel back, winded by disbelief. He's shaved off his beard and his hair is stubble-short, but I recognise him instantly. So does Esther. 'Harry!' Her glow is suddenly even brighter than before.

He shoves a second helmet at her, his eyes scanning the trees, passing right by me. 'Get on, quick!'

My shock mutates into anger and my impulse is to leap from the bushes and shoot Harry, before forcing Esther down the track into my car. But my hand is shaking too much to risk it. How deep does this betrayal go?

Esther holds the helmet against her stomach, like a basket. 'I thought you weren't coming.' Her voice shakes with emotion.

'Of *course* I was coming. Now, please, *get on the bike.*' He sounds agitated. Nervous. It's a side of Harry that Esther, unlike me, hasn't seen before.

I narrow my eyes. They've arranged this meeting somehow, right under my nose! My fury expands until I feel it will split my skin. I must stand very still now; one tiny movement and I will surely explode.

Harry revs the engine and as Esther gathers up her skirt, the pale skin of her calves is revealed. I feel sick.

Harry holds out a hand. 'Come on, grab hold.'

But Esther stops. Shakes her head. 'We can't just leave them here. Felicity needs to –'

Harry's voice is urgent. 'We have to go *now.*'

This is the moment for me to act. Now, while she's hesitating. I aim my gun at Harry. But it's so dark where I'm standing, and rage is making my hand tremble. I can't be sure I'll hit him.

'I promise they'll be out tonight,' says Harry desperately, his hand stretching out. '*Please.* You have to trust me.'

Esther stands very still, frowning, and then to my dismay she nods. 'Okay.' She takes his hand and swings her leg over the bike, her skirt hitching up around her thighs.

My horror roots me to the ground, unable to do anything but watch as Harry drives off with Esther – *my Esther* – sitting on the back of his bike, her arms wrapped tightly around his waist.

It's not until they're out of sight that I think to pull the purple glass bottle from my pocket. My hand is shaking so much that the liquid nearly spills as I take a sip. My surroundings fade, and then Esther is standing before me, encircled by light. The first Esther, from the photograph. My vision.

'*You're angry,*' she murmurs, her voice like distant chimes.

'Of course I'm angry!' The tonic mingles with my blood, making it burn. 'They *betrayed* me.'

'*There is no time for anger. It only immobilises you. Great change is coming and we need to be ready,*' the vision says, raising her hands. '*Very soon the Special Ones will move to a new level of being. The entire world will know and revere us. It's what we have been striving for.*'

I am *fury*, but her words quieten me a little. Ease some of the tension in my muscles. I find myself barely even breathing, for fear of missing a single word.

'*This Esther doesn't need to be renewed. You have seen that for yourself. She is still full of her wonderful spirit.*'

'But what has happened to her?' I ask. 'Why is she being so difficult and disobedient?'

'Everything is about to change,' the vision explains. *'This change will bring wonderful things, although the journey will not be easy. You need to forget everything you knew about the Special Ones. Leave it all behind.'*

'Not the farm!' My muscles start to tense again.

The vision nods. *'Yes, the farm and the other girls too. Harry is completely irrelevant, of course.'* Her hands stretch up above her head, her beautiful hair streaming back, liquid silver whipping wildly in the wind. *'Leave everything behind – everything except Esther. She is the one thing you must not lose. You need to collect her again – alive – and take her home.'*

'I will,' I vow. 'I will.'

The vision rewards me with a smile, beautiful and powerful as she fades, leaving me with a feeling of intense joy. I hurry to my car, hidden in a little clearing nearby, and begin to drive off in the same direction that Harry took a few minutes ago. I do not doubt for a moment that I'll catch up with them. Then I will collect her and bring her home, to me.

As I drive, laughter spills unexpectedly from me. And once I start, I can't stop. This evening has not gone how I had imagined, but this doesn't matter. That's the wonderful thing about being me. When things take an unexpected turn, it usually means something better is coming.

CHAPTER SEVENTEEN

There are no lights along the dirt track but I don't need them. If I were blind I'd still be able to drive this route – I know its bends and dips intimately.

When I hear the rumble of the motorbike ahead of me, I pull back a little. I do not want Harry to see me and attempt some dangerous getaway that results in an accident. I don't want to see Harry's traitorous face again, either, for that may cause me to lose control. Satisfying as it is to imagine side-swiping Harry's bike, or picturing his body being tossed into the dirt or speared by a tree branch, I cannot risk anything happening to Esther.

I make sure to remain a bend or two behind them. Let them think they have evaded me so far.

Once we've turned onto the freeway and I'm shielded by other vehicles, I pull a little closer. The traffic is heavy for this time of night and Harry weaves through it impatiently, his bike leaning dangerously as he edges ever forward. He knows I'm there – I'm sure of it – although I'm equally confident he hasn't spotted me yet. Hiding in plain view is one of my specialities.

Esther also senses I'm nearby; each time the bike appears in my line of vision her head turns, examining the drivers of the cars around her. Would she recognise me if she saw me? I'd like to think she would, just not right now.

I try to read her thoughts, but the distance and the motorbike helmet make it difficult. All I can pick up on is her agitation, which buzzes like static in her head.

I send her mental messages of reassurance. *Have no fear, Esther. I know this is a confusing time. But I promise you won't have to wait too long until we're together again.*

Waiting is difficult. I know this because I've done such a lot of it. The worst waiting was when I was very young, when it felt endless. Waiting for Christmas. Waiting for the holidays. Waiting at the doctor's as my brother was stitched up again. Waiting to hear what my mother would say when she phoned her friends, the ice clinking in one of her strong-smelling drinks as she whispered words she thought I couldn't hear: *There's something about him that scares me.*

Waiting to learn which punishment my father, Mr Big Important Police Chief, had selected for me this time – beaten with his belt, while ash drifted down like grey snow from his cigarette, or locked in the dark cellar for hours, with nothing but that gurgling boiler for company?

But, through it all, I knew instinctively that these hardships were temporary, and that ultimately the waiting would be worth it. Something was coming that would make sense of my life. Something greater.

I sense that Harry and Esther are heading for the city, and at the next turn-off I'm proven correct. The traffic slows and merges. Sound-blocking barriers are replaced with suburban yards and houses. Where is he taking her? Back to her house? Surely not to his. I have not kept track of Harry since he left the farm, assuming he would stick to our agreement, so I do not know where he lives these days. But if his current address is anything like the one where I first met him, it would not be at all appropriate for Esther.

At the first set of traffic lights I have to fight the urge to rush up, drag Esther from the bike and bundle her back into my car. The problem is that there are far too many people about. Ordinary people are so limited in their thinking. They wouldn't understand what I was doing. That I was only reclaiming what already belonged to me.

I trail the bike through a tangle of outer suburban streets, suspicious that Harry is trying to lose me. I pull back, create a little more distance between us, and as a consequence almost do not see him turning into a car park – the car park of a police station.

I pull up around the corner, seething. How could Harry bring Esther this close to danger? I've made it very clear that the police are not to be trusted, under any circumstances.

I get out of the car, leaving the back open, and hurry quietly around to the car park. It's Friday night and the streets are crowded with people either going home or heading out. No-one pays any attention to me. I weave silently between the parked vehicles, sticking to the shadows around the edge of the lot, finally crouching behind a station wagon only a few metres from Harry and Esther.

They are standing near the bike and, although I can't make out everything they're saying, it's clear that they're having an argument. Harry is holding both the helmets, and Esther has her hand on his chest like she's trying to push him away – a sight that makes me smile, despite the touching that it involves.

I see Esther mouth a word. *Go!*

The sound of traffic blocks Harry's reply but I can tell from his expression that he's not happy.

They're distracted, I think. *I could drive up in my car, knock Harry down and grab Esther. I'd be gone before anyone realised what happened.*

My blood pumps faster at the thought of doing it – and right beside a police station too! How angry my father would be. Silently, I turn and hurry back towards my car.

CHAPTER EIGHTEEN

I'm still shaking from the journey here on Harry's bike. I'd forgotten how loud and fast traffic is, especially on a freeway. Everything was so bright, all those shiny, flashing lights zooming by. I held onto Harry with all my might, rigid with excitement and terror. Even now that we've stopped, those twin feelings swirl around inside me. But I have to force myself to concentrate on Harry's face. On what I need to do.

His arms are crossed. 'Where you go, I go,' he says firmly. He looks so different in normal clothes. His hair is short as peach fuzz, and the beard has gone too. Would I know him, if we passed each other by chance?

Nothing feels certain right now. My head is foggy from all the car fumes I've been breathing in, the unfamiliar city sounds. Some passers-by on the street suddenly laugh, and I nearly jump out of my skin.

Get it together. Focus. Appear rational and calm, even while your heart hammers in your chest.

Around me the air seems to pulse with danger. I swallow. Try again. 'Please, Harry. It's better if I go in there alone.'

Harry frowns in confusion. 'But *why?*'

I hesitate. The thing is, I'm not exactly sure why I want Harry to stay hidden for now. It seems crazy, just when we've found each other again, but it's a feeling I have – one that's squeezing my insides like a clamp. Obviously a *feeling* will not be enough to persuade Harry to go. Nor will telling him that enough people have been hurt because of me, and I can't risk it happening again. Because what exactly do I think will happen if he comes into the police station anyway? I can't explain it, but I can't shake the fear either.

'I don't know if the police will even believe me,' I say in a rush. 'I might get arrested, or questioned for hours. Felicity really needs to go to a hospital *tonight*. If anything happens to me, or the police won't help, it'll be up to you to get her and Lucille out. And then *he's* still out there ...'

The traffic is a low growl in the background as Harry thinks, his forehead creased. I can tell that he wants to argue, to refuse flat out. But I can also see that I've struck a chord with him. *Hurry*, I think anxiously. *Please hurry.*

Finally, his shoulders sag. 'If that's really what you want, I –'

He breaks off as a car turns quickly into the car park, blinding us with its headlights. I feel every muscle tense, ready to run, until I see the lights on top of the car. *Police.*

They pull to a stop not far from us. Harry is frozen beside me, his jaw taut, eyes narrowed. I can see his uncertainty, his reluctance to give me up. I squeeze his arm. 'Go!' I tell him, my voice soft. 'It'll be fine, I promise.'

But it's only when the doors of the police car open that he finally pulls on his helmet, kicks the bike's engine into life. And even though it's what I insisted I wanted, my insides drop horribly as he roars out of the car park and disappears from view.

Two officers emerge from the car. 'Is everything all right, ma'am?' one of them calls to me. 'Was he harassing you?'

I shake my head. 'Everything's fine.' I sound weird, false. 'He's – I hitched a ride with him here.'

One of the officers walks towards me. 'Has something happened? Do you need help?'

I'm suddenly aware of how I must look, standing there in my long white dress, gloves and bare, dirty feet. I start to shiver violently as they draw closer, *his* dire warnings about the police crowding into my mind.

They'll think you're crazy, or dangerous. They'll arrest you. Shoot you.

But I take a deep breath. Look directly into the nearest officer's eyes. 'My name is Tess Kershaw,' I say, 'and I've been missing for two years.'

As I say the words, there's a loud noise behind me and I swing round, worried and yet desperately hoping that Harry has changed his mind. But instead, I see a dark blue car with the window rolled down.

I can't make out the driver's face, but I catch a gleam of metal through the window. Then the car reverses with a screech and drives away.

CHAPTER NINETEEN

At first I feel very little at all. My senses are numbed by disbelief. *She is gone. Again.*

But soon the rage takes hold.

This is Harry's fault. Breaking promises by appearing when he should not be here at all. The vision told me to forget about Harry, and I know I shouldn't waste my energy on anger – but how can I let him go unpunished for this? That goes against what I believe.

A memory stirs – a chair collapsing under me at school, everyone laughing while a classmate held out a handful of bolts. I didn't react at the time; I waited. An accidental bump while he was using the bandsaw during Woodwork quickly removed the culprit from the school. More importantly, my dignity was restored.

I hurry back to my car. Harry can't have gone very far yet and I know the sorts of places he's likely to head to. But then I hear the vision's voice in my head.

'*Let him go. There are more important things to attend to. Your own wellbeing, for one thing. Esther, in her addled state, is likely to tell those idiots everything about the farm.*'

She's right, of course. A chill passes through me. 'Should I destroy it?'

I have prepared for this possibility – the petrol is ready and waiting in the cellar at home – but I had hoped it would not be necessary, and there probably isn't time to do it now, anyway.

'*You don't have time,*' says the vision, echoing, as she often does, my thoughts. '*Besides, it's more important that you destroy any pathways that might connect the farm to you and the Special Ones portal too. You must act immediately.*'

'But I need to fetch Esther, take her home,' I say. 'Although I suppose there will be other opportunities.'

'*Yes, there will be,*' confirms the vision. '*Right now, you must focus on protecting yourself.*'

I swing the car around and head home.

●

Our house was built by my great-grandfather on a large block, well back from the street and hidden almost entirely by trees. My mother used to grow roses along the fence but these are mostly dead now. Not that it really matters.

One day I intend to replace all the flowerbeds with vegetable patches. Perhaps it's something Esther and I can do together.

In the driveway, I stop to unlock the front gate. Inconveniently, but also typically, my next-door neighbour, Mrs Lewis, uses this moment to leap out from nowhere.

'Oh, I've been waiting all day to see you! Here, I baked you some brownies,' she says, forcing a plate of burnt squares into my hands. She's dressed, as usual, in faded purple yoga pants and a sparkly, hand-knitted top.

'Mrs Lewis,' I say. 'Really, you shouldn't have.'

The place next door had stood empty for so many years that I'd started to believe it would remain that way forever. But then someone came and cleared it up, and Mrs Lewis moved in. The land used to belong to my mother's family, but her father sold it off. Barely a day goes by that I don't curse him for his greed and short-sightedness.

I carefully developed a *good neighbour* persona to use with Mrs Lewis when she first arrived, smiling when I saw her, enquiring after her health. I even put a Christmas card in her letterbox just after she arrived last year – one from my mother's collection. Unfortunately Mrs Lewis responded rather too well. Now I've toned things down to civil, hoping she will get the message. So far this hasn't worked.

'Oh, it's nothing!' Mrs Lewis replies. 'All boys need someone to bake for them and I'm happy to do it. Not that you're a *boy*, of course,' she adds hastily. 'You must be nearly twenty, I guess. It's just that baby-face of yours. It brings out the nurturing instinct in me. Speaking of which, would you like me to pop over occasionally to water your garden? Those roses need some care and I've got a lot of ti–'

'No, thanks, Mrs Lewis,' I say, hurriedly pushing open the gate. There's no point waiting for her to stop talking. Experience has shown this won't happen. 'They're coming out soon anyway.'

Before she can ask anything else, I jump back in the car and drive around the back of the house, hurrying inside. I can lock the front gate later, when I'm sure Mrs Lewis is gone.

I deadlock the back door and kick off my shoes. There isn't even time to line them up next to my brother's runners. This bothers me, of course, but I can't waste a second right now. The brownies are flung into the bin. Even if today's guiding word wasn't *restrain*, I would never consume something that woman made. Who knows what could be in it?

I hurry to the study, directly across from my parents' room upstairs. Their door is slightly ajar, as always. I light a candle, although the glow from the screens is more than enough to see by. Beeswax candles cast a very soothing light when they burn, and I will need some soothing, considering the tasks that lie ahead.

I turn on the computer. Check the farmhouse. The cameras confirm that Lucille and Felicity are both where they should be – Felicity asleep in her bed and Lucille setting up the chat room. I zoom in on Lucille's face as she works, and her look of intense concentration gives me a small moment of pleasure. I was right about her, after all.

When she first arrived at the farm, I'd had doubts. Perhaps she was just too stubborn to accept who she really was. But she has settled in well now and I am sure that she would've done a good job of managing the chat this evening. Too bad that I have to cut it short before it begins.

'Goodbye, Lucille,' I whisper.

With the stroke of a key, I activate a virus in the Special Ones farmhouse systems – one I wrote for exactly this sort of situation. The virus sets off a self-destruct mechanism and disconnects the farmhouse from my encrypted server, and from the outside world. Once Esther tells the police her story, there is no doubt they will invade the farmhouse, searching through everything, and I need to protect us.

It's like stabbing myself to destroy, in seconds, what amounts to thousands of hours of work, but it's what I must do, if I am to remain in control of this situation. The only small satisfaction is seeing how well my emergency measures work.

Next I destroy all the electronic logs and records, anything that would connect the Special Ones portal to me – the chat, the donation page, the shop. *Don't think about what you're doing,* I instruct myself. *Concentrate on the task at hand*. I push my emotions down. Focus on getting this done as quickly and efficiently as I can. Tell myself that there's a sense of joyful cleansing and rebirth – renewal, really – that should ease the difficulty a little. Sometimes it's necessary to clear away the old to make way for the new.

After a couple of hours I have secured my online anonymity, but there is still work to do. Harry has betrayed me and I have no idea what information he might have already fed to the police. He doesn't know where I live – I was always very careful to keep that secret – but I need to do all I can to cover myself. Despite the warmth of the evening, I hastily build a fire in the fireplace and open the filing cabinet. It's an old wooden one that my father brought home when the police stations in his district were modernised. 'Got it for free,' he said. Its beauty was entirely irrelevant to him.

His hunting club magazines are still in the bottom drawer, along with the manual for the boiler. I haven't used the boiler at all since the 'tragedy', but I keep the manual for sentimental reasons. My father was so proud when the system was installed, and showed me the diagrams of how it worked, the safety checklist written in big red letters. 'It's important to keep the air vents clean or it can leak poisonous gases into the air,' he told me.

'I'll keep it clean,' I said, eagerly. 'It can be my job.' That was back when I still thought there was a way to please him.

He laughed dismissively. 'As if I would trust you with a task like that.'

At first I examine every piece of paper, each document, before placing it on the fire. Here's the sketch I drew, back when I was still at school, of how the farmhouse should look, and there's the rough layout for the Special Ones portal. I waste precious minutes with the first draft of Esther's remembering book, as well as my beehive designs. But time is rapidly passing, so I grit my teeth and force myself to be more ruthless, less sentimental, and begin throwing things on the fire without reading them. Sweat drips from my face, saturating my shirt and plastering it against my skin.

Then I come to the photograph and everything stops. It would be impossible to burn this. I take it from its protective leather sleeve, running my thumb down the pale border.

I found the photograph while I was waiting in the principal's office of the *very good boarding school* my parents sent me to. It had come as a complete surprise to me when my parents banished me like that, but I see now there were warning signs. All those visits to experts, all those *special vitamin pills*. And then there was all the fuss when I started going into my brother's room during the night to watch him sleep.

The school principal, Mr Mills, always wore the same wet-lipped, disapproving expression, and the same egg-stained tie. He liked to make me wait alone in his office before he swept in to lecture me. I suppose he imagined I'd sit there stewing, regretting my wrongdoings. What I actually did was go through his things. Mr Mills always had a nice little stash of medications in his top drawer, so the first thing I always did when left alone was to sample a selection of them at random.

Why was I there that day? I have no idea and, anyway, the particular misdemeanour is not important. What matters is that after I'd downed a handful of Mr Mills's meds, I saw the edge of a photograph poking out from a book on his desk. I extracted it carefully, already glowing pleasantly from the pills, hoping it might be something I could use as blackmail fodder. Compromising shots of someone who wasn't his wife, for instance. But these thoughts evaporated the moment I saw what the photograph actually contained.

Three girls, arranged in that elegant, formal way of old pictures. The fourth figure, a male, whose beard made him look older than he was. There was something instantly familiar about him.

In fact, all the figures were familiar – in a way I couldn't explain but somehow *felt*. I knew Mr Mills fancied himself as a local history buff. He'd probably unearthed the picture during one of the regular flea-market trips he was always droning on about at assembly. He probably hadn't noticed what I had – that although the figures were standing in the shade, they emanated a brightness, like the way the entire length of a candle sometimes glows when the wick is burning. The tall girl in the centre of the group particularly seemed to shine, and I held the photograph close to my face so I could examine it more carefully.

Everything around me dimmed: Mr Mills's depressing office furniture, the sound of the boys playing soccer on the field outside. The edges of the photograph stretched up and out, enveloping me. There was a breeze. Sun on the top of my head. The four figures from the photograph were before me on the verandah.

The tall girl smiled at me and spoke. There was no sound but I could read her lips. *Are you ready?*

The vision was over in an instant. But it was long enough to have changed everything.

How to describe the moment when you realise that you've lived before? That you've never truly died, but simply moved through different bodies in the same way that you might move from one house to another. A feeling of bliss flowed through me, powerful and profound.

I looked at the male in the photograph again and this time I easily recognised myself. My hand shook as I turned the photo over, already knowing what I would find there. At the bottom left were three words in faded ink: *The Special Ones.* After this came the names: Lucille, Felicity, Esther and Harry. *Esther.* Those six letters brought such heat to my chest!

Not everything returned to me on that first day, but I remembered a few important things, at least. The girls were my true family. I was Harry. Most thrilling was the deep, unshakeable knowledge that we all still existed today in some form, and that if I brought us together again, great things would happen.

•

In the end I burn almost everything, save the Special Ones photograph, and Harry's file. I am not entirely sure why I keep it, but I know that my instinct on such things is usually correct.

After I've hidden these two items beneath a loose floorboard, I drag myself down the corridor to my bedroom, which is opposite my brother's, at the other end from our parents'. It's vital that I rest for a few hours at least, but, although I am physically exhausted and mentally drained, I cannot fall asleep. There is no bed in my room – most of the furniture from here is at the farmhouse – but sleeping on the floor does not usually bother me.

Eventually I take a sip from the purple bottle and let the images begin to swirl. This time it's not my vision I see, but the real-life Esther who just slipped through my fingers today.

She smiles at me, no longer afraid, no longer wanting to escape. Her hands stretch out. *I'll be with you in the house soon,'* she whispers and her sweet words soften the boards beneath me until I feel that I am floating on a bed of cloud and feathers.

'*Soon,'* she whispers. '*Very soon.'*

CHAPTER TWENTY

When I wake at dawn, there's a tightness in my chest, like hands pressing down on me and I know instantly that Esther's story has broken. I sit up and begin to meditate. It's crucial that I prepare myself mentally for what I am about to face: my secret place ripped open for everyone to see.

This is all for a purpose, I remind myself, *a vital step that will progress the Special Ones to the next stage of existence.*

Besides, I think, *maybe some good will come from the exposure.* The entire world will soon learn of the Special Ones' existence. Millions of people will get to see our farm. How beautiful it is. How pure and perfect life was there. It makes sense that, after this, followers will come flooding to Esther and me in even greater numbers, wanting to learn our ways.

They can't ever be Special, of course. But they can try.

I flip open a laptop and check my newsfeeds. Immediately an item catches my eye.

BREAKING NEWS – PRISON FARM RESCUE!

My hands are shaking as I click through. There's an aerial image of the farm splashed across the home page of a news site, and although the image is dark and blurry, I can still make out many distressing details: the front gate lying twisted and broken on the ground, armoured vans surrounding the farmhouse, the swarming police.

Along the top of the webpage are links and I make myself click on *What we currently know*. A moment later I am watching a clip in which a reporter talks breathlessly about the *unimaginable horrors* that he has seen this morning.

My whole body begins to tremble and it takes every inch of my self-control not to smash the computer against a wall. It's as if people *want* to find the dark and the dirty in things that are pristine and beautiful.

I'm tempted to take a sip from the purple bottle and hear some reassuring words from the vision, but it occurs to me that it may be some time before I get a refill. The ingredients, after all, can only be found on the farm.

Instead, I go down to the kitchen. Drink some water, straighten up my shoes. Once my breathing is steady again, I take a TV from the pantry – an undelivered one from last week – and plug it in.

The networks are all playing the same footage of Lucille and Felicity leaving the farmhouse: Lucille wrapped in a silver blanket and Felicity on a stretcher. *What a shocking discovery this has been*, all the reporters say. *How heartbreakingly scared the girls look*. There's no denying they look scared, but I seem to be the only person who realises their fear is not from living on the farm but from having their home violated in this grotesque way.

Rage boils inside me now, surging just beneath the skin. It's so difficult to witness this evil, these lies, without losing control. To accept that this is the way everything is meant to go and that I must accept it as part of the process. We Special Ones have endured similar trials before, and will survive them again.

I spend the day inside, watching as the story spreads, my feelings swinging violently back and forth. It is, on the one hand, devastating to have my little world ripped apart like this. To hear it described so negatively. The media keeps referring to it as 'the prison farm', and this rankles every time. Yet I also feel proud – deeply so – at how strongly the world reacts to Esther. Her calm, composed face is soon everywhere. Everyone adores her.

It's late on that first, frenzied day when the networks start showing scenes of Esther's reunion with her parents. 'Emotions are overflowing here!' declares one particularly vapid reporter as the camera zooms in on the family arriving at the police station.

It's quite clear that the overflowing emotions are all coming from Esther's mother and (to a lesser degree) her father. Esther embraces her parents, but she doesn't go overboard with fake feelings. And why would she? These two people are not her real family.

Esther remains polite but reserved as the media jostle around, bombarding her with questions. There's only one point, when yet another reporter asks her *how does it feel to be free?* that Esther's expression switches over into annoyance. 'I won't be free until the others have been found,' she says, in a snippet the networks play over and over again.

'But they have been,' another reporter says.

Esther shakes her head. 'No, there are others. Ones who left the farm before.'

'What do you mean?' ask several reporters simultaneously, as the cameras flash. 'Where did they go?'

Esther's face tightens. 'That's what I'm hoping to find out.'

I have to smile. Esther looks so serious, pretending that she cares about the fate of the others. I dare say she fools the reporters, but she doesn't fool me. I know that her real interest, whether she realises it yet or not, is to reconnect with me.

●

The next day, someone discovers the link between the farm and the Special Ones portal, and the headlines change to *DAWN RAID ON CULT.* The force against my chest presses harder.

How could anyone refer to us as a cult? It's laughable. The Special Ones is a philosophy that defies any traditional definition. We don't force people join us. We don't force anyone to do anything they don't want to do. People willingly seek advice from the Special Ones and buy our homemade products – bowls, knives, aprons, scarves – from the online store. No-one, I reassure myself, could possibly see the Special Ones as a *cult*.

After this my teachings begin to appear, first circulating online and eventually appearing on the TV networks. I am confident that they can't be linked back to me, and so I allow myself to feel some small amount of pride in these films. I know our followers cherish them, even now as they're being used as base entertainment. Making the films consumed a lot of my time – not just the hours spent fast-forwarding through footage to choose the best, most inspirational scenes from the day to use, but also the compiling, the editing and uploading. Yet I always knew it was worth it.

By that evening, however, my feelings have changed. Inevitably Harry appears in some of the films, although I tried wherever possible to keep him out. Watching them now, I find myself discovering little clues as to what had been developing between him and Esther, right there in front of me. I see the feeling compressed into those three-second glances – far more powerful and concentrated than anything a lingering gaze could convey. And the *not quite* touches of their bodies now strike me as almost pornographic.

Did they think they could get away with it? Deceive me? One thing, at least, is very clear to me now. There will be a reckoning.

•

The next morning, I wake up in front of the television with an anxious, niggling feeling, unable to concentrate on anything for more than a minute or two. I do not need to leave for work until late in the afternoon, but I get dressed anyway.

The problem, I realise, is that I want to go and check on my possessions. Now, immediately, rather than waiting for darkness like I usually do. It's not that I'm worried the police will locate what I have hidden there yet, but whenever I think of the factory I feel uneasy. In the end I decide to go with my instinct and drive out there, despite the risks. Now that everything is in flux, it's time to make a decision about what to do with them. I also need to confirm that there's nothing there – fingerprints, DNA – that will link the site to me.

I take my father's car, loading it up with everything I'll need. His car is a fuel-guzzling, wasteful monster, but there's no denying it's spacious. The empty water drum and the box of supplies fit easily into the boot. It's possible to fit a person in there with room to spare.

I keep my possessions in the factory whose crumbling tower can be seen distantly from the farm – I found the two locations on the same day. Although it's probably more accurate to say I simply remembered where they were.

After I'd retaken possession of the Special Ones photograph, I began meditating, often sitting cross-legged on my school bedroom floor for an entire night – while the others slept around me – trying to re-create the experience I'd had in Mr Mills's office. Meditation, especially when combined with medication, was the best way I'd found to tap back into my former life and the lives of the other Special Ones. It brought me such joy to reconnect with them. We had come from different parts of the country, drawn together by our shared philosophy on the way a life should be lived (with purity, with simplicity, with economy), and lived together in harmony in a perfect, self-sustaining farmhouse.

But the farmhouse. Where was it? I could picture it so clearly in my mind and I ached with longing to be there.

It wasn't until after the tragedy, after I'd dropped out of school and moved back into the family home, that it finally happened. I woke one morning with a strong urge to go for a drive. So, after consuming the last of my pill collection, I took off that morning in an almost trance-like state. I took no map and paid no attention to the road signs. It felt like the car itself was deciding which direction to go.

The car drove me away from the city and, after a couple of hours of winding through country lanes and dirt tracks, I found myself on a remote piece of land. It was obvious from the tangle of weeds that grew there and the broken-down fencing that the place hadn't been used in a long time. Something drew me towards it, the shining edge of a memory.

I parked the car and walked through an overgrown garden, finding myself in front of an old wooden farmhouse – dilapidated and long abandoned, though the stone chimney stood intact. It had a big front verandah shaded by a tall, lemon-scented gum, its silvery leaves gleaming as they caught the sun.

Heart pounding, I turned around, pulling something into my mind from long ago. *There will be a tower.*

And, yes, jutting up on the horizon to the right of the farmhouse, there it was: a distant factory tower, the word *OWN* just visible on the side facing me. My entire body tingled. It wasn't just that this place was perfect for my needs. It was also that I recognised it from my meditation sessions. This was where the Special Ones had lived before. I was sure of it.

I had not cried since that very last time my father locked me in the cellar, and this time the tears fell not from anger but from relief. Instinct, guided by a buried memory, had led me directly to the Special Ones' original farmhouse. This place had been waiting for me all this time. For us to return.

The last thing I did before leaving the property that day was to gather up a selection of herbs, succulents and wildflowers, my hand drawn naturally to particular ones. I took them home and pulverised them into a liquid, which I poured into one of two small purple bottles I'd found buried at the back of my mother's cupboard.

That evening I began work on the first of the remembering books, the words flowing from me in a steady, effortless stream.

●

After I claimed the farmhouse as my own, restoring it was my first priority. But when I got around to investigating the old factory, I recognised that it, too, would be useful for storage.

The site was surrounded by *KEEP OUT: PRIVATE PROPERTY* signs but, judging from the amount of rust, I doubted the owner would be around very often to bother me. I climbed in through a hole in the fencing and stood for a moment, admiring the tower. On the other side, the word *FAMILY'S* was spelled out in bricks, vertically from the top of the tower down. *FAMILY'S OWN*. I wondered briefly what had been made here. Biscuits maybe, or soap. Not that it mattered.

I scouted the space inside the main building first, with its heavy wooden doors still firmly attached to their hinges. People made things to last in the olden days. The space, although beautiful, with light filtering in from small, high windows, was too open for my needs. Even the tower was not suitable. But what piqued my interest immediately was the vast storage area under the floor – the sort of place where things could be hidden and not found again. This is where I keep my possessions.

CHAPTER TWENTY-ONE

The first time I was in this police station – just after Harry left, only days ago – everyone treated me like I was the most important person in the world. They fussed around, couldn't do enough for me. Someone brought a cup of tea and a chocolate biscuit, draped a coat across my shoulders. And everything, every tiny thing I had to say, was vitally interesting to them.

That's all changed now.

I've made Dad drive me here and as I walk in, two of the officers hurry over to bar the door against the crowd that's followed us from the house. The sergeant comes out of his office when he hears the commotion. 'Hello, Tess,' he says, his cheerfulness sounding a little forced. 'Back again so soon! You can just call me, you know. Probably easier that way.'

His eyes flick over to the people outside calling my name and trying to take pictures of me on their phones.

'I did call,' I say. 'Lots of times. But they kept telling me you were busy.'

The sergeant gestures to his office. 'Well, come in. Let's talk.'

My dad starts to follow me in, but I stop him. 'Can you wait here?'

'Really?' he says. 'Are you sure?' He's relieved, though, I can tell. He clearly hates hearing about what happened.

'I'm sure.'

'Well, I'm here if you need me,' he says as I walk into the office. The sergeant clicks the door closed behind me.

'I've had some more ideas about where he might be keeping the missing girls,' I tell him before I've sat down. 'It'd have to be somewhere –'

'Tess,' says the sergeant, taking a seat behind his desk. 'What I'm going to say will sound blunt, but I need you to understand. There's very little chance that those girls are still alive. We believe we're dealing with a psychopath here, and in our experience, once a victim has ceased to be of interest to someone like that, they tend to be disposed of pretty quickly.' He presses his fingertips together and points them at me. 'We are searching for bodies, Tess, not living people.'

I shake my head. '*I'm* still here,' I point out. 'I survived.' *And so did Harry.*

'Luckily, yes,' agrees the sergeant. 'But you're probably the only one.' He leans back, gives me a searching look.

'Have you remembered any more details of how you made it from the farm to the city?'

I force myself to hold his gaze. 'Just what I've already told you. Someone happened to come past and I hitched a ride.'

The sergeant nods, but doesn't smile. 'It's just such a pity that the person who gave you the ride didn't come into the station and make a statement,' he says. 'It would've been extremely helpful. Are you sure he didn't give you his name?'

'No,' I say, hoping the sergeant doesn't notice how my face is heating up. 'I mean, I didn't ask.'

'Okay. And can you tell us anything else about your *arrival* at the farm?' the sergeant presses.

My head automatically swivels to see where my dad is. He's on the other side of the waiting room, talking to an officer. There's no chance of him overhearing, but I still lower my voice. 'I told you everything I can remember.'

The sergeant regards me silently for a moment. 'It's just strange how different your story is to the statements we took from the other two girls,' he says slowly. 'It's not how these perpetrators generally operate. They usually follow the same rituals every time.'

I lean forward, grasping the edge of the desk. 'But that's the thing about him!' I say urgently. 'I don't think he's like anyone else you've ever dealt with. And that's why I want –'

'Listen, Tess.' The sergeant presses his palms into the desk and stands up. 'You've been through a highly stressful experience. Right now, you should be focusing on recovery. Get your life back in order, that's the most important thing. You've been very helpful to us and we appreciate it. But you've done enough. We can take it from here.'

He goes over to his door, opens it and beckons to my father. 'Tell your daughter that it's time for her to relax,' he says in a loud, jovial voice. 'Hang out with her friends. Have some fun. Try to go back to being a normal teenager.'

My dad stands up. 'We're working on it,' he says.

I stay in my seat. The sound of the crowd outside the station is audible again now that the office door is open. In a minute I'll have to push through all those people, any one of whom could be *him*. Like that guy in the sweatshirt and jeans, or the one looking at his phone. He could be the one with the band T-shirt, drinking a bottle of water. He could even be one of the police officers in here.

The sergeant seems to sense what I'm thinking. 'You know, we believe he's probably fled the country by now,' he tells me. 'People with this profile don't tend to stick around. But he'll surface again somewhere else before long, and when he does, we'll be waiting for him.'

I shake my head. 'He's still here.'

'How do you know?' The sergeant's voice is suddenly sharp. 'Has he contacted you?'

'No. But I can feel him watching me.'

The sergeant barely contains a sigh, and then ushers me out of his office. 'Listen, if by some small chance he's still around, there's no need to worry. We have an officer permanently stationed outside your house, and you can always call. Believe me, you're very well protected.'

CHAPTER TWENTY-TWO

Usually I don't pass a single other driver in the last stretch out to the factory, where the outer suburbs have given way to farmland and scrub. There is nothing around here to draw people off the highway. But this time, even though I don't actually see any cars, I have the constant sensation of being followed.

I switch on the radio – something I never normally do – just to distract myself. A news bulletin blares out.

'The manhunt for the mysterious figure behind the so-called Prison Farm kidnappings is intensifying, with federal agents now joining the search. While investigators are remaining tight-lipped about any leads, a spokeswoman said that finding the perpetrator was a top priority. Evidence seized at the farm –'

I quickly turn the radio off again. I do not want to listen to what must be lies. There was nothing at the farm that could lead them to me.

But as I drive along in silence, doubt creeps in. Maybe the virus hadn't wiped the chat-room server completely clean. Or maybe Harry has said something. I had the impression that he was hiding, like a coward, but how do I know he hasn't been working with the police all along?

Suddenly there are flashing lights in my rear-view mirror, and glancing back I see a sunglassed, blue-uniformed figure indicating that I need to pull over. My foot instinctively begins to press down on the accelerator. But I stop myself. There is a better way to approach this.

I slow and pull over, quickly dragging my yellow work jacket on over my shoulders. As the cop walks up to my window, I take the gun from my bag and slip it under my seat. Just in case.

'You're in a hurry,' he says. His voice is neutral, unreadable.

I give a nasal, high-pitched laugh. 'Was I speeding? Sorry, mate. It's been a long day,' I say. 'I just need to get this last parcel delivered.' I point to a parcel sitting on the back seat, one I haven't yet got around to selling.

'Long way to come for a delivery.' The cop's mouth is as thin as the slot of a ticket machine.

'We go anywhere,' I tell him, shrugging. 'Company policy.'

'I've never seen a delivery guy drive a Lexus before.'

'Van's in the shop, mate.'

The policeman's face doesn't reveal if he believes me or not, and I cannot seem to get into his head to read his thoughts. He asks me for my licence and I cheerily provide him with one of my false ones. He turns it over in his hand and I feel him consider whether it's worth going to check it. *Don't*, I instruct him. He hands it back to me.

'This road's blocked ahead,' he says curtly. 'You'll have to go back to the main road, find another way through.'

I thank him for his help, and keep driving until I'm just out of view. Then I quickly turn off into the bush. I'll just go cross-country.

•

As the tower looms into view through the trees, I park my van among some bushes, take the items I'll need from the back, and make the rest of the trip on foot. I move from shadow to shadow, stopping every now and then to listen. Check I'm truly alone.

There's a dark silence as I pull back the wire and climb into the factory grounds. The silence of sleep, or of death. It usually soothes me to be here – the solitude it carries and the simple, sturdy beauty of the mossy stone walls. But today I'm on edge and, even though the cop is far away now, the feeling that someone is close by, watching, has returned, more intensely than before. I crouch in the shadows for a long time, listening for footsteps, scanning my surroundings for anything unusual or out of place. I stiffen at a crackling sound, but it's just a bird or a rabbit. Eventually I decide that it's safe to unlock the door. As always, I pull a balaclava over my face and slip on my gloves before moving any closer.

The rusty padlock pulls free with some resistance and the door creaks open. The musty, cool air from inside curls around me, drawing me in. It's like stepping into somewhere sacred; even though I'm on high alert, just being there eases my tension a little. The roof is very high and shafts of light slice downwards, catching the swirling dust. Tiny specks billow up around me as I walk over to the trapdoor in the corner. I have a sense that the cellar below was once used as a storeroom for this factory, though you'd easily miss it if you weren't looking for it.

Sweat drips from me as I remove the pile of rubble I've heaped across the entrance and unlock the trapdoor underneath. It's wedged tightly shut and the ring slips from my gloved hands several times before I manage to yank it open. The air from below instantly floods out, the powerful stench nearly knocking me over. Once I've steadied myself, I drop down the boxes of supplies and the ten-gallon drum I've brought with me. Then, taking a final deep breath of above-ground air, I pocket the padlock and lower myself into the darkness, pulling the trapdoor shut above my head. Normally I leave it open, but today I feel like it needs to be closed.

The darkness is thick and I fumble for my torch in the box, wishing I'd remembered to clip it to my belt before descending. When I switch it on I give a yelp of shock. There's a face, barely inches away from me, the eyes fixed unblinkingly on mine. It's one of the ex-Lucilles – at least, I think it is, because I only see it for a second before I drop the torch.

As I bend to pick it up, I am sure I hear muffled sniggering, and the gentle clinking of chains. I stand up straight, gripping the torch firmly. This is the problem with renewal. Once a Special One's soul has vacated a body, what remains is far less pleasant and dignified.

Most people in my situation would not have bothered to keep these leftovers at all – they are simply husks now that the Special Ones' spirits have passed through. It says a lot about the sort of person I am that I have collected them all here, allowed them to live. Besides, up until this point they have been somewhat useful. Now that the Special Ones shop is closed, however, that usefulness has come to an end.

'Show yourselves, all of you!' I say. 'Line up in front of me.'

There's movement and some more clanking, and when I shine the torch around again, all four of them have gathered in a bunch – two ex-Lucilles and two ex-Felicities. It's a tragedy to see them. They're nowhere near Special any more. They're barely even human, with their knotted hair and pale, scabby skin. They stare at me and, though I know they can't see me, their expressions make my skin crawl.

'Well, what have you made for me?' I ask, as though everything is normal. 'Supplies are running low.'

One of them scuttles off into a dark corner – as far as her leg chain will allow her to go – and comes back with an armful of things: skirts, headbands, scarves, all of which she drops at my feet. I pick up one of the skirts and examine it. The standard of their work has been going downhill recently. Even so, were the shop still running these items would be snapped up.

I kick one of the supply boxes towards them. 'There's more material in there,' I tell them. 'Back-up batteries for your work lamps, if you need them, too.'

None of them move to collect the box. 'We're hungry and thirsty, Harry,' whispers one of the ex-Felicities suddenly, and an echo of whispers starts up around her, like wind through long grass. *We're hungry, thirsty.*

Annoyed, I push the other box over to them with my foot. Their manners are appalling. The four of them fall on it, tearing it open to get to the food. It's a very generous amount this week. The supermarket skip was fuller than usual. 'Better not eat it all at once,' I say.

They are too busy gorging themselves on biscuits and stale white bread to listen. I would never consume such things myself – they contain no nutritional value – but it's good enough for husks to eat.

While they stuff themselves I do my rounds, making sure everything is correct. As I thought, there's nothing at all down here that could link back to me – no boxes connected with the depot, nothing. Still, it's shocking the state they keep this place in, with no interest in tidiness at all. I order the two ex-Lucilles to funnel the contents of the toilet buckets into the ten-gallon drum I've brought with me, and then they push it over beside the other drums in the corner. It makes only a minor change to the smell, which seems to have permanently seeped into the floor. It clings to the husks themselves.

I jump when one of the ex-Felicities speaks from directly behind me. 'We're still hungry,' she whimpers. 'And cold. How can we work when we're so cold down here?'

'I brought you blankets last time. They should be enough.'

'But they're not!'

It's the tone of voice that bothers me most. These possessions of mine used to be so anxious to please, so full of fearful respect. But that's changed. Now it often feels like they are laughing at me.

Enough. I've been far too patient. Too kind. Slowly I reach down into my bag and feel around for my gun. But it's not there and I realise with a stab of disappointment that it's still under the seat of my car. How could I make such a stupid mistake? It's not like me at all.

Just leave, I tell myself. Once I'm out of here, my head will clear and I'll get myself together again. It's being in this stinking hole with these nightmares that's confusing me.

I start collecting my things and as I do so, one of the ex-Felicities curls her dirty little fingers around my arm.

'Bring us something new to copy,' she whispers. 'Something that the ones on the farm have made.'

I leap back from her, nearly tripping on her chain in my haste. None of them have ever dared touch me like this before. The feeling of her cold, spidery fingers on my skin is beyond disgusting and, besides, I don't want any of my DNA under her nails. This creature can't be any older than nine or ten, but her face, caught in the beam of my torch, looks like that of an old woman.

'You don't need new things. Continue making the same items until I say otherwise.' The sharpness in my voice makes the ex-Felicity retreat into the gloom, but my ill ease grows.

The others slink away too, but a moment later one of them whispers at me from the darkness. 'How is the farm? How are the *Special Ones*?'

'That's none of your business,' I snap.

A thin, mocking laughter starts up. 'We know something's wrong!' one calls back in a singsong voice.

'You don't know anything,' I retort.

'Yes, we do. We can read your mind.'

'That's not possible,' I say and then, to try make them be quiet, I add, 'You won't be down here for much longer, anyway. *He*'ll be letting you out soon, if you behave.'

They all seem to find this hilarious. 'Do you know what happens if you're locked in the darkness for long enough?' one of them hisses from the gloom. 'You learn how to see the future. So we already know we'll be getting out soon. And we know what will happen to you too.'

I fold my arms, raise myself up to my full height to show them that I'm not at all affected by this deranged nonsense. 'And what is that, exactly?'

'Bad things,' they giggle gleefully. 'Very bad things.'

I cannot stand being here any longer. Not for another minute, not for another second. I bundle everything up and hurry for the stairs. The husks laugh in that horrible, scratchy way and one of them even touches my leg as I climb.

The air in the factory above, which seemed a little musty when I first came in from outside, now seems blissfully sweet and clean. I close the trapdoor over the monsters below and bolt it. *You're safe now*, I tell myself as I carefully rub the padlock with a handkerchief to make sure it's free of fingerprints. I am still wearing my gloves, but you can never be too sure. Then I heap the rubble back over the trapdoor.

An urgent need grips me: *I have to get out of here.* I can almost hear the vision in my ear, urging me to run. And so I do – hurrying back to my father's car without taking nearly as much care as I should.

Once I'm back in the driver's seat, I close my eyes and take a little sip from my purple bottle. Get my breathing under control. The tonic spreads through me, cleansing and soothing.

The vision answers my question before I even let it form properly in my mind. *'You're done with them now,'* she says. *'You can leave them there to rot.'*

CHAPTER TWENTY-THREE

When I arrive at work, Mack is lounging around in the loading bay with the front-office girls, who are on one of their many cigarette breaks. Mack is a couple of years older than me – twenty-two maybe, or twenty-three. He's tall – the sort of figure who could easily be intimidating, but his slumped shoulders and high, nasal voice reduce him to harmless. I've modelled my delivery guy persona on him.

A tabloid newspaper is spread out on top of a crate. The radio is on, turned up way too loud, as usual. *'Police now believe that a number of other missing girls could be victims of the Prison Farm cult, as well as the three already released ...'*

'Jeez,' says Mack, bending over the newspaper. 'What kind of a monster does stuff like this?' He shoves it in my face as I walk past. 'Have you *seen* this?'

There's a photograph taken from inside the farmhouse – but looking nothing like how I last saw it. How it's *supposed* to look. The orderly, spotless parlour is now completely chaotic. Furniture tipped over, mess everywhere. The copy of the Special Ones photograph, which usually hangs over the mantelpiece, is gone.

'Looks like hell, doesn't it?' says Mack.

Below it is another image – crime-scene investigators in white disposable coveralls dusting the kitchen for fingerprints. *They won't find anything*, I reassure myself. I have always been very careful about wearing my gloves when I went to collect my tonic.

'I try not to look at that sort of thing,' I say, moving away.

'It's just *awful*,' says Judith from the front office. 'I hate to think what happened to those poor girls while they were in there.'

Judith, whose skirts are always too short and whose necklines are too low. She has feelings for me – I can tell from the way she watches me, when she thinks I'm not aware. Of course, the feelings are in no way reciprocated but I am careful not to be rude to her. She never blinks an eye at the frequent 'lost parcel' or 'invalid address' forms I submit to her and never mentions when these undelivered items 'mysteriously' disappear from the company's database.

'They were starved for days on end. Woken up during the night to perform weird rituals,' says the other front-office girl, Petra. '*And* they were brainwashed into thinking they were reincarnated saints.' She looks around, her owlish eyes even wider than usual. 'You know the worst bit for me, though? That they were forced to chat with people online and give out advice, *every single night.*'

Judith nods. 'It's just *awful*,' she says again. 'Can you imagine? Wondering the whole time why no-one's realised what's going on and raised the alarm. I know I would've, if I'd ever used that site.'

I don't say anything, but I have seen our office's IP address on the user logs for the Special Ones site more than once. And I have definitely spotted a scarf in the lunchroom that could only have come from the Special Ones shop.

I've been trying to stay out of the discussion, loading my orders into the van, but I can't stand it any longer. 'We shouldn't believe everything the media tells us,' I say, as evenly as I can. But no-one is listening.

'I can't stop thinking about the others,' says Petra, leaning over the newspaper. 'The missing ones. Have you seen this?' She taps at a row of photos of the ex–Special Ones, all blurry screen grabs from the education films. Harry's photo is there too. *Interesting*, I find myself thinking. *So the police don't know where Harry is yet.*

Petra shudders. 'I guess they're probably dead, but who knows? Anything's possible with a creep like this.'

'I think it looks like a pretty incredible place to live,' I say tightly, tearing my eyes away from the newspaper. 'You can tell that a lot of care and effort went into making it.'

The others seem to think I'm making a joke.

'Yeah, it looks *real* cosy,' guffaws Mack.

'And so safe with that great big fence all around it!' Petra titters.

Mack swigs the last of a takeaway coffee and stands up. 'Well, I wouldn't worry about it,' he says. 'They'll find those missing ones soon enough – or what's left of them. And they'll find the nut-job behind it all and lock him up for life. They always do in the end.'

Nearby on the packing table is a staple gun. My fingers twitch, longing to seize it and close Mack's mouth permanently. But instead I just slowly shake my head.

●

When my shift ends, I don't return the van to the depot straight away. But I don't go home, either. I go somewhere I haven't been in two years.

The suburb where Esther's parents live is the sort of place I usually despise – ugly modern glass boxes built so close to one another that their roofs nearly touch. Each one has a pseudo-oriental garden in the front – a combination of white pebbles and stunted trees. There is, of course, not a water tank to be seen.

But still, I feel a certain warmth as I near her block. This place is important to me. It's where I first saw Esther, while delivering parcels for that shopaholic mother of hers. There's a park nearby that holds special memories for me, too – I followed Esther there once, after I first spotted her, and watched while she played with her dog near the fountain. How I longed to walk up to her right then! I wanted to tell her how our lives were linked. But I knew I needed to hold back. Wait.

There's a mind-your-own-business quality to Esther's suburb that I can also appreciate. People don't try to chat if you pass them on the street. They don't make noise after 9 pm or create any kind of disturbance. Which is why it's such a shock when I turn into her street to find it blocked by a wall of people and vans.

There are camera crews and photographers pressed up against Esther's fence, boom mics raised and lights flashing. There's even a group of girls mooching about who have made themselves up to look like Esther in long, floating white dresses, their hair pinned back.

I don't bother to stop. I thought that I would at least get a glimpse of Esther. It even crossed my mind that she might take the family dog for a walk, like she used to, and that I might use the opportunity to collect her. But clearly I will have no chance to do that this evening, and so, deeply irritated, I return the van and head home. Esther's popularity is proving inconvenient.

For once I manage to evade Mrs Lewis and, after quickly preparing something to eat, I go directly to the study. It's occurred to me that Esther might still have the same computer, in which case I may be able to watch her through her webcam, just as I used to. But, although her original computer is still part of her family's network, she never has it on. It's frustrating, but at least I am able to access the other computers in the house. Surely Esther will come into view eventually.

First I take control of the laptop in the kitchen. The webcam is angled so that all I can see are the fridge and rubbish bin. But I can hear voices too. At first, with a rush of excitement, I think it is Esther's voice, but it turns out to be her mother.

'– get rid of anything connected with that place,' she is saying. 'So she can just forget it ever even happened.'

'Really?' a male voice answers. Esther's father, I suppose. 'But the doctor said that we should –'

'Well, I think he was wrong.' The mother's legs stomp into view; the lid of the rubbish bin flips open and something white and crumpled is shoved in. Esther's leaving dress. Something else is thrown in on top of it. A comb of some sort.

'Does Tess know you're throwing her things out?' asks the father.

'She's asleep.' Off-screen, I hear the mother sigh. 'Look – it's just that I'm worried about her. She feels *responsible* for what happened there, and for those missing girls – like she has to be the one to find them.'

The father mutters something. 'I know,' the mother replies, her voice cracking. 'She's constantly on the phone with the police, giving them every bit of information she can think of – I caught her calling them at 3 am the other day. She's obsessed. You know what she asked this morning? She wanted me to borrow a bunch of books from the library about cult leaders and psychopaths.'

'Oh, god. What did you say?' asks the father.

'I said no, of course.' Hands reach down into view and yank the liner from the bin. The mother says something I can't hear over the crackling of the bag, and then: '– going to completely drain herself otherwise.'

Then there are footsteps, the sound of a door opening. I picture her pushing the rubbish bag, containing the leaving dress, into an ugly green bin like it's something worthless. But I do not allow myself to feel angry, because I can see this for what it is: an opportunity.

CHAPTER TWENTY-FOUR

It's so strange being back here. In my room. On my bed. It's like being in a time capsule, where everything looks exactly as it did two years ago. My books lined up in the bookshelf, my clothes hanging in the wardrobe. Minnie lying on the rug, her ears pricking hopefully every time I move.

But everything *isn't* exactly how it was. When we first moved in, I refused to put anything up on the walls – a kind of protest about being here. But someone has hung pictures in my absence, mostly just of me. By the door is a big family portrait in a black metal frame. It was taken a very long time ago, back when my hair was much fairer and I was still willing to say 'cheese' for the camera. I'd like to take it down – take *all* of the photos down – but Mum would want to know why.

The girl in the photographs is so naive-looking, so gullible. Is that why he chose me? Not just because I resembled a girl from a hundred years ago, but because he could see how easily

I'd believe whatever he wanted me to? It's hard to fight off thoughts like this, thoughts about *him*, about who he actually is. On the farm he was just a voice – a bodiless shadow – but now he's taking on an actual form and every day that form becomes a little more solid and real. Whenever I see a crowd of people, I automatically scan the faces, wondering if he's there, disguised as an ordinary person. I often think I can feel his eyes on me, watching for a chance to grab me again.

I have other ugly thoughts, too. About how it was that I ended up at the farm. I try to convince myself that it was the same way the others came to be there, but I know that's not true.

I sit up on my bed. I need something to do. Something to distract me. On the farm I had a household to run, but now I'm stuck in my room with everything done for me. My days have no structure, no guiding word, no tasks. Worst of all, no-one listens to me any more, not seriously. It's like my thoughts don't really count.

Down the hall, I can hear the TV. I know I should go and join my parents on the sofa. They are so desperate to make things right. It's hard for them, I know that. But I can't just pretend – like they're trying to – that the last two years didn't happen.

The phone rings and I hear Mum answer it. 'Absolutely not,' she says crisply. 'And it doesn't matter how many more times you people ask, the answer will always be the same.'

I can guess who it is. Yet another reporter requesting an interview.

'She needs to put all this behind her and move on,' I hear Mum say before hanging up.

She and Dad are trying to protect me, I get that. But they're also trying to squeeze me back into a memory. Into the shape of the little girl I once was.

Yesterday, Dad triumphantly presented me with a hamburger. 'Your favourite!' he said. I wasn't hungry, but he was so excited that I made myself take a bite. Instantly, my mouth was flooded with so much grease and salt that I grimaced, and had to force myself to swallow. Dad made a joke of it, but I could see he was crushed. I felt bad, but also frustrated. I mean, who cares about whether I do or don't like hamburgers any more when there are four girls missing? I hurried to my room before I said something I'd regret.

'What's the point of escaping from a prison farm if you spend all your time locked in your room?' I overheard Mum say as I shut the door behind me.

Now, I close my eyes and think for the thousandth time: *If only Harry were here.*

I miss him, even though I insisted that he go. And deep down, though I could never tell anyone, it frightens me that I haven't heard from him since I came home. I wish we'd made some kind of arrangement – a way to communicate secretly – so that we could figure out what to do next, together. But we didn't, and now all I can do is hope that he's safe somewhere, waiting until the time is right to come out.

Or maybe I have to accept that I won't see him again, no matter how much I long to. Who is it exactly that I'm missing, anyway? The Harry I knew on the farm, with his pipe and his beard, is gone for good. What do I even know about the guy who met me outside the gates? For all I know, he's not even really called Harry.

But that's not important. He's still the same on the inside, I'm sure of it. That calm, kind person who sat across from me in the evenings, fixing things, doing his best to make life easier for us, who might not have said much, but what he did say was heartfelt – he still exists, no matter what he's called or how he looks.

I miss him.

I get up from my bed, pad across the room. I keep the comb Harry made for me hidden at the back of the wardrobe, on top of the folded-up leaving dress. I'm not sure what to do about the dress. I thought about burning it, but then I remember the effort Lucille put into making it and it feels wrong.

But the dress isn't in the wardrobe. The comb is gone too. Feeling sick, I run down the hallway to the lounge room. Mum and Dad look up from the TV, startled, as I burst in.

'Where are they? My things from the house?'

'I threw them out this afternoon,' says Mum. She looks a little nervous, but her chin juts out defiantly.

'Why would you do that?'

'Because you *have* to forget about that place.'

The kind of wild fury I used to feel begins burbling up inside me, but before it tips out, I find myself slipping into Esther-mode, drawing on her self-control, her dignity. 'You couldn't possibly understand what it was like,' I say, in Esther's slow, cool tone. 'I'm not a child any more, Mum. You don't get to make decisions for me like that.' Then I hear myself add, 'And the next time one of those reporters calls up about an interview, please tell them yes.'

My parents exchange an anxious look. 'Tessy, do you really think –' Mum begins.

'The police have given up on those girls,' I tell her. 'I want to talk about it on TV. Make everyone understand that they could still be alive, and that we can't stop searching yet.'

I mean what I say, but I don't mention the other reason I suddenly want an interview. That by doing it, maybe I'll be able to get a message to Harry, asking him to let me know if he's okay at least.

Then, bracing myself, I go out the back of our house. The bin isn't where it usually is. It must be rubbish-collection night, which means it's been wheeled into the lane. I'll have to leave the confines of our property if I want to check its contents. I hate the way I instantly start shivering at the thought of this, but I do my best to keep it together, opening the gate and slipping into the yard. I hope there's no media people lurking out here – or anyone else.

The bin is on the other side of the laneway, illuminated by a streetlight. I hurry over and open it, pulling at the top bag. Rubbish spews from it, and I see there's a slit down the length of the plastic, like it's been deliberately sliced open. Harry's comb clatters to the ground, spaghetti strands caught in its teeth. There's no sign of the leaving dress. Not in this bag, or any of the others.

I stand there for a moment, hands slimy with rubbish, surrounded by empty dog-food tins and toast crusts, trying to work out what's happened. And then, out of the corner of my eye, I see something move. It's to my right, out of the streetlight's reach.

I freeze. Maybe it's just a cat. Or a shrub, being blown by the wind. Maybe it's nothing at all. But a blind panic seizes me and I feverishly wrench the back gate open, almost tripping over in my haste to get back inside, back into the house, back into my room, where I can lock the door and window and try to breathe again.

CHAPTER TWENTY-FIVE

I place the dress in the lounge room, being careful to touch it as little as possible. The odour of rubbish clings to the fabric, but it holds Esther's scent too and I do not want to lose any more of that. Whenever I feel doubt about our current situation, I kneel in front of it, imagining the day – surely not too far away now – when its folds will be filled out by Esther's form.

●

'I really like Esther's style,' says Petra, during her afternoon cigarette break the next day. 'Long skirt and high collar – it's elegant. And that French knot thing she does with her hair – very cool.'

Judith takes a puff on her cigarette. 'She might not look like that any more, you know.' Her own hemline, I've noticed, has dropped a little lately. 'Most of the footage they're showing now is old stuff, from the portal. No-one's seen her since she was rescued.'

'Which is why tonight's interview is going to be *so* interesting,' says Petra, sipping her coffee. 'I can't wait! I might even go out to the studio and see if I can get a glimpse of her arriving.'

'You idiot!' laughs Judith. 'It was filmed this morning. And I bet you couldn't have got near the place anyway.'

She couldn't have. I know because I tried myself and found the studio door completely blocked by gawpers, weirdos and security. All I could do was hang in the background, my gun tucked into my work jacket.

'You know, I'm surprised she's doing the interview at all,' muses Judith. 'The other two are still in hospital.'

'It was probably the money,' says Petra. 'I heard that one network offered her two million for an interview.'

'I heard three,' says Judith. 'But I don't think it was the money. People who've gone through this sort of thing almost *never* go on TV, especially not so soon afterwards. There must be something else going on.'

Petra's eyes gleam. 'I can't wait. The promos say there are going to be *explosive revelations*, whatever that means. Maybe they've worked out who the creep behind it all is. I heard there've been thousands of calls to Crime Stoppers –'

'Are you okay?' Judith interrupts, glancing back at me. 'Did you just staple your thumb?'

'No,' I say, through gritted teeth. 'Everything's fine.'

Judith stands, takes a final drag on her cigarette and then stubs it out on an old saucer. 'Well, like I said, whatever ends up happening tonight, I get the feeling it's going to be interesting.'

●

The only chair left in the lounge room is a purple vinyl recliner – it was too modern, too ugly, to go to the farm. It was in this very chair that they found my mother, I believe, with my brother and father on the sofa nearby, the gas heating turned up to the highest setting, as usual. None of them could've cared less about conserving energy.

Usually I just sit on the floor or on a milk crate, but it feels appropriate to sit in my mother's chair tonight. She used to watch *Tina Talks It Through* religiously. The show promotes itself as an 'in-depth conversation' between the host and whoever they've coerced into appearing. As far as I can tell, the main goal of the show seems to be to get the guest to cry.

As the theme music plays, the camera shows Tina arranging her notes and planning, I assume, today's strategy for extracting tears. Opposite her, on the brown leather couch provided for the guests, is Esther.

Her back is straight, hands folded in her lap. I recognise the expression on her face. It's how she used to look during verification. Radiantly calm, inwardly focused. Composed. How I used to love watching her standing there! But her expression is almost the only familiar thing about her. She's wearing jeans and a T-shirt like she's some ordinary teenager, and her face has been so caked with make-up that she's barely recognisable. It hurts me to see her like this, but I take solace in what has remained the same: that serene expression, her beautiful long hair.

Looking at her makes me realise just how much I've missed being able to see and speak with her every day. To know what is in her head. I try to read her thoughts but it's difficult through the television screen. All I am able to detect clearly is her immense discomfort.

I lean forward and focus on her image, in particular her forehead, pushing my words in. *Do not worry, Esther. I am here, guiding you.*

The show begins with the same old footage of the police ransacking my farm, followed by the shots of Esther returning home. There's the nauseating voice-over telling us about the *terrible lives the prisoners led under the ever-present watch of their captor* and Esther's *daring escape from certain death*. There's no mention at all of Harry.

When it's over, Tina turns to Esther with a concerned smile. 'The whole world has seen the terrible footage of that place, Tess. You were there for two years – no electricity, no contact with the outside world, continual hard labour. It would've broken a lot of people. How did you cope?'

Esther moves uncomfortably. 'I coped because I had to.'

'Well, I think I can say on behalf of everyone that you're a pretty incredible young woman,' says Tina. The studio audience claps and whoops and there's a shot of some girls in the audience, Esther lookalikes, who smile and wave at the camera.

'So what have you been doing since you returned home?' asks Tina, when the camera focuses on her again. 'Are you picking up your studies? Reconnecting with old friends? I guess you've got a lot of TV to catch up on, right?'

Esther looks a little taken aback. 'Um, no,' she says. 'I've been trying to help find the ones who are still missing. They're out there somewhere, and –'

'Really?' says Tina, her eyebrows lifting. 'Haven't you been through enough already? I would have thought you'd leave that to the police.'

I can tell from the way Esther's mouth forms a grim line that she still shares my opinion of police capabilities. 'I just pass on anything I remember that I think might help,' she says.

Tina arranges her expression into one of concern. 'And have you had any contact with the other two survivors from the prison farm yet?'

'Well, no,' says Esther, frowning. 'Felicity – I mean Zoe – is in hospital, isn't she, and I don't think –'

But Tina silences her with a dazzling smile and then turns to address the camera. 'We're going to take a short break now, but stay with us because we'll return with something very exciting – a special reunion here on *Tina Talks It Through*.'

During the commercial break I pace up and down the hallway as I cannot bear all those advertisements for useless, landfill-producing items. When I hear the theme music, I hurry back in. There are now two other people sitting on chairs next to Esther. One of them I recognise straight away as the last Felicity, but it takes me a few moments to realise that the other girl – with blonde, straight hair – is the last Lucille.

There's something in her face that gives me a strong feeling of foreboding. Her expression is compressed, like there's something simmering there. Sitting beside her is Esther, looking tense, and I see her eyes flit to the side, like she's looking for a possible escape route.

Tina is sitting up in her own chair, looking very pleased with herself. She speaks to Felicity first, asking how she's feeling.

'Much better, thanks.'

'I hear you went back home this morning, right? That must have felt good.'

Felicity nods. 'Yep, it was great. Although one of the rabbits died while I was away.'

Tina leans in a little closer. Tilts her head. 'So what was it like on the farm?'

'It was okay,' says Felicity cautiously, 'so long as you remembered about the pretending.'

'Pretending?'

'Like, I had to pretend we all lived in the olden days and my name was Felicity. I almost started to think I really *was* called Felicity, but I know that's not true now. They told me at the hospital.'

This is disappointing. *The brainwashers have got to her too.* It's a shame that these girls should so easily be convinced of their ordinariness, but on the other hand it's further proof that Esther and I will be better off on our own.

Tina nods. 'And what were the others like to live with?'

'Well, Harry was my favourite.'

Tina smiles sadly, then prompts, 'And Tess?'

Felicity looks blank.

'Esther.'

Felicity gives a little grin at Esther. 'She helped me a lot. She always reminded me that my name was Felicity and she made sure I got up early so I would have time to do all my chores before bedtime.'

'And was she fun? Did she play with you and give you hugs?'

Felicity looks shocked, as well she might. 'Of course not! She wasn't allowed.'

Lucille breaks in and I'm struck by the spiteful gleam in her eye, bright as a blade. 'Esther was very cold,' she says. 'She didn't feel anything. She used to freak me out – it was like she was dead sometimes. She could do these terrible things without reacting at all. It wasn't normal.'

The camera cuts to Esther then, probably hoping she'll get angry and start arguing with Lucille. Esther sits up straight, her face flushed. 'You know I *had* to act that way! It wasn't how I felt inside.'

Don't be rattled by this nonsense, I urge her. *Stay calm.*

'I got locked in the cellar once for days and days without food,' Lucille continues, talking over the top of Esther. 'And when I was finally allowed back up – literally starving – she just hands me a bit of bread and says, "Here" – like, *get on with it, don't complain.*'

There's a murmur of disapproval from the studio audience. I grind my teeth in irritation. Fasting is a necessary discipline for a Special One. It strips away what is unnecessary and hones the mind for work.

Lucille shakes her head, looks down. Wipes some undoubtedly fake tears from her cheeks. Tina turns to Esther. The look in her eyes is much cooler than before. 'That sounds incredibly difficult. Would you like to comment, Tess?'

Felicity jumps in before Esther can answer. 'We were *all* punished!' she says. 'But only when we'd done something wrong.'

Lucille looks up again, eyes flashing with anger. 'We weren't *all* punished,' she snaps. 'You were, Zoe, and I was, but Harry and Esther were *never* punished. And they broke rules all the time.'

'Hey!' protests Felicity. 'That's not –'

But Tina cuts her off. 'It sounds,' she remarks, 'like the four of you weren't really equal.'

'We weren't even *close* to equal!' Lucille snaps. 'Esther and Harry were in charge. We had to do what they said, or we'd get in trouble. And you know something else? Everyone keeps saying that Harry is dead, like the other girls who were renewed. Well, I don't believe it. Esther was renewed and *she's* still alive.'

Tina swings round to Esther. 'Do *you* think he's still alive?'

Esther is very quiet for a moment and the camera zooms in on her face, waiting for her reaction. I lean forward too, wondering if she'll finally come clean about Harry. 'I don't know,' she says carefully, 'but I hope so. And I hope he's okay.'

Lucille snorts. 'Of course he's okay – he's probably in hiding! He's the one who kidnapped us all, so he's not going to give himself up to the police when he's a criminal.'

Tina crosses her legs. 'Let's talk about that for a moment, as clearly things with Harry are more complicated than we've all been led to believe.'

Lucille jumps in again. 'It's not complicated. Harry kidnapped me, although he and Esther called it "collection". He told me he was a talent scout for a movie and invited me to visit the set.'

Tina nods. 'And you believed him.'

Lucille closes her eyes for a moment, the colour rising in her cheeks. 'He seemed so … nice. I trusted him.'

Tina swings back to Felicity. 'Did Harry *collect* you too?'

Felicity nods. 'I was walking home after school and he said he had some baby chickens to show me.'

'But that was also a lie, right?' says Tina.

'No, he really did have baby chickens,' says Felicity, earnestly. 'On the farm. We ate one – after it grew bigger, of course.'

Lucille turns sideways in her chair, arms tightly crossed, her narrowed eyes fixed on Esther. 'Why don't you ask *her* how she was kidnapped by Harry? I'd love to hear what she says.'

Esther suddenly pales and I sense her tensing up. The camera seems to sense it too, and instantly her face fills the screen.

'How did Harry kidnap *you*, Tess?' asks Tina.

I feel my own body tighten a little, but from excitement rather than fear. What I've seen in this interview has tested my trust in Esther, though her glow is still there. Like Lucille, I'm very curious to hear how she'll answer the question. If she'll tell the truth. There's no harm in the world knowing, after all.

Esther's voice is steady, but firm. 'Harry didn't kidnap me.'

Tina frowns. 'So how were you taken to the farm? Were you forced at gunpoint? Or tricked somehow?'

There's a moment of silence and, although I can't read her actual thoughts, I can tell that Esther's struggling with what to say. *Just tell them the truth,* I advise her. *There's no shame in it.*

I know that this message gets through to her because Esther looks directly into the camera and answers steadily and clearly. 'No-one made me go there. It was my choice.'

CHAPTER TWENTY-SIX

The show cuts to another ad break and I take the opportunity to prepare a snack. I'm feeling exultant. Ugly make-up and bad clothes can't disguise the fact that Esther is still the same inside. She has told the truth. Announced to the world that she came to the farm because she wanted to be there. Knew that she needed to join me. The bond between us feels so strong right now. I can't believe I ever thought she was growing away from me.

When I return to the living room with my cucumber slices, there's a shot of the studio audience on the TV. The girls dressed like Esther aren't waving any more. Everyone seems very quiet.

'Tess,' says Tina, seriously. 'We've just heard some very disturbing accusations against you and Harry. I'm going to ask you this straight out: are you the leader of the Special Ones cult? In conjunction with Harry?'

'Of course not!' snaps Esther.

'Well, then, who *is* the leader?' asks Tina.

'I – don't know.'

'But you must have *seen* him?' pushes Tina. 'He must have come to the farm to check on you.'

'He watched us through the cameras,' Felicity pipes up.

Tina's disbelief is quite apparent. 'What kind of cult leader doesn't live with his disciples? Surely that's the whole point?'

Esther returns Tina's suspicious gaze without flinching. 'I guess he's different.'

Without realising it, I have assumed a kneeling position on the ground in front of the television, close enough to the screen that I can feel warmth emanating from its surface.

Yes, I am different. I listened to you, Esther, when no-one else would. I understood you, when no-one else could.

Esther's face suddenly turns so that she's looking directly into the camera. Through the screen – at me. Once again she's heard my words, I'm sure of it.

'And so the leader of the Special Ones asked you to join him?' asks Tina.

'Yes.'

'Didn't you just tell us before you'd never spoken to him?' It's apparent from her tone that Tina thinks she's just caught Esther lying.

Esther maintains her composure. 'No. I said I never saw his face.'

'He sent you emails?' asks Tina.

'Letters.'

'But how did he *know* you?' the irritating woman persists. 'What made him choose *you*?'

It's such a ridiculous question. I didn't *choose* Esther. I simply found her again.

'I don't know,' says Esther, sounding frustrated. 'An envelope just appeared on my windowsill one day with my name on it.'

'How did you write back?' presses Tina.

'I left my letters in the same place I'd found his.'

'And what did he write about?'

Esther frowns for a moment, looking down at her hands, and I sense that she's reluctant to share the contents of our correspondence. 'All kinds of things,' she eventually says. 'His philosophies, how he felt about the world. He hated the way most people waste their lives. He said he wanted to live differently. To do something important and valuable and – *special*. He told me that we'd lived before and that we'd live again.'

I lean forward, so that my face is not far from hers on the other side of the screen. My heart is racing, alight with joy. I remember the excitement of that period so well, those early exchanges. The bond between us was instant, of course, and I desperately wanted to tell her why, about how we'd known each other in a previous life. But I knew I had to let this information come gradually.

Drop by drop I reminded her about her past. Our shared life. Then I began to let her know what her future held. In the final letter I instructed her to leave her window open that night when she went to bed. The last sentence I wrote was: *When you wake up, your new life will have begun.* Over the final full stop I placed a little white pill.

'You believed it?' asks Tina. 'All that reincarnation stuff?'

Esther closes her eyes. She looks very pale. Drained. 'I was a lot younger back then. Things were ... so hard at that time. Or at least I thought they were. I was very naive.'

Poor Esther. She looks so uncomfortable and I don't blame her. It must feel terrible to have to lie like this.

Tina lets out a rush of air, almost like she's disappointed. 'So what's going to happen now, do you think? If this leader is still out there, is he going to go and kidnap a whole new bunch of people? Start a new branch of the cult?'

'No,' says Esther firmly. 'That won't happen.'

'How can you be so sure?'

Again Esther turns and looks directly at the camera, and I understand that what she's about to say is intended for me. 'Because I am going to find him first.'

My heart expands with joy. She's searching for me! I lean forward and press my face against hers through the screen.

It's what I used to do sometimes when I watched her in the house, so I could feel closer to her.

Don't worry, my most precious one, I promise her. *We'll be together again very soon.*

CHAPTER TWENTY-SEVEN

We haven't spoken about it yet. The interview. In fact, we haven't spoken at all. Mum and I drove back from the studio in total silence. Not the comfortable sort, either. When we arrived home, the people waiting outside had to leap out of the way – it was clear Mum wouldn't slow down as she drove through the gates.

Once we were inside, she stormed off to her room and slammed the door while I found myself heading to the kitchen. I needed to *do* something – active and mindless.

My first urge was to start scrubbing – to clean the oven, for instance, but ours is used so rarely that I knew there wouldn't be much satisfaction in it. After searching through the cupboards and finding flour and an ancient sachet of yeast, I decided to make bread.

Yet even kneading dough didn't stop my thoughts entirely. How could I have been so stupid? Had I really believed that

I'd be able to appear on prime time and talk only about the missing girls? That I'd be able to get a message to Harry somehow? I remember what those news shows are like. I feel like an idiot for thinking it'd be different for me.

I also feel guilty about the way Harry was slandered. I should've done more to defend him. But even as I was trying to stick up for him, I found the same terrible thought creeping into my head that has been pestering me for days now: *How much do you truly know about him?* I don't want it to be there. But I also can't seem to get it out.

On the farm, I never thought about who Harry had been before he was Special, just as I tried not to think about who I'd been either. I'd never even considered *how* he came to be there. There were more important things to focus on, like surviving.

I squeeze the dough between my fingers, the frustration ballooning inside me. I wish so much that I could see Harry – even for a short time, or speak to him at least. I have so many questions.

●

I'm taking the bread rolls from the oven that evening when Mum finally comes out of the bedroom. Her face looks blotchy.

'Was life with me and your dad really that bad?' she blurts out. 'So bad that you thought joining a cult would be better?'

I know I shouldn't feel annoyed, but I do. Wasn't this covered in the interview? The one she's heard twice, now?

'It was a mistake, Mum.' Tendrils of steam curl up from the bread. 'I was dumb. And I didn't know I was joining a cult. I thought I was doing what I was destined to do. I believed I was ...' I trail off, unable to say the word.

Mum shakes her head. I'm not sure she's even heard me.

'When you disappeared, the police kept referring to you as a runaway,' she says tightly. 'But I said that no, you'd never do that. I insisted you'd been kidnapped.' She covers her face with her hands so that her words are muffled and distorted. 'You told the police, didn't you? That you'd gone to that place by choice.'

'Yes.'

'But you didn't tell us.'

I say nothing. What *can* I say?

Mum straightens up, her eyes suddenly as hard and cold as the kitchen counter. 'Tell me the truth, Tess. You went to that place because of Harry.'

'No!' I say, suddenly shrill. She hasn't changed. Not one bit. She still won't listen to me. 'I didn't meet Harry until I got there. You have to believe me. I'm your daughter.'

'Well, it'd help if you acted like you were!' Mum yells, her face red. 'I feel like you're some stranger who doesn't want to be here – who disapproves of everything we say and do!'

I must look shocked, because instantly Mum covers her mouth. 'I'm sorry,' she says. 'I didn't mean it. I'm just – it's all so – oh, *Tessy!*'

She rushes towards me, arms outstretched. Instinctively, I flinch and pull back. Mum freezes, arms midair. Then she lets them drop and bursts into tears.

I stand there, feeling awkward and terrible. I know I should say something, or even just hug her – that's what she wants more than anything. But I can't. It would feel fake. Talking should be easier than hugging, but the trouble is there's too much to say. I want to tell her I'm still discovering how much being on the farm has changed me. What it's like obsessing over why he chose me. Why he wrote to me and me alone, making me believe that I wasn't just some ordinary girl. And always, *always* having to live with the feeling that maybe I can still do something to make it right again. Survivor's guilt, I guess they'd call it. But this is so much more complex than that. My head is too full. My heart is too guilty.

'I promised myself that if you came back, I would never get mad or argue with you again,' says Mum. She's stopped crying but her voice is awful – all strangled-sounding. It makes my own throat ache to hear it. 'I told myself I would agree to everything you wanted, all your opinions. But that was never going to work.'

I think about the promises *I* made too, during sleepless nights on the farm. Those deals with fate. I would be the perfect daughter. Smile for photographs. Hold back my criticisms of the way my parents live. *I'll do anything.*

'I guess it's not that easy,' I mumble.

Mum reaches out a cautious hand and puts it on my shoulder. It's hard, but I manage not to move although I feel it there, heavy as a rock. 'The important thing is that you're back here. Safe.'

'Yes.' But as I say it, I find myself remembering something from the night I last saw Harry, outside the police station.

A car.

The glint of metal from just inside the window.

The feeling, like a constant prickle in my neck, that someone was watching me.

Safe is the last thing I feel.

CHAPTER TWENTY-EIGHT

'There was something about that girl – Tess – which is not to be trusted. Even I could see that, on my terrible old TV.'

Mrs Lewis is sitting in my kitchen, perched on a plastic crate. I am sitting opposite her, also on a crate, with her laptop open on my knees. I am still not quite sure how she ended up in here, other than that she somehow got to the front door (I must have left the gate unlocked – a careless mistake), and I quickly understood that it would be more dangerous to forbid her entry than to let her in.

She will only be allowed to stay for a short while, however. I finally have a day off work and there are many more pressing things to do than help Mrs Lewis discover what's wrong with her laptop. From what I can tell so far, the short answer to this appears to be *everything*.

I look up from the computer. 'What do you mean, "not to be trusted"?'

Mrs Lewis purses her lips. 'She's holding things back, that one – picking and choosing what she reveals. Did you notice how she hardly looked anyone directly in the eye? Very suspicious. And as for this mysterious "him" who she claims is the leader of the Special Ones – well, I don't believe he even exists. It's obvious that Harry is the one in charge – no matter how much she denies it.' Mrs Lewis leans closer. Close enough that I can smell her stale cigarette breath. 'She's in love with him. That's why she won't say where he is. She's trying to protect him. Classic Stockholm.'

A dust storm whirls inside me, blurring my judgement. But although I'd like to wring her skinny neck right now, it's not really Mrs Lewis I'm angry at. It's Harry. This, after all, is his fault. I had been so fair to him and he broke his contract.

From the moment I first saw the photograph, I knew that *I* was Harry and that I would eventually live with the others in the farmhouse. But as it got closer to the time when I was to move in, a niggling doubt began to grow inside me.

Eventually the vision appeared before me during a meditation and confirmed what I already suspected. *'It is not the right time for you to move into the house. Your role is to watch over the group, keep it safe, keep it controlled, while remaining on the outside.'*

As the vision said this, I knew she was right. There were still so many things that needed to be organised. The Special Ones portal, for instance.

But there was one thing that still troubled me. 'Does this mean that I won't ever live with Esther?' I asked. It had taken months of back-breaking work to bring the farm to a livable state – even after I acquired some help. It was a terrible blow to think I might never live there.

'*When the time is right, you and Esther will be together,*' the vision had assured me. '*But there are many things you must do before that is possible. Bring the Special Ones back together, and choose someone to stand in for you, until it is time to take up your rightful place.*'

I nodded. It was what I had already felt to be true.

The vision raised a hand, streams of light billowing from her as she moved. '*It's important to choose your stand-in very carefully. Someone who won't ever question you. And be sure that he doesn't stay too long. Otherwise he may begin to believe he is more important than he really is.*'

•

'Mrs Lewis, your computer is past repair,' I say, handing it back to her. This may not be true, but I've wasted enough time. 'You'll need a new one.'

'Oh no!' wails Mrs Lewis. 'But they're so expensive! Could you help me find a cheap one somewhere?'

It's so tempting to shout at this insufferable woman. Order her out of my house and tell her I have more important things to do than help her shop. But it seems wasteful to destroy my carefully constructed *good neighbour* persona, especially when I am about to bring Esther here. The last thing I need is an offended Mrs Lewis spying on me.

'Hang on,' I tell her and, going into the pantry, I grab one of the undelivered laptops from the pile and hand it to her. 'Here. You can have this.'

Her eyes bulge. 'How wonderful! How much do I owe you?'

'It's a gift.'

Mrs Lewis looks like she might cry or, worse, hug me. 'I am so *blessed* to have you as a neighbour!' she gushes. 'Let me at least cook you dinner as a way of saying thanks. I often think, *that poor young man must be so lonely all by himself, stuck in that place where such a terrible thing happened.* You come round and I'll cook you some spaghetti.'

'That's really not necessary,' I say firmly, and usher her, as quickly as I can, out the door. I hurry around to the garage and get in my father's car. I should wait until she's gone, but I'm impatient to get on with my work so Mrs Lewis has only just reached the front gate when I drive up. She hurries to swing it open for me, her purple yoga pants almost snagging on a protruding twist of wire in her haste.

'Where are you going?' she asks, when I get out to lock the gate again behind me.

'Just catching up with an old colleague,' I tell her. And then I drive off quickly, before she can delay me any further. Nestled safely in the glove compartment is my gun.

●

It's almost amusing how obsessed the world seems to be with finding Harry at the moment. All this fuss for someone who amounts to so very little! Crime Stoppers keeps replaying grainy footage of Harry from the house; they've even produced an identikit photograph that makes him look twice his actual age and three times his weight.

One national paper – the *Morning Star* – publishes an article describing all that is known about Harry (basically nothing) and where he might be (basically anywhere). A psychic appears on daytime TV claiming that Harry has committed suicide and his spirit is sorry for everything he did. Several people come forward claiming to be him. I hear a police spokesman say that they've received so many calls it may take weeks to go through them all.

Of course, I am also very interested in finding Harry, and unlike the media and the police I have a lot of useful information to hand. Not just facts, either, but detailed insights into how his mind works and what his weaknesses are. This is why I head for the part of town where the lowlifes hang out – the thieves, the drug dealers, the criminals.

It's where I first found Harry, and no doubt where I'll find him again.

I drive slowly around the litter-strewn streets, getting out occasionally to stare down a dark alley or to ask someone if they've seen a dodgy-looking guy who seems like he's hiding from something. One drunk laughs in my face. 'You just described ninety per cent of the people around here,' he says.

Eventually I come to an empty doorstep – the very one where I first spotted Harry, all those years ago. He hadn't looked like much back then, sitting there with another wasted guy, both of them drugged-up and dirty – but he bore a strong enough resemblance to the Harry in the photograph for me to stop and watch. When the other man had said, 'Pass us the bottle, Harry,' it felt like a clear sign.

I hadn't needed to use force with him in the beginning. The promise of some cheap gear was enough to lure Harry out to the farmhouse, where I locked him in the changing room with a bucket of water. He was in a sorry state when I went back a week later. Battered and bruised. Shaking from the withdrawal. I stood over him and breathed in his fear. It smelled good.

When the worst of it was over, he took to work at the farmhouse better than I'd anticipated. He seemed to genuinely enjoy it – sleeping out under the stars, eating simple food and drinking nothing but water. After a month, he told me he wanted to stay. I remember the eagerness in his voice. His sincerity. 'It's really changed me, being here.'

I smiled but did not say what I was thinking: *people like you are incapable of change.* Instead I said, 'That is very good news.'

It was then that I showed him the photograph, explaining that I wanted him to stand in as Harry for a while, until I was ready to take over myself. I told him that I would pay him – a pittance, but it was steadier work than he'd ever had. It was obvious he would've done it for free, but I wanted to be clear that this was just a job for him. That he wasn't *special.* And he agreed.

It was soon after this that I finally spotted the first of the Special Ones – a Lucille – coming home from a dance class. Her hair was the wrong colour but the set of her features and the way she moved were instantly familiar to me. Excitement leapt in me. *It's definitely her.* I had always imagined that the first collection would be Esther, but I saw now that it didn't really matter. I would collect them as fate and fortune allowed.

I remember the excitement of that first collection so vividly. I had driven Harry into town that evening and I could tell he was nervous, as well as confused. We parked near the dance school and waited until the blonde girl came out.

'I know her,' I told Harry. 'Can you go tell her that her dad is in trouble and we need her help? I'll wait for you both around the corner.'

Harry looked mildly uncertain as he hopped out, but did not question me. I parked around the corner and popped the boot. From under my seat I pulled a blanket – an old favourite of my brother's – and pulled on a balaclava. I'd felt jittery with excitement until I heard the vision counselling me. *Stay calm, stay in control.*

A few moments later, Harry and the girl entered the lane. I saw him gesture to my car and she peered forward, trying to see me through the tinted windscreen.

'Is my dad okay?' she said, looking worried.

'I'm sure everything's fine,' Harry told her. 'He just needs your help.'

A thrill passed through me as the girl came closer. Finally my little family was coming back together! The moment she turned away from the car, I stepped out quickly and threw the blanket over her, swaddling her tightly. Muffling her cries.

'Help me lift her into the boot,' I said to Harry. My voice was calm, but I made it clear he had to obey me.

Harry stood fixed to the spot, staring at me with an almost comical look of horror on his face. I had to heave her in by myself.

'What's wrong with you?' I snapped, when the boot was securely closed. 'You're paid to help me.'

'You lied to her!' His voice was strained.

'She belongs on the farm,' I told him. 'She just doesn't realise it yet.' From within the boot came the sound of muted yelling. 'Let's go,' I said, striding around to the driver's seat.

'No!' said Harry. He had the nerve to sound angry. To doubt what I was doing. 'You have to let her out!'

I knew that I did not have to justify my actions to this temporary fill-in, but then he made a move towards the boot. I pulled my gun from my jacket and pressed it to his chest. 'If you open that, I will shoot you and then I will shoot her too.' I spoke slowly and clearly so he would understand how serious I was. 'Get in the car, and let's go.'

●

I trawl the streets for hours, my frustration and irritation steadily growing until they threaten to spill out. I uncover no sign of Harry – not a trace. As far as I can tell he hasn't checked into any of the boarding houses he used to frequent when he could cover the rent, or the doorsteps he'd sleep on when he couldn't. No-one seems to have any information, not even when I threaten them or offer money.

I feel bone-weary by the time I start driving home late that evening and I am sorely tempted to take a swig from the purple bottle – but the contents are getting low and I am not sure when Esther will be back to make me a new supply.

When I stop to unbolt the front gate, I find that a newspaper has been shoved between the bars. It's almost definitely been *passed on* from Mrs Lewis. It falls to the ground as I swing the gate open and I see the front headline: *HUNT FOR HARRY HEATS UP.*

Reading it, I have a revelation. Why should I bother searching for Harry anyway? There was the attraction of personally making him pay for his betrayal, but, just as the vision warned, searching for Harry is taking up too much of my time – which is ridiculous when there are so many others who are more than willing to do the job for me. They just need a little assistance.

When I get inside, I go straight to the loose floorboard and pull out the only file that was not burned during my purge. Harry Fernard's file. My instinct to keep it was correct. It contains all the information I have collected about my former employee. I decide to scan only the police file with its accompanying mugshot, and the document that Harry wrote out and signed when he began working for me. The contract which stated that once Harry's two years of working for me had finished, he would disappear and have no further contact with me or any of the girls from the farm. If he'd just stuck to this, everything would've been fine. But he didn't, and so now he must endure the consequences.

There are many other things I could include, but this is enough to get things started. Then, using a fake address and a proxy server, I shoot off an email to the editor of the *Morning Star.*

CHAPTER TWENTY-NINE

I've come down to the kitchen for some water and no-one
is about. Dad is probably at work and maybe Mum has
gone out, although that would be unusual. I think they've
decided that one or other of them should always be here
with me. As protection, I guess. Or maybe to stop me from
disappearing again.

I take the opportunity to go through the bin, as I've
suspected for a while that my parents are hiding mail. All I've
received are some cards from people saying they *admire me*,
although they don't actually say what for. I'm positive there
must be other things being sent – maybe even something,
heavily disguised, from Harry.

Sure enough, shoved into the back of the bin is an
envelope with my name on it. It's not from Harry, though.
And it's definitely not a fan letter. The opening line, written
in angry block letters, accuses me of being a witch and of

sacrificing the missing girls for my black magic. *You do know what used to happen to witches, don't you?*

Feeling unsettled, I'm just hiding the letter back in the bin when I notice the newspaper on the kitchen bench. It's strange, because my parents generally don't buy papers. Then I see the headline:

HARRY PAID TO BE ON FARM!

Below the headline are two photos of a boy, one taken face-forward, the other in profile. With a shock, I realise it's Harry. He looks much younger than when I first met him, but that's not the only reason he's hard to recognise. The boy in the photo seems sick and dirty. His shoulders slump, his expression is closed. He's nothing like the Harry I knew on the farm. Shaking, I start to read.

For Harry Fernard, life on the prison farm was not a daily battle to survive. He did not need to fear that the smallest mistake would result in punishment or even death. Fernard was not one of the so-called 'Special Ones'. His place on the farm was secure. For two years, at least.

Many have questioned Fernard's exact role within the cult. Some have suggested that he is in fact its spiritual leader. But recent documents obtained by the Morning

Star *indicate that Harry's role filled a more basic need.*
For Harry Fernard, the prison farm was simply a cushy
live-in job.

Feeling dizzy, I scan the page. Halfway down is a photograph of something written out by hand. It seems to be a kind of contract.

'I, Harry Fernard, agree to keep the Special Ones
safe from intruders. I will also ensure that no-one
leaves its confines, unless I have received other
instructions ...'

For Fernard — former ward of the state, drug-addict
and petty criminal who had lived on the streets since he was
thirteen — this job must have seemed like a dream come
true. His duties included light farm work and a little bit of
eavesdropping. His main task was to make sure that any
misdemeanours, insubordination or disrespect were swiftly
dealt with.

And then, of course, there were the 'renewals', as they
were euphemistically referred to. No doubt these took a
little more effort, but Harry was a model employee and
carried them out without complaint. And when his two-year
contract ended, he simply walked through the gates and left
the others to their fate.

Even before I've finished the article, I am positive that *he* is behind it. He's leaked information about Harry – his last name, details of his past – to help identify him and lead to his capture. But I can tell that's not the only motivation, or even the main one. This is a message for me. It's meant to convince me that I too should give up on Harry. Stop defending him.

Of course it's a shock to read that Harry was paid to guard us, but in my heart I still believe that he's a good person. And I am positive that it wasn't just money that kept him with us on the farm. You can't live as closely with someone as I did with Harry and not be able to know something of how they think and feel. Harry probably didn't realise what he was getting involved in when he wrote that contract – it's not so different from what happened to me, after all. Perhaps I'm the only person in the world who could understand that, but it's still the truth. And no matter the mistakes either of us made in the past, the bad decisions, the wrong turns – neither of us should've had to go through what we did. We shouldn't be blamed for the things *he* did.

The more I think about it, the angrier I get. Not just because of this attack on Harry, but because of how *he's* still trying to manipulate my thoughts and feelings. He obviously believes he has control.

I stand at the kitchen bench, motionless except for the rapid pumping of my heart. *Does* he still have control? Am I still letting him shape my life?

Maybe.

But, I decide on the spot, *not any more.*

It's not that I'm no longer afraid, because I am. But now I also feel a white-hot fury that *he* has made me feel this way for so long. I scrunch up the newspaper and shove it in the bin. There's a tingling in my fingers, little pricks of adrenalin, which quickly spread across my body. *I'm not giving up.*

It's only then that I become aware of people yelling outside.

CHAPTER THIRTY

The media pack outside Esther's house is as dense as it's ever been. The crowd of gawpers has doubled too, although there's a noticeable absence of Esther lookalikes. As I pull up I'm aware of some kind of commotion, but it's not until I park and open the door of my van that I hear the woman screaming.

'Where is my daughter? Tell me what you did with her!'

Over the top of the crowd I can just glimpse a pair of hands gripping Esther's front gate, rattling it vigorously. The screaming rises like a wave once more. 'I know you know something. You and Harry!'

I grab a random parcel from the back of my van and go and stand by a man in a tracksuit with a dog on a leash. 'What's going on here, mate?' I ask. 'I've got a parcel to deliver to that place.' I do my *vaguely curious bystander* act smoothly, but inside I'm seething. These people are in my way.

'You know those prison-farm girls, from the cult?' says the man. The dog lies down with a resigned grunt.

'Hard not to have heard about it.'

'Well, the girl who got out first – the tall, spooky one – she lives in there with her parents.'

'And who's the crazy person shaking the gate?'

'Steady on, mate – that's the mother of one of the missing girls,' he says, looking at me strangely. 'Can't blame her for being upset. I'd be exactly the same – wanting some answers.'

I make the sort of noise people make when they're agreeing, then I move away – the sooner I am gone, the sooner I am forgotten. I work my way to the front of the crowd – close enough to see the hysterical woman's blotchy face: her red, watery eyes and monstrously swollen nose, glistening with moisture. It's so repulsive I can barely look. It's hard to believe that anyone would let themselves be seen in public looking so undignified, so out of control.

She rattles furiously at the gate again. 'What are you scared of, Tess? Why won't you come out and face me?'

On the other side of the gate is Esther's mother. She's changed a lot from that first day when the TV cameras recorded her *emotional reunion* with Esther. It's not simply her deflated hairdo and make-up-free face. There's something dark about her now.

She marches up to the gate. 'The police are on their way.' She glares at the group outside her house. 'Why can't you people leave my daughter alone? Can't you see what this is *doing* to her?'

The woman on the other side of the gate explodes. '*Your* daughter! *Your* daughter is safely at home with you. What about *my* daughter?'

Esther's mother bunches her fists. 'That's not Tess's fault.'

'Yes, it is!' shrieks the woman. She sounds like a seagull. 'It is her fault! She kept my daughter there, didn't she? Tricked her into believing a whole pack of lies. She and that Harry Fernard. They could've done something to save her.'

It's hurting my ears, the way this woman keeps going on. It's so tempting to go over and tell her the facts. *Don't waste your breath. Your daughter is almost certainly dead by now.*

Even more irritating is that all this nonsense is delaying my plans. On the drive here I had been in good spirits, picturing Esther running down the driveway to greet me, smiling with joy. But owing to this lunatic woman, I may not even *see* Esther today.

There's a noise at the house and I see the front door swing open. Esther appears. She looks pale and tired, but her back is straight as she walks towards the front gate.

The crowd, which has been noisy and jostling, falls silent. The woman stops rattling and screaming and the journalists stop yelling out questions. Esther has that effect on people. She glides down the path and stops at the gate, directly in front of the crazy woman.

'I'm so sorry,' she says, 'but I don't know where your daughter is.' She doesn't raise her voice, but somehow it's loud enough even for those of us standing near the back of the group to hear. I notice a new tone to Esther's voice; a hardness. It's not surprising. She must be as tired of these people as I am.

'You're lying!' the woman yells at her. Her voice is strained to the point of hoarseness. 'Don't pretend you had nothing to do with it. You know way more than you're letting on.'

Esther shakes her head, frustrated. 'I *don't know* where she is yet, but I am going to find her and the others. I promise you.'

'You're holding things back,' spits the woman. 'I can see it in your face.'

Esther's shoulders look high and tense. 'Why would I lie to you?' she says, her voice leaping upwards in pitch and volume. 'I have told the police everything I know, *every little detail* about the missing girls that I can remember. I lie awake at night, wondering where they are, if they're okay. How do you think *I* feel, knowing that I couldn't save them?' Her eyes flash with a look that would be almost murderous if it wasn't so agonised. 'I can't even leave my house without being swooped by that lot,' she adds, gesturing wildly towards the media pack. 'I'm more trapped out *here* than I ever was at the farmhouse –'

Esther's mother rushes over and takes her arm, pulling her back towards the house. 'It's okay,' she tells her. 'You don't have to –'

Esther rips her arm away, her chest heaving. 'It's not okay, Mum!' she shouts. 'Don't you see? None of this is okay.' Then she storms towards the house.

'Yes, you go back inside, where you're nice and safe with your family,' the woman hurls at her. 'While my daughter is out there somewhere, *all on her own.*'

Esther pauses mid-storm, her entire body suddenly rigid, and she turns back to the woman. Her eyes are wide and the fury from a moment ago has been replaced by something exceedingly strange. She stares at the woman in silence and then she runs back inside the house, slamming the door behind her.

●

I drive home, nerves jangling. There was something in Esther's face just before she turned and ran that has disturbed me. Something unfamiliar and dangerous. Being at home calms me a little and I distract myself by making sure everything is in order. I straighten up the shoes at the door and reorganise the cutlery drawer. And then I remember that there is an important task I need to complete – one that will definitely make me feel better.

One way or another Esther will be arriving here soon, and I need to prepare.

To begin with she will be down in the cellar. It's not where I want her to be but I don't expect that she will have to stay down there for long. Just until she has readjusted to life under my control.

I haven't been down in the cellar since the investigators came to examine the boiler after the tragedy. 'The air intake shafts are full of dust and dirt,' I heard one mutter to the other. 'The fumes would've seeped up through the floor and out of the heaters.'

I'd hung in the background, the grieving son and brother. They passed on their condolences and their advice: pull the whole system out and have a new one installed. 'Although you probably won't want to stay here anyway, right?' they added. 'Too many memories now.'

But of course I was going to stay. Why on earth would I leave just when I had the place to myself? I didn't bother to replace the boiler, either – I just kept it off. Heating is unnecessary and wasteful.

The cellar is not the most inviting of spaces – there is no natural light and it is even dustier and grimier now than when my father used to lock me down there – but it has the benefit of being almost completely soundproof, which may prove useful while Esther readjusts. I spend an hour or so sweeping and rearranging the clutter. I spread out an old rug that I find rolled up in the corner. From my father's camping gear, I select a sleeping bag, and dust down a cushion for a pillow. It looks quite cosy now. I think Esther will be pleased.

As a precautionary measure I take a length of chain, add a pair of my father's handcuffs to one end and bolt it to the wall. I sincerely hope that I won't need to use the cuffs, but it's best to be prepared.

When I return upstairs it is with the feeling of tired satisfaction that comes with knowing you have done something well. I make myself some food – salted popcorn as a treat – and go into the lounge room to watch some TV. It's not something I normally do but I definitely deserve a reward.

At first I am not sure what I am seeing on the screen. It appears to be a live cross to a crime scene – there are lights flashing, the wail of an ambulance and people rushing around. It's dark, but there's still something familiar about the location. For a moment I think they're back at the farm, but then there's a new camera angle and in the background I see a tower, illuminated by the bluish glow of police lights. Then the true horror of what I'm seeing hits me.

They're at the factory.

'Unbelievable scenes here tonight,' says a reporter, coming into shot. 'Four young girls have been found, chained up in the cellar of a deserted factory. Police have issued no statement as yet but they are believed to be the four missing girls connected with the Special Ones cult. All four appear to be alive but in a critical condition.'

There's a cut to the newsroom, and a question from the anchor. 'Do we have any idea how the girls were located?'

'Nothing is confirmed at this stage,' replies the reporter, 'but the unofficial word is that the information came from Tess Kershaw.'

I know I should turn the television off. Watching this will just infuriate me more, but I cannot seem to move away from it. Initially there is some anger, of course – strong enough to make me hurl my plate against the far wall, where it explodes, sending popcorn flying like tiny dust clouds into the air.

But by the time the press conference comes on, my anger has dissipated a little. Instead, I now feel wounded by Esther's actions and puzzled by what it is she is trying to achieve. I had never for a moment believed she was sincere when she said she wanted to find the missing girls. I had assumed it was one of those things you have to say, not because you mean it but because those around you apparently expect it. Like 'your baby is beautiful' and 'I'm so sorry to hear about your wife'.

So when Esther appears on the press stage, along with a gang of smug-faced police staff, I turn up the volume. I want to see if I can discover what could have motivated her to do this. There's something else bothering me too – how she found out. A disturbing possibility has begun to nag at me. Maybe the reason I have struggled to access her thoughts recently is that she has discovered how to access mine.

CHAPTER THIRTY-ONE

During verification, I used to pick a point somewhere ahead of me to focus on while we stood there. It helped keep me calm, stopped me from panicking. I automatically try to do the same thing now, during the press conference, fixing my attention on the edge of the door behind the crowd. Block out all those cameras and microphones. But my eyes keep slipping down and meeting the curious stares of the people before me. Even when they know that I've seen them, they continue to look, blatantly, as if I'm not a person but some artefact on display.

It's so hot and stuffy in this packed little room. The smell of many different shampoos, of sweat mingled with deodorant, of coffee and perfume and foot odour, all seem to coat the inside of my lungs, making it difficult to breathe. There's something else in the air too. Something hostile and unfriendly. But I am not sure if this is coming from them, or from me.

Just get through this, I tell myself as the police commissioner talks about how the girls were found, making it sound like it was almost entirely his own work. I concentrate on keeping my breathing steady, remind myself that I've agreed to do this for a reason. *Maybe Harry will be watching.* And if he is, I'm hoping he'll see in my face how much I need to talk to him.

Someone in the front row calls out a question. 'Why wasn't the factory searched earlier? It can be seen from the farm. Wouldn't that have been a fairly obvious place to start?'

'The factory was a considerable distance from the main crime scene,' the commissioner replies quickly. 'It wasn't, in the department's opinion, an obvious site to search extensively.'

'But isn't it true that the police *did* search there, a week ago, and found nothing?' another reporter presses. The crowd murmurs in agreement.

The commissioner shuffles some papers uncomfortably and concedes the point, but says with the volume of tips they'd received, they'd 'had to rationalise certain aspects of their investigation'.

I start to seethe. Nothing about this investigation has seemed rational to me. I had to fight for them to take me seriously, to listen to me at all. Yesterday, when I rang to say I was sure the girls were hidden in the factory somewhere, I could practically see them rolling their eyes at each other. In the end, I think they only agreed to go out there because I swore I would stop calling if they did.

'Check underground,' I pleaded. 'He used to leave us in the cellar.'

Suddenly, the police commissioner reaches out and claps me on the shoulder, making me jump. 'We have this remarkable young lady's persistence to thank for their eventual discovery,' he says heartily. 'She insisted that we search the factory premises again. Said she had a hunch. We went back with thermal-imaging equipment and, sure enough, there they were beneath the floor. The entrance was completely obscured by rubble.'

I fix my eyes on the edge of the door again, praying that no-one will ask me anything. It doesn't work.

'Tess – can you explain to us *why* you thought the girls were there?' someone calls from the back of the room.

It's what I've been dreading – because I know I can't explain it in a way that sounds believable. How as that woman had screamed at our gates, I'd suddenly remembered the tower I could see from the farmhouse, the word *OWN* spelled out in bricks up its side. If I say that, someone will probably accuse me of claiming to have visions. 'We used to get locked up in the cellar as punishment,' I say, keeping my explanation as short as possible. 'And I often used to look at that tower from the farmhouse. It seemed the logical place for him to take –'

'I'm sorry, Tess,' someone else butts in. 'But don't you think that's just a *little* too coincidental?' It's a guy in a grey suit and although his tone is polite, his expression is unbearably smug.

Everyone goes quiet, waiting for my answer. When I first emerged from the farm, these same people swarmed around me, congratulating me on my escape, acting like I was a hero. Now it feels like they can't wait to trip me up and pounce. I wish I'd been better prepared before I came here. I could've worked out my answers, like I used to do for evening chat. But unlike Esther, I have no remembering book to help me with this sort of thing.

'Not to me, it doesn't,' I say evenly.

The guy in the grey suit continues to push. 'You know, some people are saying that this proves you knew where they were all along. And that you've only revealed where they were being kept because you think it'll help your leader.'

'People can think what they want,' I retort. Irritation and frustration are starting to seep through my wall of calmness and control. 'The important thing as far as *I'm* concerned is that the girls are out of there. Now we can focus on the next step: finding *him*.' My face burns as I swing around to face the police commissioner beside me. 'I have a question too.

What are you doing to find the person behind all this? Have you got any closer?'

The commissioner starts off on a long-winded, evasive reply, but I don't bother to listen. I already know the answer. They're no closer to finding *him* than they were when I first left the farm.

My only hope now is that Harry is watching this and that it's as clear to him as it is to me that we can't rely on the police to help us.

'Of course,' adds the commissioner, 'the crucial factor in our further investigations is Harry Fernard making himself known to us.'

There's no doubt from his tone that the police still consider Harry their number-one suspect. If he were to present himself now he would be arrested, I have no doubt at all. *Don't do it, Harry,* I mentally will him. *Stay away.*

My fury finally breaks through the delicate walls of my self-control, flooding out like a deluge. Because of all these people and their stupidity, I may never get to see or speak to Harry again. And I've had enough of being bombarded with questions. I'm tired of everyone assuming I have all the answers. Without really being aware of it, I find myself pushing back my chair and storming out of the conference, chased by the persistent flash of cameras.

CHAPTER THIRTY-TWO

What am I supposed to make of what Esther's done? What she went on TV and said? Her actions are almost impossible to interpret. There's less than a finger's width of liquid in my purple bottle now but my need is great and so I allow myself three drops on the tip of my tongue. The vision flickers before me like a faulty light bulb, her voice barely louder than a whisper. *'Don't you see? This isn't a bad thing. This will help us.'*

I think I detect a note of annoyance in her tone, though I can't be sure – then she fades altogether. But her words give me hope and as I continue to watch the news reports that evening, I see that she's right. That despite my initial shock, the discovery of my possessions does indeed work to my advantage.

When the girls are asked who kidnapped them, they say, of course, Harry. But even better and more unexpectedly, when they're asked who put them – and kept them – under the factory, they say that was Harry too. Clearly, my vigilance in keeping my face in darkness when I visited paid off. Or maybe this is what they were told to say by the police when their statements were taken – I am sure such things go on. Whatever the reason, it is a piece of excellent fortune for me.

It's enough to put anyone in a good mood.

●

The next time I access the computer in Esther's kitchen, there's another good sign: Esther is sitting there drinking a glass of water. She isn't facing the screen completely, but she's so near that it feels like I could touch her! I am careful, however, not to come too close. If she can indeed see my thoughts, I must be careful. Her glow is even brighter than usual, but the expression on her face is dark and glowering.

She has a pencil in her hand that she taps on the bench, first on one end, then on the other. *Tip, tap. Tip, tap.*

'Come on, Tess,' says the mother, refilling her cup. 'You need to put this behind you. Start enjoying your freedom.'

'I'm not *free*,' mutters Esther. 'I can't even go out the front door without someone taking my photo.'

'Then why don't you do a bit of shopping online? Order some new clothes. I already said you could use my card.'

'I'm not in the mood for shopping.'

I hear the mother sigh – the sort of long, drawn-out sound that people make when they want others to know of their frustration.

'Have you checked the mail today?' asks Esther, glancing at the clock. 'It's usually arrived by now, right?'

The mother gives a little nervous cough. On the computer screen, I see Esther frown. 'I know you've been holding back my mail.'

'I've been checking it, yes,' admits the mother. 'But now that we know Harry got you interested in the cult by writ–'

'That wasn't Harry!' snaps Esther. 'Doesn't anyone *listen* to what I say?'

'Well, I haven't found anything from him, if that makes you feel better,' says the mother. 'All I've been holding back are the letters from obsessive weirdos. You wouldn't believe some of the stuff people send. The other day someone sent a stinky old wooden pipe!'

Esther inhales deeply. 'Mum – has anything arrived for me *today*?'

The mother hesitates for a moment and then I hear her clacking off out of earshot. A minute later, her footsteps grow louder again and a parcel appears in the camera view – a rectangle wrapped in brown paper and secured with a frayed-looking piece of string.

'I was actually planning to take it to the police,' says the mother. 'It looks very –'

But Esther, ignoring her, has already begun to rip off the paper. The mother's head comes into view as she leans in to see. 'Oh! You bought yourself a phone!' she exclaims delightedly. 'Well, that's –' She's interrupted by the sound of her own phone ringing faintly in the background, and gives Esther a squeeze as she hurries off.

Esther sits very still, the box in her hands, a strange look on her face. Slowly, she opens up the lid. The phone is a temporary prepaid one, the sort used by travellers and drug dealers. As she removes the phone from the packaging, something falls out. It appears to be a small, tightly folded piece of paper.

Esther picks it up and flattens it out. Her breathing, I notice, has suddenly changed and I strain to see what's on the paper. It's a twenty-dollar note.

Esther stares at it with a very strange expression on her face. One that I, even with my intimate knowledge of her facial arrangements, can't fathom. Perhaps she's wondering, as I am, why anyone would send her money. But that doesn't seem quite right. There's something else in her eyes – excitement.

Then I know. I know who sent this parcel to her, although the significance of the money is a mystery. And something else is clear too. Despite everything that I've revealed about Harry, the truth about his sordid background, the fact that there was never anything *special* about him, somehow Esther is still very much under Harry's spell.

Heat begins to rise from my chest, creeping steadily up my neck, across my face. How much more of this can I be expected to stand? Esther's glow is suddenly so bright that I can hardly look at her. And there's a sound too – her heart beating, steady and true. I lean in to listen to its music, hoping that I might have confirmation that I am her deepest devotion, after all.

But her heart's rhythm is not for me. There's not even an echo of my presence in there. I, who have done so much for her! Who revealed to her the pathway of her own immortality, who brought devotees flocking. Who dedicates every moment of his current life to freeing her from a mundane existence and showing her who she truly is. Instead, her heart beats for that impostor. The fill-in has somehow forced his way into the place where I belong.

My bitterness transforms into something fierce and venom-filled. I have been cheated of what belongs to me – what has belonged to me since the beginning of time. It is too much to stand.

I lift the purple bottle to my lips and drain it of every last drop.

The vision comes on strongly, her aura burning with a dark-red intensity that pushes me back. She swells in size until I am enveloped in a shining cloud of her wrath. Her hair whips and lashes around her face as she raises her hands, hands curled into tight knots, eyes narrowed into dark slits.

'You have let Harry take advantage of us. He is nothing and you are everything, yet you have let him outsmart you.'

Her anger and my own are intertwined, spinning and merging. I try to calm her, calm myself, but we're too caught up in it, too tightly wound. The feelings come from somewhere dark and deep. I'm a child again with a struggling puppy in my arms. I'm locked in the cellar with a boiler hissing in the corner – a monster that can only be kept at bay by throwing huge handfuls of dirt at it.

'Harry has not beaten us yet,' I insist. 'No-one believes in him. Everyone thinks he's a criminal.'

'Not Esther.' This vision is merciless; her darkly glowing eyes bore into my head, melting my skull and turning my brain into bubbling lava. 'Nothing you have done has made any difference to her feelings. You are losing your hold on her.' Her voice is like the howling of a bushfire wind, an invisible wall of hot fury that spews white hot sparks into the air. 'Don't you understand what that means? Once we have no hold on her, once she no longer belongs to us, her soul will become mortal and the Special Ones will cease to exist.'

The storm is inside me too – a whirling, devastating gale growing with intensity with every passing moment, fuelled by so much hurt, so much betrayal, by an irreparable sense of loss. Esther, who had seemed so close, is now further away than ever. She's changed and I am no longer sure I'll be able to change her back. Sorrow washes over me. *I wish that I could start over.*

And then, just like that, it's suddenly so obvious: starting over is exactly what I must do. There's no point trying to force this current version of Esther to go in the direction I want. She's a tree who's grown past the point where mere pruning can help maintain her shape. She needs to start from a seed again. And I need to accompany her on the journey – from the very beginning.

I do not even need to say my thoughts out loud for the vision to hear them. 'Yes,' she breathes, an angel once again, shimmering and gold. '*Yes. You are right. If the Special Ones are to survive, then you and Esther must renew together.*'

My heart rate quickens. I am not afraid of dying – it would be ridiculous to fear something so temporary. My excitement comes from understanding that I have found the answer. All my frustrations melt away and even though I am not sure exactly how it will be carried out I have not a single doubt that it will be.

It's almost as if it's already happened.

CHAPTER THIRTY-THREE

There's a knock at my door and then Mum pops her head in. She lights up when she sees me sitting at my desk, my old laptop open in front of me.

I was actually about to shut it just before she walked in, having tried and failed to see if I can trace the phone's origins. My computer seems unbearably slow. Plus it's still almost impossible for me to sit in front of a screen and not expect a message from a follower to appear. Or worse, from *him*.

'You're charging the new phone, I see!' Mum says, spotting it next to me as she comes in. She sounds so thrilled. So relieved. Laptops and phones symbolise normality to her. A return to my former life.

But, for me, the phone means something very different. It's finished charging now, so I unplug it and show her. 'What do you think?'

'Is it meant to look retro?' she says doubtfully. 'It's kind of ugly.'

She's right. It's chunky and old-school. But it's also the most beautiful object I've ever seen. *Harry sent this*, I think, looking at it in my hand. *He's going to call me on it.* It's hard to believe these words are true, because I'd started to accept that he'd disappeared forever. And who could blame him, given all the terrible things that have been said about him?

'Well,' my mother says brightly, 'I'll leave you to make some calls. Dinner will be about an hour, okay? Dad's bringing home pizza.'

Pizza again. I'd offer to cook, but whenever I do Mum acts like I'm criticising her. So I just say, 'Great, yep,' until she pulls the door shut behind her. Harry might call at any minute and I don't want to be arguing with her when he does.

Speaking on the phone to Harry. My heart thumps at the thought of it. What will I say?

That I miss him. That we can't blame ourselves for everything that happened, even if the rest of the world does. And that I have to see him again. We need to talk about what to do next.

I've set the phone to vibrate rather than ring. When it starts to shudder beside me, I snatch it up so quickly that I almost knock it to the floor.

'Hello?' My pulse thumps.

'Hi. Tess. It's … me.'

Tess. It's the first time I've heard him use my real name. For a moment, I can't speak.

'Are you okay?' he whispers, sounding concerned.

'I'm fine. I just – I haven't –' I take a deep breath. Channel a little bit of Esther and pull it together. 'It's really good to hear your voice.'

'Yours too,' he says, and I can hear – *feel* – his smile. 'I'm so glad you answered. I've been trying to work out how to get a message through to you. I didn't think you'd be online and I figured your parents were probably checking your mail, but I thought I'd try sending the phone anyway and hope that you'd get it.'

'I got it.'

I close my eyes, blotting out my bedroom, eradicating the phone, pretending that he's actually here beside me, close enough that I can feel his cheek against mine. The gap that silence formed between us has disappeared. But my happiness and relief falls apart with Harry's next sentence.

'Tess – I'm calling to tell you I'm on my way to hand myself over to the police. I should've already done it, but I wanted to speak to you first.'

My mouth goes dry. 'What? Why?'

'Because I'm tired of living this way.' The pain in his voice is raw and hard to hear. 'Hiding from everyone, staying quiet. I hate everyone thinking I'm too scared to face up to what I've done.'

'Harry, no!' I say in a panic. 'You'll get blamed for everything. They'll put you in prison! And if I try to stick up for you, they'll say you've brainwashed me.'

'Maybe you have been brainwashed,' he says with a sad chuckle. 'Maybe you're the one not thinking straight, and everyone else is right about me.'

'No.' Tears have risen dangerously close to the surface. 'I know you, Harry. You're a good person.'

'Yeah,' he says bitterly. 'Kidnapping a bunch of girls is a really *good* thing to do.'

I can't stand hearing him talk like this. 'But you had no choice! He would've killed you if you hadn't. He's obviously insane!'

'I should've stood up to him anyway,' Harry growls. 'I bet you would've, if you'd been in my position. You've got this determination about you. A kind of toughness.'

I feel my face flush. 'No, that's Esther, not me.' There's a pause.

'I think,' Harry says slowly, 'that in some ways you're more like Esther than you realise.'

That stops me. It's something I'd never considered before. I'm not sure how I feel about it.

Harry sighs deeply. 'Oh, Tess, I'm going to miss you so much. I hope you'll visit me sometimes.'

It's then that I know I've got no chance of convincing him to stay hidden. Not over the phone, at least. My voice comes out louder and fiercer than I'd intended. 'Well, I have to see you before you do anything. Privately, with no-one else around. Once the police have got you, who knows when we'll get the chance again? There will always be people watching. I need to have at least one time when I can talk to you without someone listening in.'

On my desk, my old laptop starts to whir loudly. I glare at it pointlessly, and reach out to close the screen. 'Tess,' says Harry, and I pause, hand midair, waiting for him to continue. His breathing is loud, shallow, and I know he's battling his desire to see me with his desire to keep me safe. I've no intention of making it easy for him. 'It's not a good idea –'

'Please, Harry. Just for a few minutes. To say goodbye.'

I'm sure he's thinking the same thing I am. Remembering how it felt when we were pressed together on the bike. How everything had to stop before it even began. He must feel that same longing.

We've never even kissed.

But saying goodbye is not the real reason I want to meet him. A plan has started to form in my head.

He gives a long, slow exhalation, one that tells me I've won. 'But where would we meet?'

'There's a park not far from my house – just around the corner,' I say, speaking rapidly. 'I could meet you there – near the fountain in the middle.'

I'm half out of my chair, leaning on the laptop screen, almost rigid with the tension of waiting. But this time the pause isn't so long. 'Now?'

Through my open window I hear the front gate's mechanical whine as it opens, followed by the scrunch of tyres on gravel. Dad's home with the pizzas. 'No, later. When it's dark.'

'Around ten?'

'Perfect. See you then.'

I slam down the laptop screen, cutting out the fan, feeling victorious but also unsettled. Harry has let his heart make the decision rather than his head. It's what I wanted him to do, to give me a chance to convince him of my plan. Once again, I get my way. But for some reason it's put me on edge.

At dinner, I force down a slice of pizza and then tell my parents I'm having an early night.

'Oh no – really?' my mum says, disappointed. 'I thought we could watch a movie or something. Like we used to.'

Poor Mum. I know she wants things to go back to how they once were, long ago. Impulsively I go over and hug her, and her face flushes with pleasure. 'Oh, that's a nice surprise,' she says.

'Tomorrow I'll watch a movie with you guys,' I promise. 'I'm just really tired tonight.'

My bedroom has its own bathroom and I go straight in and lock the door. I need to prepare. I take a pair of scissors from the drawer and quickly begin to hack at my hair, letting it fall to the floor in long strands around me. It's only when it's all gone that I even think to look in the mirror. I got so used to not having one on the farm that I still often forget to use it.

I stare at my reflection, barely recognising the girl I see. My face has changed in the two years since I left home. It's thinner, my skin as pale as porcelain. Now that my hair has gone my eyes suddenly dominate my face. The look in them is strong. Determined.

Back in my bedroom I dress as if I were a jogger or a cat burglar: black leggings, black hooded top, sneakers. Leftover clothes from a former life.

Quietly I open my bedroom door. Down in the lounge I can hear the hum of the TV. I slip back into my room and out the window, keeping as close as I can to the wall as I make my way around to the back of the house. There are fewer media trucks camped out the front these days, but I'm not giving the ones left a scoop.

I can't tell if I'm shivering from nervousness or from the cool evening air. When I reach the back fence I climb over it as quickly as I can, terrified that someone next door might choose this moment to step outside. But no-one does and I land on the ground with a quiet thud. Scrambling to my feet, I dash down the side of the house until I reach the main road, and then I slow my pace just a little, controlling my movements so I look more like someone exercising and less like someone trying to escape.

There is a trickle of people in the park when I get there – joggers and a dog-walker and a couple trailing along, holding hands. There's a bright-yellow van parked near the entrance and I see a delivery guy organising boxes in the back of it. No-one pays any attention to me.

My pace picks up as I start to jog through the park, impatient now to reach the fountain at the centre. I round a bend and see it, a large white circle with a twisted central stem like some kind of strange plant. The spout has been turned off for the night and the water in the pool is completely still, shining in the moonlight.

I sit on one of the benches to get my breath back. It feels so familiar, waiting to hear Harry's footsteps approaching, but of course this time it's different. This time we're both on the outside, and no-one is watching.

I'm excited but also nervous. What if he's changed? What if he doesn't recognise me? What if it doesn't feel like it did the last time? Worst of all – what if he doesn't turn up?

But even as I think this there are footsteps, quicker than I remember them but still familiar. My head turns, almost of its own accord.

It's Harry, it's definitely Harry. Thinner than I remember, with an expression that's wary and sad in a way that makes me ache, but when our eyes meet, his face breaks into the broadest, most Harry-ish of smiles.

'*Tess.*'

I had vowed on the way here that I would try to maintain a little dignity and poise. No crying, definitely no throwing myself at him. But the moment I see that smile, I'm on my feet, running over to him, and suddenly there we are. Together.

His arms encircle my shoulders and mine fold across his back, pulling him close. I press my head against his chest for a moment, breathing in his smell of sunshine and grass, hearing the rapid beating of his heart within his chest. Can he feel mine? Surely he must, it's pounding so hard.

I lean my head back and look into his eyes. Neither of us says anything. We just look. Three seconds. Four. Ten. It's like we're under a spell. Like we'll be this way forever and visitors to the park will find us here tomorrow frozen in place, like two new statues.

Harry's hand slides slowly up my spine to the back of my neck, making me shiver as he pushes his fingers gently into my short hair. 'You cut it,' he says.

I pull a face. 'It's ugly, isn't it?'

'Nothing about you could ever be ugly.'

Impulsively I lean forward and press my lips to his. I had thought that it might feel strange to kiss Harry. Strange and dangerous and wrong after all that time when we couldn't even look each other in the eye for more than a few seconds. But it doesn't at all. It feels perfect and also familiar, like it's happened a thousand times before.

We stand there, pressed together for a very long time. And then I can't hold it in any more. 'Harry, don't go to the police,' I tell him in a rush. 'Not yet. We've got to catch him first.'

I have it all worked out. Harry knows more about him than anyone, so together we can track him down. Capture him. And once we've handed him over to the police, Harry's name will be cleared. The world will have to apologise and finally they'll see him as I do.

Harry shakes his head. 'Tess,' he says softly. 'I've been trying, believe me. I can't find him anywhere. It's just better if I tell the police what I know. Work with them. I want to do things the right way from now on.'

I frown. 'But the police are never going to catch him. He's too smart. We've got the best chance – especially if we work together.' I had planned to lay this out for him in a logical, unemotional way, but the kiss has dazzled me, pushed me off-balance. The words come out in a rush, more pleading than decisive.

Harry strokes my cheek. 'Oh, Tess,' he says. 'You don't have to be the one to catch him. You've done enough. You need to focus on other things. Finish school. Make new friends. Go to university, or travel – something like that. I've always imagined you doing something amazing with your life. I used to think about it all the time when we were on the farm – what you might do one day.'

I begin to cry. There's another vow broken. 'I don't want to *make new friends* and I'm not interested in going to uni. What's the point?'

Harry grips my hands very tightly and looks intently into my face. 'The only way I'll be able to live with what I did to you is if I see you get past it.'

'But you didn't *do* anything! You were a prisoner too, in your own way,' I say, my voice thick. 'If you hadn't been there, things would've been a lot worse for us.' And then I blurt out something I haven't admitted to anyone else. Not to the police or my parents because I know everyone would think I'm crazy. 'Sometimes I actually miss being on the farm. And the reason I miss it is because you were there.'

Harry says nothing. He simply pulls me close and we kiss again because we both know there's nothing else we *can* do now. Nothing either of us can say will change the other's mind. I close my eyes, fold myself into the moment. Try to hold it for as long as possible.

I don't remember hearing a bang. What I do remember is the sound Harry makes – a kind of surprised gasp. His eyes fly open and he looks at me, face frozen in shock and lips still holding the shape of a kiss. His hand goes to his shoulder and a dark stain blooms beneath it, spreading slowly across his shirt. I grab him as he staggers forward.

'Harry? What's happened?' My voice doesn't seem to belong to me at all. There's a sharp burn in my arm and when I touch it, my hand comes away wet and sticky.

What's going on?

Harry crumples from me. 'Tess. Run!' His voice comes out in a strangled gasp. But I'm not leaving him. No way. My whole body is shivering; my teeth chatter as if the temperature has suddenly dropped. I can only think in short bursts. *Call for help. Phone? In my backpack.*

It's as I lift my head that I see a guy wearing a bright yellow delivery uniform, standing behind Harry. He's holding something, pointing it directly at me. Something gleaming and metallic.

A gun. He's got a gun.

I'm too shocked to be afraid. 'You shot him!' I say, crouching down protectively next to Harry. 'We have to call an ambulance!' Harry is silent, but his face is contorted in pain, his eyes squeezed shut.

The delivery guy takes a step towards us. 'He's not important, Esther. We're done with him.'

I know that voice. Harry knows it too. His eyes have opened and are fixed on mine, full of horror.

'Stand up, Esther.' I look up to find myself staring directly into the barrel of the gun. 'Stand up or I'll shoot Harry again.'

I hear a noise from Harry. He's trying to talk but his voice is weak. I make out one word. *Run* ...

But if I ran, how far would I get before I was shot? Before Harry was shot again too? No, I'm not running away. This is a chance to get even. Get my revenge.

'Come on, Esther. Let's go.'

It's a terrible thought, once again choosing to leave with this – *person* – but it's what I need to do.

He steps up beside me, lips parted in a thin smile as he presses the gun into the small of my back. 'Good girl. My van is on the street.'

My hands are slick but my mind is strangely sharp, despite the pain in my arm.

'Let's walk.'

I take a few steps forward and then turn, hoping that Harry is looking my way, hoping that he can see in my face that I'm not really deserting him. Behind me, *he* stops abruptly and for a moment I wonder with a stab of fear if I've accidentally said my thoughts out loud. Then I feel the gun slide away from my back and I know that something terrible is about to happen.

I whip my head around to see that he's pointing the gun at Harry again. 'No!' I scream, and shove at him, 'No!' but he stands firm and fires.

Harry, who has somehow staggered back to his feet, slumps to the ground.

'He was just a fill-in anyway,' *he* says, dismissively.

•

The pathways are all empty now. The joggers and dog-walkers have gone, the strolling couple too. There's no-one to scream to for help. The worst thing – way worse than being caught like this – is the thought of Harry lying alone on that dark, cold path, his blood slowly pooling around him.

I'm forced along the pathways at a rapid pace, the barrel of the gun ever present in the small of my back. His breathing flickers with excitement. We reach the road, which is also frustratingly deserted, and he directs me towards a van. It's the one I passed before, cheerfully yellow and so ordinary that it's hard to believe it's connected with *him*. The back door squeaks as he opens it with one hand, the other still training the gun on me.

'Get inside, Esther,' he says in his flat, unemotional voice.

My muscles tense. If I could just make it around the corner … Just get into someone's driveway … But I'm starting to feel weak now. Dizzy. The wound in my arm pulses and throbs.

Harry is dead. Is Harry dead? I don't believe it. It can't be true.

He pushes me with the gun and I stumble into the van. The door slams closed behind me.

The sound of the engine and the smell in here – musty, airless – triggers a memory. The sensation of lurching from side to side. Darkness. A fog-filled head. I've been in this van before, when he took me to the farm, clouded with medication. But the difference is that last time I wanted to be here, believing I was heading for a better life. This time I definitely do not.

Time passes. Ten minutes? An hour? I can't tell. We finally stop and I hear him get out of the driver's seat, the engine still rattling. My breathing is loud and panicked in the pitch-black, but while the van is stopped I hurriedly try to feel my way to the back doors. They are locked, of course, and there are no windows to smash through. Even if there were, I can barely raise my arm.

Outside, there's the whine of a gate opening. My heart thuds painfully. *We're back on the farm* ... But no, that can't be possible. He wouldn't go back there, not now it's become so public. But where else could he take me?

The van sags slightly as he gets back in the driver's seat. We move again for a few seconds more, and then we come to a complete stop. The engine cuts out. A moment later the back door creaks open and he's there.

With a smile he reaches out to me. 'We're finally home!'

I stare at his hand, at him. *Home?*

'Don't worry,' he says, misinterpreting my expression. 'You are allowed to touch me. I am the real Harry. You must remember that, Esther, from our last life together?'

I can't do this, I think, wearily. *I can't pretend to be* her *again. Pretend to remember things that never happened.* When I don't accept his proffered hand, he reaches into the van and wraps his fingers around my good arm. Pulls me out, all the while with that awful, fixed smile.

He seems to be gaining more strength by the minute – or maybe it's just that mine is failing. The sensation in my arm – somehow both burning hot and freezing cold – is spreading up my neck and down into my elbow. I trip as I leave the van and he hoists me to my feet, fingers gripping into me like a claw.

'I need to see a doctor,' I tell him, my teeth chattering. 'You shot me. I think the bullet is still in me.'

'You're fine,' he says. 'Let's go inside. Then we can relax.'

Before us is a large brick house, rising like a shadow out of the ground. It's the last place I want to enter. There are probably other houses nearby. *If I scream, maybe someone will hear …*

But again he seems to know my thoughts and clamps a cold hand over my mouth before pulling me in through a door. There are shoes just inside, lined up in a neat row, and it crosses my mind that there might be other people here too. But as I'm led down a chilly corridor, that thought quickly vanishes. This place is empty of all living things. I can feel it.

There's a strong smell to it that I know in my gut is bad. He pushes me into a room and closes the door behind us. The toxic stench is stronger in here. Now that we're *safe*, he finally lets me go. His grip leaves a sting like nettle-burn.

I look around, trying to make sense of the room. It's hard to turn my head, though, and my body feels so heavy that I long to sink to the floor. But I can't. I have to stay upright. Focused.

My eyes dart around, seeking something to help me. Something I can snatch up and use as a weapon. But the room is almost completely empty, except for an old television and a worn-out purple chair. It's a bleak, unloved space. Frayed curtains drape the window. A single globe hangs from the ceiling. I see what I think is a person, crumpled in a corner, but then I realise with a lurch it's Esther's leaving dress. The sound of my breathing seems to ricochet from one bare wall to the other.

In the middle of the room are some small plastic containers, grouped together.

'I'm sorry for having to hold you so tightly,' he says, with that awful smile. 'But you understand, don't you, Esther? Sometimes it has to be like that during a collection.' He seems much more relaxed now we're inside, and yet his excitement has also intensified.

'Where are we?' I need time. To think. Plan what to do. I wish my body wasn't throbbing so much. It makes it hard to concentrate.

'We're in our house,' he says. 'I had prepared another space downstairs for your arrival, but plans have changed. I won't need to keep you down there as we're going to be leaving here very soon.'

I feel a little surge of hope. *We're not staying here.* There's still a chance of escape.

He hands me the leaving dress, stained and stinking of rubbish. 'Put this on,' he says, then goes and sits in the purple chair, facing me, his arms folded in his lap.

The idea of wearing the dress again is so repulsive that anger flares. 'I'm not putting this on.'

His odd smile vanishes. 'Why not?'

'Because I –' Then I think of Harry. That pool of blood. If I die now, there's no chance of Harry surviving. No chance of defeating *him*, or making him pay for what he's done to me and all the other girls. 'Because I can't lift my arm,' I say finally, which is true. The whole side of my body is damp, although I'm not sure what's blood and what's sweat. The pain is so intense that I can barely move my fingers.

He rises from the chair and comes swiftly, eagerly, over to me. 'I will help you, Esther.'

'No, really, it's okay,' I say, filling with dread at the thought of him undressing me. 'I think I can do it, after all.'

I begin struggling out of my clothes as quickly as I can, kicking off my shoes as the pain shoots up through my arm. But he stands in front of me, unzipping my bloodstained hoodie, slipping it over my shoulders. I stand very still and brace myself. The only thing I can do now is get this over with as quickly as possible. As he lifts my T-shirt, his hand grazes the bare skin of my stomach, and nausea churns inside me.

'And now, time for the dress!' There's a tremor in his voice as he holds it up, its heavy layered skirts and petticoat folded like a drooping flower.

'Please don't do this,' I beg him. 'Don't make me put that on.'

'Don't be silly,' he tut-tuts. 'You look beautiful in it, Esther. Like a goddess.'

As the dress passes over my head, I feel like I'm falling into a deep, dark well with slippery sides, from which I'll never escape, no matter how much I struggle.

'Now turn around so I can do you up.' His breath is against my neck as he starts to button me up and I feel his hands move like bony, white spiders across my back. I press my arms against my side, hands gripping my legs, trying to make them stay strong and supportive.

Through the layers of the skirt I feel something solid tap against my knee, something within the dress itself. What is it? While he is fiddling with the buttons, I slowly slip my hand into the pocket. My fingers touch something metal – smooth and hard, sharply pointed at one end.

My scissors from the farm. They're still there, where I hid them the night I left. I curl my fingers around them.

'There!' he says, taking a step away from me. 'Let me look at you.'

I keep my eyes down while he examines me, praying he won't notice the sudden flush in my cheeks.

'You look beautiful,' he announces, 'except for your hair, of course. It was wrong of you to cut it, especially so close to the end. But there's no time to correct that now.'

My hand, holding on to the scissors, trembles. *Do I dare?* I'm not sure at first where to aim. Then it comes to me. *In the chest. Through the heart.*

But I can't seem to do it. Can't draw my hand and the scissors out of the pocket.

He fusses around, making adjustments to my clothes and hair. Then, brushing a final wisp away from my forehead, he nods. 'Now we're ready to move on together.' He doesn't seem to have noticed that blood is already seeping through the white material, the stain growing larger and larger.

'Move on where?' I croak. My throat feels like it's full of husks, scratchy and dry.

When he looks at me, his eyes are all anticipation. He takes hold of my uninjured arm, just above the elbow. 'Onto the next life, of course. You and I, together. This existence has become far too complicated. The next one will be much, much better.'

Oh my god ... Panic overtakes me and I scramble frantically for the door. But he moves faster and quickly takes hold of me again, dragging me back to the centre of the room with the gun shoved hard under my ribs.

'Don't spoil this, Esther. Not when we're so close.'

He keeps the gun trained on me as he hurries over to the plastic containers and unscrews the lids. The strong chemical smell is coming from the liquid inside. 'I've already done the rest of the house,' he says, like we're preparing for a party.

My hand has crept back into my pocket, the metal solid against my leg.

'It needs to be thorough,' he says as he splashes the petrol around the room, one hand holding the plastic container, the other the gun. 'We don't want anything left behind. No remains. That way we'll transition into the next life quickly.' In one corner of the room he suddenly stops, tucking the gun into his jacket pocket as he bends down and prises away one of the floorboards. He lifts out a small photograph and before I even see it I know what it is. The original image of the Special Ones.

'Isn't it wonderful?' he says, staring at the photo in his hands. 'Everything we've been waiting for – it's finally happening.' I'm not sure who he's addressing – me or the people in the image. 'The wait has been hard for us. But that's all behind us now. And this time when we return, we'll be together right from the start, with no obstacles blocking our way. Just you and me: Esther and Harry.'

I tighten my hold on the scissors. *How can you possibly believe you're Harry?* I want to say scornfully. He looks nothing like the figure in the photograph. He would never pass a single verification. And with a rush I remember the feeling I'd had after reading that article about Harry. How I'd promised myself that I would never again let *him* control and manipulate me. My panic disappears and something else flares in its place. Defiance. Fury.

I didn't deserve any of this.

He lays the photograph on the ground and from the hole in the floor pulls out a box of matches. 'Would you like to start the fire?' he asks, as if he's offering me the first chocolate in the box.

None of us deserved this.

My breath catches. *My chance.* 'Yes,' I say steadily. 'Give me the matches.' And I take a step towards him, not hurried, keeping my mind clear of thoughts as I reach out for them.

But just as I touch the matchbox, his expression changes and he yanks it away, scowling. 'I'll do it,' he says sharply.

He seems to be talking to someone behind me. Someone I can't see.

The match lights on the first strike, fizzing and flaring into life, making the grim, dingy room glow for a moment. He strides over to the door, opens it and flings the match away. Almost immediately I hear the *whoosh* of fire. Then he strikes another one and this one he throws into the corner of the room we're in. Instantly a fire flares and crackles, dancing up the walls.

Even as the flames take hold I feel strangely calm. It's like there's a voice in my head, telling me what to do. *Don't let him see your anger.*

'Come and kneel with me, Esther,' he says, holding out his hands. 'We should be together as we make this transition.'

Remember what's in your pocket.

The flames are leaping around the room and the air is rapidly filling with smoke. My eyes stream and every breath is a struggle. I stumble over to him and, as I kneel down, I pull the scissors from my pocket, keeping them hidden in the folds of my skirts.

His face, blurred by smoke, glows in the light of the flames. 'Oh, Esther. We are going to be together forever.'

The heat is ferocious, but it doesn't seem to affect him the way it's affecting me. And he's clearly not afraid. Behind me, something explodes and I turn my head to see that the TV screen has shattered. 'Don't worry,' he chides me gently, reaching over and putting his hand under my chin. 'Look at me.'

My skin feels like it's blistering, yet I am still calm. *Now. Do it now.*

It's almost as if someone else is controlling my hand, pulling the scissors from my skirts, lifting my arm up above my head. Does he see the gleaming metal through the smoke? My hand is so swift and sure that he doesn't even realise what's happening until the blades are buried deep within the flesh above his collarbone. I drive them in with all the force I have left.

'I'm – not – Esther!' I scream above the roar of the fire. 'I've *never* been her! Do you understand that? I'm not *special* and none of it was real!'

Now he's screaming too, his face contorting like a nightmare, but I can't hear it. The volume has suddenly muted. His hands flail about, first going to the scissors, then to grab at me as I scramble to the door and try to turn the handle. But the door doesn't move. Is it locked? Jammed? Maybe I'm just too weak.

I feel his footsteps and when I turn, he's stumbling towards me, the scissors flashing at his neck. He is wheezing, like the air isn't flowing through him properly. *'Esther!'*

Desperately I slam against the door, over and over, and even though I'm giving it everything, nothing moves. I should be in pain too, but I can't feel a thing. My body is numb. He lunges out at me, a hand connecting with my arm. His skin is still so cold, despite the heat. I kick out at him and he buckles. Finally the door gives way.

The corridor is full of thick, black smoke that fills my lungs and makes my eyes stream. I drop and crawl in the only direction not already engulfed in flames, the heavy skirts catching under my knees. The air is almost solid in the heat, too hot to breathe, and I'm sure that I'm about to die.

Then, unbelievably, there's a loud banging noise and a voice, strong and commanding. *'We're coming in!'*

At first the voice seems to be coming from somewhere inside and I look around, trying to see if someone else is in here, hidden by the smoke. 'Help!' I shout, but my voice is barely more than a whisper. Then I realise that I've reached the end of the hallway, and ahead of me is the front door.

'One, two ...'

I manage to roll away just as the door explodes. People in uniforms flood through. *The police. Firemen.* Someone grabs me and drags me outside, where I gulp huge mouthfuls of cool air. I'll never get enough to fill my lungs.

There are so many people out here, yelling and running around. There are lights blinking – red and blue, red and blue – and the crackle of police radios.

'Stretcher here!' yells the guy who's dragging me.

And instantly there's a woman with a heart-shaped face leaning over me. *She'd make a good Felicity*, I think foggily, *except she's way too old.*

'It's okay, sweetheart, everything's fine,' she's telling me. 'Lie down, please.'

But I can't lie down yet. Now that I can breathe again, I have to tell someone about Harry. As I start to explain this to the ambulance lady, there's a commotion near the house and I see two big policemen dragging *him* out through the front door, covered with ash and blood, the scissors still in his neck. He's screaming.

'We've got you now, mate,' I hear one of the policemen shout.

'You've got me?' he roars. *'Don't you realise what you've done?'*

'We know what *you've* done,' the other policeman says grimly. 'You've been stealing from your employers. One of your colleagues has been keeping us up to date.'

The nice ambulance lady has started cutting the leaving dress off me, ripping away the blood-soaked material. 'Now, hold still,' another medic instructs as he tries to stick a needle into my arm.

But I wrench my arm away. 'I need to talk to someone.'

'You will, you will.'

'I need to talk to someone *now*!' I yell, as loudly as I can.

Another woman appears beside us. She is dressed in purple yoga pants, but she speaks with a cool, efficient authority. 'I'm Detective Lewis from the Fraud and Extortion squad,' she tells the ambulance lady. 'Can we take her down to the station?' Without waiting for a response, she looks at me and says, 'What's your involvement here?'

I am gaping at her, shaking my head. What she's saying makes no sense.

'Well?' she says briskly. 'Who are you? Do I have to put you under arrest too?'

I struggle to sit up again. 'I'm Tess Kershaw.'

'What?' she barks.

'My name is Tess Kershaw.'

Her eyes widen as she registers the name, and then I see a thought strike her. 'Is this guy connected with that prison farm?' Her tone is less cool now, but just as urgent. 'Is that Harry?'

'No. That's *him*,' I say. I'm trying to speak as few words as possible because my tongue has turned to porridge and I want to say the thing that matters. 'Harry's been shot. In the park near my house.' I start to cry. 'Someone has to help him.'

Detective Lewis starts speaking into her radio and shouting instructions at the other police. People are rushing around and I realise I can still hear *him* screaming, until a car door slams and his screams are cut short.

Relief floods through me. Finally, someone will go and look after Harry. I lie back down on the stretcher and look up at the sky while the needle is pushed into my arm. There are stars above me. Nowhere near as many as I saw that night with Harry on the farm, but still beautiful.

A fire engine arrives – or maybe it's been there all along – and an ambulance leaves, and there are more lights, more sirens. I feel calm. More relaxed than I've ever felt in my entire life.

'Right. Let's get you out of here,' says the grown-up Felicity and they slide me into the back of an ambulance. It's so bright in there and full of machines. It's like the farm's chat room.

'Everything's going to be fine,' someone says blurrily. *'You're going to be fine, don't worry.'*

And somehow, despite everything, I know it to be true.

EPILOGUE

We always hug first – tightly and silently. Every time we meet, I notice how she's grown. Her head is now almost level with my shoulder. Her parents hover twenty metres away. I wave and, in return, her mother points meaningfully at her watch. *One hour* ... I nod and smile politely. At least they're letting us meet.

'So, Zoe.' I rarely stumble over her name any more. 'Ice-cream or walk today?'

'Walk,' she says decisively.

As we wander through the park, we talk about what we know.

That she and I are here – not just alive, but thriving.

That the scars people notice on us – the burns on my skin, the angry mark just above her knee – are nothing compared with the hidden scars, tucked away inside us. But those, too, are fading. Slowly.

That *he* is locked up and will be forever. At some point during the afternoon, Zoe will say, 'It's really true, right?' and I'll say, 'Yes, it's really true.' It's part of the ritual. Like somehow repeating it strengthens the bars, makes the locks on his cell ever stronger.

That even though we now know *his* name, we're not going to say it. Ever. Not because we're afraid of him, but because we don't want to. Don't need to.

Then we focus determinedly on positive things and on the future. Zoe's going to start high school. Her birthday is coming up and she's asked for chickens. I'm still deciding about uni next year. I'm going out. *Meeting new people.*

•

Today we arrive at the fountain as dark clouds are gathering overhead. A cool wind begins to whip up around us. Zoe picks a tiny white daisy from the grass and drops it in the water. We watch it float there for a moment, bobbing and twirling, and then we look around for a bench. They're all full, but an elderly woman sitting alone stands up and gestures that we can take her place.

'I'm leaving before the rain starts,' she explains. Then she adds with a smile, 'How beautiful you both are! Are you sisters?'

It's strange how often we are asked this. Today we answer simultaneously. 'Almost.'

We do not talk about Harry. It's a forbidden topic – partly because Zoe's parents won't allow it, and partly because I still find it so hard myself. It's painful to remember that night, and as time passes it's more, not less, confusing to sort through all the feelings I have – the ones from before and the ones from now.

My therapist brings the topic up sometimes, gently pointing out that there were so many limitations on what we could say to each other, that we were so locked into our roles. 'The situation made it impossible for you to truly know each other,' she tells me.

But she's got it round the wrong way. As I keep trying to explain to everyone – including my parents – the situation meant that we knew each other better than anyone else. Because we couldn't hide behind words. We knew each other from the things we didn't say. From the space between the words.

The skies open up and the rain begins falling. Everyone around us scuttles for shelter, shrieking and laughing, but we stay on our bench, reluctant to waste our hour. Who knows when we'll see each other again? It's not like I get regular visitation rights. Besides, after living on the farm, neither of us will ever feel anything but relief at the sight of rain. The flower in the fountain rocks from side to side as raindrops disturb the surface of the water.

Then I look at Zoe, see how wet she's getting, and feel guilty. Even though she is perfectly fit and well these days, I still worry about her. *Esthering*, Zoe calls it, with an eye-roll. But just as I'm about to suggest we leave, Zoe turns to me.

'You know what I miss most about Harry?' she says, and she gives me a look – one that defies me to stop her.

But I don't try, even though my heart begins to pound. *Maybe it's time.* 'What do you miss the most?'

'I miss how funny he was. He could always make me laugh, even when I was in the most terrible mood.'

'What else?'

'I miss his smile,' she says and instantly I see it, that broad, slow smile of his. 'And I miss how safe I always felt when he was around. Like nothing could go wrong, you know?'

I nod. Because I remember feeling like that too.

'My parents say that he wasn't a good person. That it was just an act and he didn't really care about me at all.' She looks at me, her eyes serious. 'What do you think?'

'He *definitely* cared about you,' I say. 'You were his favourite.'

Zoe pulls a face. 'Don't be dumb! *You* were his favourite. I was his second-favourite.' She bats a pebble on the ground thoughtfully with her foot for a moment. 'Sasha sent me a card. You know, Lucille. She's pretty nice, really.' Zoe squints up at me. 'Do you think she'll ever speak to you again?'

Some questions are easy to answer. 'No.'

Then Zoe looks around, checking for her parents. Her time is nearly up. 'Do you think I'll ever get to see Harry again?' she says quickly. 'Now that he's out of there?'

'I don't think so. At least, not for a very long time.'

Her face falls, but only a little. She must have known this would be the answer.

Around a bend in the path her parents appear, sharing an umbrella. They won't be impressed that I let their daughter get so soggy. Maybe it'll be the last straw and they'll forbid us from meeting again.

At first I think this is why Zoe flings her arms around me. That she's worried it will be a while before we see each other. But she presses her mouth to my ear and whispers, 'Can you say hi to him from me? And tell him that I'm still his friend?'

Then she jumps from the bench, runs to her parents and soon she's out of sight.

●

It's later that same afternoon – after I've gone home and changed out of my wet clothes, and checked in with my parents so they don't worry – that I get a chance to pass on Zoe's message. Since Harry got out, he's moved into a flat on the other side of town. It's on the ground floor, of course. The physio says that one day he'll be strong enough to manage stairs again, but it won't be for a while yet. Nearby is an Italian cafe that is always dark and full of old guys playing cards and smoking in the doorways. If they recognise us, they aren't interested in showing it.

This is where we meet. To sit and hold hands across the table. Often we don't say very much. Not because we don't have anything to talk about, because the opposite is true.

The rain is still thrumming outside and I look at Harry, wondering if he too imagines the water tank and dam filling up on the farm. Not that those things even exist now. The place has been bulldozed.

But we're not here to talk about rain, or water tanks. Or even the farm. Today I have news. I grab my bag and pull out an opened envelope and lay it on the table between us.

Harry glances at it, and then at me. 'Foreign stamp,' he comments.

'Yes.'

'The letter's from that university, isn't it?'

I nod. Slowly.

'And you were offered a place.'

'Yes.' And as I speak I realise I've made up my mind about it. 'I'm going to accept it.'

Harry reaches across and squeezes my arm. He doesn't say anything and a moment later his chair scratches across the tiles as he stands up.

'I'm not leaving for another two months!' I say in a panic, and he laughs. A couple of the old guys look around from their card game and smile at us briefly.

'I know.' Harry grins and holds out his hand. 'But this deserves a celebration.'

I take his hand and stand up. He leads me through the tables towards the front door.

'You can come and visit,' I point out.

'Yes,' he agrees, even though we both know he probably won't. He pushes open the front door and then we're standing on the footpath in the cold.

'And it's not like it's forever,' I add, even though we both know it might be. I shiver as a droplet falls down the back of my neck. 'Where are we going, anyway?'

'Just here,' says Harry.

I give him a half-smile, not understanding. And then he pulls me in towards him, one arm around my back, the other still holding my hand. 'You missed out last time,' he murmurs. 'This is to make up for it.'

He wants me to dance in the rain with him, I realise. But I'm not sure I can do it. Act silly. Clown around in the rain outside a cafe in the late afternoon.

Yet Harry persists in that slow, patient way of his, which has become slightly slower but no less patient since that night in the park. And, before I know it, I'm part of it too. Part of the dance, part of this moment. Dancing with Harry as the rain falls around us.

ACKNOWLEDGEMENTS

Many thanks to everyone at Hardie Grant Egmont, in particular Hilary Rogers and Marisa 'the scissors' Pintado who were both endlessly encouraging and who helped guide this book into the shape it needed to be. Thanks also to Charlotte Bodman for enabling my book to reach international readers and for the kids' birthday party advice, Penny White for being the project editor and Emma Schwarcz for the scrupulous copyediting. Much gratitude to the HGE book reps, in particular Mandy Wildsmith who has always been such a great promoter of my work. Thanks to Erin Gough for the legal advice on Harry's behalf and to Astred Hicks for creating the gorgeous cover. And finally a very heartfelt thank you to Matt and Mads for their patience, understanding and encouragement while I was working on this book.

HIGH VOLTAGE READING
FROM ELECTRIC MONKEY

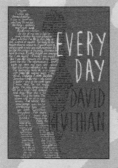

EVERY DAY
DAVID LEVITHAN

FRONT LINES
MICHAEL GRANT

EUGENE LAMBERT
THE SIGN OF ONE
ONE FOR SORROW, TWO FOR DEATH

ELIZABETH WEIN
CODE NAME Verity

SEED LOVES HER
SEED
WILL NEVER LET HER GO

LYNN WEINGARTEN
SUICIDE NOTES FROM BEAUTIFUL GIRLS

ANDREW SMITH
GRASSHOPPER JUNGLE
LOVE, GIANT BUGS AND THE END OF THE WORLD

THE #1 RULE FOR GIRLS
Love is all you need?
RACHEL McINTYRE

IN ANOTHER LIFE
YOU ASKED ME TO COME, SO I'M HERE. I WILL FIND YOU.
LAURA JARRATT

 @EMTeenFiction

 @electricmonkeybooks

 ELECTRIC MONKEY

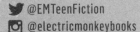